Rádé

Adekunbi Rowland

 Pyxidia House Publishers

Rádé

Request for information on this title should be addressed to

Adekunbi Rowland

Lagos, Nigeria
Email: kobbiekoo@yahoo.com

Library of Congress Cataloging-in-Publication Data

Adekunbi Rowland
RÁDÉ
ISBN-13: 978-1-946530-18-9 (Paperback)
ISBN-10: 1-946530-18-2 (Paperback)
1. Fiction 1. Title
Library of Congress Control Number: 2019943390

Edited by Winnie Aduayi

Published in Dallas Texas by Pyxidia House Publishers. A registered
trademark of Pyxidia Concept llc. www.pyxidiahouse.com
info@pyxidiahouse.com

Printed in the United States of America

For Claire Rowland,
You asked me to write a book.
It's here but you're not.
I wish upon a Star ...

Aknowledgement

To the Lord Jesus, who chose me even before I became palpable matter.

You write alone but draw strength from many...

A heartfelt thank you to everyone who contributed even in the smallest way to bringing this book to being. My family for the love and support. My Friend, Dr. Leke Oshunniyi, the first I dared send this manuscript many years ago, then cover page. Imonide David, Eme Bassey-Ezeliora who read the manuscript at different stages and gave the necessary feed back. My friend Dr. Adenike Ayiedun (PHD) who got the manuscript with much excitement but could never give her feed back before changing address to one in heaven.

I acknowledge all the admirable women in my life who inspire me, and the ones transitioned too. My Editor, Winnie Aduayi, for getting so involved in this project, she sometimes slipped and would call me by the book title.

Contents

What makes the Desert beautiful is that somewhere it hides a Well. The possibility of discovering that Well makes life interesting...

Chapter One

*I*t was the final working day of the week, and on that particular day, a thick cloak of heat hung defiantly over the Metropolis. The temperature was soaring! It was a typical Friday afternoon in the commercial hub of Nigeria, Lagos, and Lagosians were bustling about in a hurried frenzy. A palpable smell of impatience permeated through the veil as passengers waited impatiently for buses at the designated and makeshift stops. Some banking halls were overflowing as customers shuffled their feet impatiently and grumbled at the sluggish services.

"The network is slow," customers were told over and again.
But the customers were convinced they were trying to prevent them from coming into the

banking halls and forcing them to use the online mediums as more people hurried to make last-minute service payments. A lot of the people were very wary and still conducting their transactions the old fashioned way.

"Cashless society, my foot," they scoffed.

Anticipations for the weekend were high; the airwaves were pulsating with radio personalities propagating the obvious with creative, upbeat and a few lacklustre programs, TGIF!!! Thank God it's Friday!

Muslims were hurrying off to attend the Friday Jumat prayers; most were dressed up, the men wore caftans, tunics with matching trousers and caps, women with headscarves, wrappers and blouses or Ankara dresses; even the non-Muslims followed suit. Some employees played hooky and snuck off work early, while for others, especially those in the government agencies, it was an official half-day. The air was laden with audible sighs of relief for the brief respite from work. There were colourful fantasies about Saturday sleeping in, perhaps even breakfast with the family for some.

If an invincible, wide view camera were placed over the city, it would show that more than a few children were allowed to leave their home assignments from school for at least one day. The pathological party-goers and crashers were gearing up for the weekend as they made final arrangements with friends, acquaintances and even enemies.

There were a few tears running through the City as victims of devious tailors stared in horror at their marred Aso-ebis. Suffice to say, the culprits took on more than they could handle, but the recovery process would be swift and back up mode activated immediately. The job seekers loved the weekend because it ensured a level playing ground as they could blend in with the rest of the world and pretend they had imaginary jobs to take a break from.

Drivers were heading out of the Island hurriedly to beat rush hour traffic. Some of the less fortunate ones waited impatiently for their bosses, while they inwardly cursed them and bemoaned their own unlucky lives. Early drinkers were heading out to the bars. Beggars were on the rampage; begging for alms and ready with their most creative prayers which occasionally turned to jeers if they weren't obliged.

At 7pm, a popular commercial street, in Victoria Island that housed a spattering amount of high-rise apartment blocks, a reasonable number of glistening office buildings, restaurants and banks was stirring with a different type of activity as official business of the day had wound down. The air was brimming with the Friday evening energy of Lagos.

On the top floor of one of the high-rise buildings sat a lone figure in an over-furnished office, the fingers fiddled with a paper cutter while scowling at a display screen. The computer's battery was running low, power had gone out, and all the UPS were shrilling in a bizarre cacophony.

"Good God!" Rade muttered, running small boned fingers through her hair. She took several deep breaths but still felt as though her mind was coming apart in seams and she yearned desperately to scream out in frustration. She, however, directed her irritation at the closest target, her telephone. She jabbed a finger at the most frequently used button on her intercom and bellowed.

"Sade, how long does it take to print out a report you claimed was ready, please disappoint me for a change, so we don't go through the same tiresome, daily routine!"

She sensed her Assistant's movement before she appeared with a scowl on her face and dropped a heavy folder on the table with a loud thud. "There you go, madam." The "madam" title was reserved for days when she wanted to derisively show her disapproval.

Rade rolled her eyes heavenwards and groaned silently. "Don't take that tone with me, Sade. It is completely unnecessary."

"I'm sorry, Miss," she apologised.

"I've been waiting for a while, and I did specifically indicate I wanted a hard copy. Is there something the matter?" Rade asked.

"It's nothing, Miss Doherty, but its Friday and well past closing time, you…"

"Is that the problem?" Rade cut in before Sade could finish. "You had prior notice we would be staying overtime, and you agreed. So please, why are you then complaining? And you get paid for the extra hours. You should have outrightly informed me of your unwillingness to continue instead of torturing me."

"Don't be upset with me Miss Doherty; it's just that I'm a little tired today, it's as though I'm coming down with malaria, I feel funny…" Rade's eyes widened in amazement; she couldn't believe Sade's audaciousness! Adopting the malaria line again so soon. She had used that one twice already within a short period. Sade always developed a touch of something when she didn't want to work; it was on the tip of Rade's tongue to advise her to get far more ingenious excuses if she wanted to continue being lazy and a liar. She had a few suggestions she could recommend, like herpes, toothache, but decided against it. She was too weary.

'It's all right, have yourself a malaria-free evening," she said instead.

"Can I get you anything else?" Sade asked coyly.

"Have a good evening Sade, before you get on my already frayed nerves, I just wanted us to finish the report before they shut down the backup power supply. I guess it's too late for that now."

Sade smiled back unremorsefully as she switched off the UPS and hurried out of her boss's office to do a quick tidy up in hers while doing a mental calculation on how long it would take her to get home, take a shower, get dressed and head back to the Island to hit the nightclubs. She had bungled her evening plans by not preparing for her night out; else she wouldn't have to go home first.

She didn't feel bad about leaving her boss behind. Who in their right mind stayed hours on end after work each day looking for imaginary work when there was none? She was convinced her boss didn't have a life. Fortunately, she did, and no one was going to put a damper on it. Why should she be suffering for the sins of a workaholic boss? Rade let out a pent up sigh; the day hadn't been great. She knew she probably owed half the staff an apology and would have to make it up to them somehow. She was an easygoing girl on any other normal day, but today she seems to have woken up on the wrong side of the bed.

She had woken up late after a night plagued with meaningless dreams and couldn't find the energy to do her stretches nor usual morning devotion. She stormed into the office late to discover the Production Manager had called in sick. Her Assistant, Sade, whom she was sharing temporarily with another Director, chose that day to be extra sluggish, chugging along heavily and annoyingly, fueling Rade's anger. Sade is usually slow, but she does her work well, when you can get her engine started and when she isn't feigning malaria.

With her anger already fueled, she snapped at everyone, and the surprised expressions on their faces at the usually composed and pleasant Rade irritated her even further. She was aware they were whispering behind her back and observing her warily like a freak show.

The clients they were waiting on still weren't ready to part with their monies, and she wondered why they had arranged the meetings. Everything was loose ended; no sealed transactions just more demands for reassurances, which she had given a dozen times already, and had to offer again through gritted teeth accompanied by a plastered fake smile that said: *"Make the commitment already and stop wasting my time!"* She had felt like howling like a Coyote more than a few occasions and at times like that, she wondered if she was cut out for her job; or perhaps, it is near that time of the month, a little voice said. She made for her phone to check her monthly cycle app but got distracted and fumbled with the top buttons of her silk shirt instead.

"I must have been crazy to wear this shirt," she muttered.

It was a very hot, humid day and the airconditioner was off due to a power outage. Her shirt clung irritably to her back, and her hair felt hot and heavy against the nape of her neck as she searched the insides of her chaotic Hermes tote in vain for a hair band.

She went over to the windows and stood by it forlornly wishing she was anywhere but her office in Lagos. She gazed down with a slight frown at the activity below and made mental notes as she observed the smaller figures from her elevated view. She loved watching people and curiously observed a newly formed group made up of a few of her company drivers and other faces she didn't recognise. They were engrossed in their conversation, complete with wild gesticulations, loud guffaws and raised voices. A passerby suddenly reached out to someone in the group, and the recipient's face lit up with recognition as they exchanged pleasantries and a unique form of handshake excitedly, while the others cheered on.

She watched as Sade breezed out excitedly and waved to the group of drivers who responded enthusiastically and watched her derrière sashay hypnotically as she hurried across to a waiting car and by a man, who in sharp contrast walked with a weary countenance, drooping shoulders and shuffling feet, completely oblivious to his surroundings. Watching him made Rade want to cry. She pressed her head against the window pane and felt an overwhelming need to open the window and stick out her tongue at them all, to Sade, the people below and to Lagos itself if possible. She resisted the urge, imagining the roar of noise that would hit her, and no one would notice her anyway except maybe she called out to them. "Look at me," she would say, "I'm sticking out my tongue at you all." She smiled a little at the thought and decided she was definitely losing it.

Maybe her job was driving her mad! Whenever she felt this overwhelming apprehension about work, she immediately directed blame at her mother, but thinking of her father, she would only prove him right if he saw her like this.

****

Moradeyo Doherty, fondly called Rade by her family and friends, had lived twenty-two out of her twenty-seven years in London. Rade Doherty is attractive; though she thinks her nose is a little too broad and her teeth too widely spaced. Her slim, petite, 5ft 3in sculpted figure is enviable; her waist is miniscule, and her nicely shaped legs are one of her best features in her opinion. She is light complexioned and her skin prone to occasional breakouts with a pair of large, dark brown eyes that sparkle when she smiles. She has long, full, baby soft hair; category 3C or 4A is how two different hairdressers had described her hair type. She's fashion savvy and forward; the go-to person for fashion tips within her circle. She is a self-assured woman in her own right and well-liked and admired amongst her peers. She is a city girl and very proud of it.

She had only returned home due to pleas and a consistent harangue on why she should return to Nigeria from her mother, Juliet Doherty. Mrs. Ju, as she is referred to is a bubbly, light-skin tone, tall and full-figured, Itshekiri woman. She's cultured, elegant and very stylish, with long, black natural hair that is well cared for; she is in her mid-sixties but does not look a day older than fifty; her gap-toothed smile made her an instant charmer. Determined and set in her ways, she often has a way of getting exactly what she wants.

The family's textile business established by her father and his father before him was on the verge of going under. She was startled at the news as she had always been so sure the business was as solid as a rock.
"Everything is falling apart!" Her mother had dramatically told her over the phone.

"Please darling," Mrs. Doherty had cried, "you need to make it back home. Don't you ever get homesick?"

"Mom, how can I be homesick when this is my home! Home is where the heart is."

Her mother scoffed and muttered several expletives in Itsekiri language, her mother tongue.

"Rade, England is not your home! You are a pure African, Yoruba-Itshekiri girl, and all this silly talk about the heart; home is where family is. My dear girl, today is not the day we have the conversation on the sad truth about your British identity as I don't want to burst your bubble, but when the chips are down, you'll realise that soon enough!"

"Thank you for the gloomy disposition, mom. You really should refrain from playing the divisive race card. The last time I checked, my international passport still indicates I'm British; I pay my taxes, I love the royal family and the Prime Minister too, though some think me crazy," Rade added with a chuckle.

Her mother wasn't amused.

"Whatever you say, it doesn't matter if you're Chinese at this point, you've got to come down here where you can really make an impact and not just one out of an increasing number of immigrants;

you need to see how fast Doherty Textile is going down."

Rade was exasperated, "Mom, I know nothing of daddy's businesses. More so, this one is his baby; he knows this business probably better than he knows his children, besides he has good hands; many competent experts work for him. Perhaps the old man is just tired and needs a break, and if that's the case, why don't you make Bisade this offer and see if he'll oblige," she said referring to her elder brother.

"No!" Mrs. Doherty said, "Bisade isn't the one; we both know he's an Academic, not a businessman. I haven't even mentioned any of this to him, I don't want to intrude into his life, the fact that he's trying to settle in one place and not travel so much is a miracle in itself, and please refrain from referring to my husband as an old man."

"Well, well, mom, what makes it okay for you to intrude into my own life? I have a good, well-paying job I enjoy very much, my friends live here, and there's Aunt Jo. Moreover, I don't think daddy will even want me coming down to Nigeria to run his business."

"Oh dear! You can be so headstrong, aren't you even a bit curious about how Nigeria is after all these years?"

"I admit, I am a little curious," Rade replied. That's the entire opening her mom needed.

She pounced.

She asked Rade to imagine the grand reunion she'd have with her old friends, how she could make new ones and start a new life in Nigeria. She made her feel guilty by reminding her that they "her humble parents" could be reason enough for her to be returning home.

"Mom, please!" She felt cold fear creep into her heart as her mother was beginning to wear her out and weaken her resolve.

"How do you call people I went to nursery school with friends? Maimuna is the only childhood friend I've reconnected with, thanks to social media, and that's good enough for me."

Rade begged her mom to drop the subject, but when Mrs. Doherty starts on something, she never stops until she sees the end of it.

Rade grimaced when she remembered her mom telling her that her father was aching to see her, but she had overheard him in the background telling her mother to speak for herself.

"You can set the business right," her mother kept saying, "I feel it in my heart."

"Why mom? Just because I have joint honours in Business Administration and Economics doesn't mean I can…"

"Tut, tut, Professor Bateson won't be too happy to hear you now; remember how disappointed he still is that you haven't returned to pursue your PhD as intended. I will never forget what he said to me about you: *Your daughter has one of the brightest minds I've ever encountered, Mrs. Doherty.* He said it so matter of fact; I had goose flesh." She interjected, referring to one of the most respected professors in Rade's department who happened to be Rade's mentor. "Don't underestimate what you were taught and what you've learnt."

Mrs. Doherty was convinced in her heart that her daughter could turn the business around and kept preaching it. She mentioned that Rade's father wanted to slow down but would die before admitting it to anyone.

She reeled out some of Rade's good points to her, "you have a good head on your shoulders, you're young, you have a lot of positive energy and drive needed for this job; I've read your professional profile. Besides, you told me you're not in a relationship, so there is no man issue; in any case, there are a lot of good men in Nigeria."

"Mom! Now you're pushing it. This is blackmail! Where was dad anyway when that Managing

Director was turning the place upside down?"

"He was overworking himself to death, and I made him take an impromptu vacation. We went to Jos where we spent six days then proceeded to Calabar for the rest of the vacation. We had a wonderful time but returned to bad news; the M.D. was nowhere to be found. Your father had a series of meetings with the Finance Directors and other members of the board, and after an Audit, they discovered the scoundrel had taken off with more than half the money for a proposed capital project which was going to rake in hundreds of millions in foreign exchange for the company." She emphasised the millions again for full effect.

"The accounts were overdrawn; he has been diverting funds for a while and was paying himself outrageous allowances. It seems unbelievable he's just being discovered, almost as if he cast a spell on everyone. Your father blames himself repeatedly as he was his Protégée and he trusted him completely."

"I can't imagine he is actually capable of such poor error in judgment," Rade said with veiled sarcasm.

"No; you can't," her mother replied, "Moradeyo, I won't have you taking that slightly sarcastic tone when talking about your father. He has faults like all other human beings, but he's a hardworking, kindhearted man. All he's ever done is to give back to the Society. Do you know how many people are in Doherty Textile's employment and what will happen to them if the Business were to fold?"

"Now you're bringing out the big guns. What if the board doesn't want me? There is someone next in line for this position I presume?"

"The company needs new blood, someone completely unbiased, trust me; your father is a hands-on Chairman, the board will do anything to get out of the mess everyone's in; things are still run the old fashioned way."

"And you wonder why there is a problem? I don't know how you can think me an unbiased solution, mom; I'm the Chairman's daughter."

Mrs. Doherty had an answer to all her daughter's queries, and Rade wondered why her mother wasn't taking the job herself; she knew nearly everything about the business.

Her mom reminded her, they had never asked anything of her as parents and had left her to run her life as she pleased. She asked her to consider the offer carefully, and asked her to tell her aunt to ring her immediately she got back into town.

Mrs. Doherty spoke to her twin sister that night and asked her to speak to her niece who had been under her care since she was a child.

"So you want to take my favourite niece away from me?"

"Yes Jo, I want to see my daughter; it's been too long," Mrs. Doherty cried, "we see her only on our holidays abroad, I don't think you know how much I miss having my baby around, but as my twin and a mother yourself, you should understand."

"Yes Ju; I, more than anyone, understand how you feel."

"Please talk to her; you are more of a mother to her than I am anyway, she'll listen to you." Rade's mom said as they slipped into their Itshekiri mother tongue.

Aunt Jo, whose full name was Joan, spoke with Rade the day after.

She had her own guilt trip, and Rade knew her mom had worked her magic on her twin sister. She lamented and blamed herself for not encouraging Rade to visit home for her own selfish reasons, forgetting that her relationship with her mother was equally as important and she needed her too.

"What's all these needy talk about, Aunty Jo. What about what I need and me? Is this even about the job or about returning home, as they both seem intertwined now? Mom doesn't need anyone. She has dad; I wish Jade were around, then she wouldn't be so needy."

"It's not that," Aunt Jo replied, "even before your sister left for South Africa to settle, she was already married and started a life of her own. I know it's difficult for you, but you must remember that your parents aren't getting younger; you need to establish a better relationship with them. And deep down in you, there is a slight curiosity about the offer your mother's extended. I know you like work, and that's all that matters; that tiny bit of interest. Why settle for the regimented, predictable life you have here? Embrace this challenge, go out there and explore new things; this is an opportunity for you to travel to a different environment and implement all the knowledge and experience you've acquired here over the years."

Rade had a smile lurking at the corners of her lips; her mom had played the most successful card - Aunt Jo."

"What if I can't do anything about the crumbling business? Doherty's used to be a successful business, they are set in their traditional ways, and it's full of old people who have been working there since I was born, and now that it's bankrupt, I'm supposed to just waltz in and wave a wand! I don't have any real experience to take on that kind of heavy responsibility; I am scared Aunt Jo!"

"It's natural to be a little scared, but I know I don't have a cowardly niece. Not only are you great at your job from your yearly reviews, but you do also have more than sufficient work experience, and if you can handle your current portfolio, think of this as a slightly bigger one, and if you don't like it there, you gather your stuff and return home."

Rade laughed despite herself, and her aunt had brushed off all the other feeble excuses she had tried to make. She had always believed her aunt should be a motivational speaker.

Her mother's scream when she called her two days later to inform her she was considering the offer almost deafened her.

Eight weeks later, Rade found herself with Aunt Jo at the International wing of the Muritala Mohammed Airport, Lagos, Nigeria.

She smiled fondly when she remembered the tearful meeting between the sisters. Aunt Jo and Mrs. Doherty were as alike as the most identical twins that shared a sack could be; the only difference was Mrs. Doherty was gap-toothed while Aunt Jo wasn't.

Rade and her mom hugged each other so tightly

that her sides had hurt. It must be the fact that she was in Nigeria that made the meeting so surreal because her parents either visited her or they travelled together nearly every holiday, even Mr. Doherty who was trying very hard to stay aloof had a sloppy expression which he hurriedly replaced with a stern one.

Mr. Yinka Doherty is a tall distinguished-looking Yoruba man in his late sixties. His face has the same defined structure as Rade's, a determined, slightly square jaw and a definitive cleft in his chin. The thick, grey hair on his head is set back on a high, noble forehead. He is lean and quite fit for his age, his back not at all stooped. He is a man that works hard, takes care of his immediate and extended family and never takes his stress out on others. His relationship "currency" is thoughtful words and careful deeds. He is extremely loyal to his relationships but very wary of change.

"Ladies!" he said brusquely.

The women turned to him, just remembering he was there. Around his eyes were laughter lines in just the right amount.

"Dad!" Rade said going over to him and hugging him tightly. As odd as the relationship between Rade and her father was, they were always happy to see each other. Mr. Doherty patted his daughter a little too heartily on the back, which made her start coughing incessantly in between much laughter.

Mrs. Doherty reminded her husband that Rade was a lady, not some young man he could slap on the back the way men did. He shrugged and went over to his wife's twin to embrace her.

"So good to see you old boy," Aunt Jo said.

"Same here, girlie," Rade's father said as they all burst into laughter.

"You look frail," Mr. Doherty said to his daughter, "if I didn't know better, I would say your aunt hasn't been feeding you well!"

"Come on," Aunt Jo said, "Rade isn't that frail; it's just that she's so slim she looks smaller than she really is."

"She's thin!" Her father replied vehemently.

"Now, that's enough," Mrs. Doherty said, "don't talk about my daughter like she's not here. It's your genes; you're quite tall," she said, referring to her husband, "but the women in your family are very small boned. I am well above average, which makes me tall too! How tall are you dear?" Rade's mom asked her.

"5ft 3 inches" replied Rade, "Would you like to know what I weigh too?"

"That's not very tall but compared to your father's

mother, my beloved mother-in-law; God rest her soul, who was four feet ten inches and weighed just a little more than cotton wool, you're alright." Though secretly Rade's mom was worried; she had to admit Rade was quite frail looking and she wondered if she could handle the pressure that awaited her.

"Wow!" Rade replied, "guess I have dad to thank for my fine structure then," looking up at her father's worried, unimpressed expression and cracking up with laughter. It was a happy reunion.

Chapter Two

Two weeks later, Aunt Jo returned to London, and Rade felt like she had lost her best friend. She got teary-eyed as she felt things were going to change from that point onwards and they did drastically.

Rade came out of her thoughts with a sigh. She picked up her bag, smart access car key and exited her office; the elevator was out of service as power still hadn't been restored, it was taking longer than envisaged to fix the major fault that had affected a small section of that business district. The backup power generator had been scheduled for maintenance service for that day; so most people had long left the building. By the time she walked down the flight of stairs, waving her weak beamed flashlight while guiding herself with the handrails of the balustrade like a blind person, she was perspiring heavily.

She made her way across her office building to the supermarket in a shopping complex where she usually shopped; and while paying for her groceries, she asked after Lateef, a hanger-on she had taken a liking to. He often hung around and organised affairs at the taxi pool by the supermarket and good-naturedly assisted people in carrying their supplies to their cars and got small tips if people were feeling generous. A shop assistant promised to help lookout for him, and Rade decided to add some items to her shopping cart while she waited.

Rade dabbed irritably at her sweaty brows despite the air conditioning; maybe she was coming down with something, she thought to herself worriedly. "It must be almost forty degrees," she muttered, and as she glanced up, she noticed the man standing near the counter, their eyes met briefly then they both looked away simultaneously. His face wore an amused expression; she thought he looked familiar, but couldn't quite place the face. It was probably her flustered sight that amused him, she thought with chagrin, then chided herself not to be absurd. She moved on to pick an item and was startled by the sound of her name or at least the caller's version of it. *"Aunty Raid! I hear say you dey look for me!"* The voice called out in Pidgin English.

It was Lateef.

She hushed him, "Why do you have to be so loud? Moreover my name is not 'Raid' the way you pronounce it like the insecticide, my name is R-á-d-é; Moradeyo in full," she stressed, spelling it out to him.

The man at the counter's amused look had turned to a full grin; he was openly listening to their conversation.

"Ah!" Lateef said, *"am sorry o, don't vex for me!"* She raised her hand in acceptance before he carried on and there would be no stopping him.

"I no know say na Yoruba name," he said in his usual broken English. "So you be Moradeyo? *That is better na! I always tink it's American name."*

Rade smiled in spite of herself.

"Could you recommend a taxi man from the taxi pool outside instead of me ordering a pick up, as I'm really tired and I don't feel up to driving? I'm going to leave my car in the office parking lot."

"Wot?!" He exclaimed, trying very hard to sound like Rade. *"Nooo o; Aunty, you cannot lif that kain fine car fo car pak fo weekend o!"*

"Hmmm!" Rade sighed, thinking of the white pearl

coloured, latest model LH 500 Sedan Lexus her mother had assigned to her, which had been a gift to her father from one of the major Toyota dealerships.

"The security guards work all weekend, so why can't I leave the car just for tonight?" Rade asked in frustration.

"In spite of that," a deep voice behind her interrupted, "they still put up a '**Cars parked at owners risk**' disclaimer."

She turned round to identify the speaker, it was the man with the amused expression, and he was still standing close to the counter. He had a nice voice, she thought but ached to tell him to mind his business, but good manners prevented her.

It didn't stop the icy stare she gave him though. Typical Nigerian, she thought; they could never mind their business. It was one of the first of many shocks she'd received and was still trying to come to terms with it. People interposing into other people's conversations without being invited, asking personal questions like they had a right to the minuscule details of your personal life, invading your personal space; the latter still startled her. They were tactile like they needed to feel you to communicate effectively. She put a reign on her thoughts and stepped back in time to miss Lateef's spittle as he stepped closer to her and bellowed, "Exactly!" Feeling quite pleased for using such an appropriate word. He hadn't quite gotten all that the man had said, but he had had a general idea and concurred.

"What do I do?" She asked as she beckoned him to a secluded section. "I am dead on my feet." Then she quickly corrected herself when she saw the dismay on Lateef 's face, "I am tired, I drove myself to work today because my driver is unavailable."

Theirs was a funny relationship because he usually didn't understand her immediately; she'd have to repeat herself severally; it was worse when she used complex words. His pidgin English wasn't any better for her, she felt it was bad Pidgin English if there was such a thing, it sounded different from the others she'd heard, but they managed to get by somehow.

"I can fit to drive you anywhere," he said smiling at her.

"Really!" She replied, "but do you drive well?"

"Ah!" He exclaimed. "I dey drofe trailer and molue, danfo, bifo bifo," he replied importantly, gesticulating with his fingers.

"Do you have a license?" she asked.

"*I get, but e don expaya o!*" He said, grinning. He

seemed to like showing off his large off-white teeth with the many gaps between them.

Lateef had the most infectious grin, and when he grinned, sometimes unnecessarily, you impulsively grinned along with him as Rade did now.

"*I go like renew am but, no pay...*" He went on to tell her a colourful story of how he came about driving trucks and the popular Lagos commercial buses, Molue. He wanted to renew his driver's license but didn't have spare money for that. Rade didn't understand the concept of license renewal but promised to assist him whenever he was ready much to his delight.

She ordered Chinese takeout on the phone while waiting to pay for her groceries and was trying to give them the address to deliver the food, but Lateef motioned to her wildly that he would go and pick it up. She smiled a goodbye at the girl at the counter after making her payment while still waiting on hold for her food bill. She hurried out with Lateef to put the items in the car. Then walked over to her regular hairdressers in the same vicinity and exchanged pleasantries with the manager. She explained her appointment was for Saturday, but she had decided on the spur of the moment to have her hair done now. She didn't think she would be leaving the house all weekend. The manager checked for cancellations and decided they could fit her insince she just wanted to wash and blow-dry her hair.

"Your regular girl is busy, Miss Rade, so someone else will wash your hair since there's an opening."

Rade pulled her best 'you-can't-resist-me,' puppy face. "I'd really prefer she does the washing and I honestly don't mind waiting if she won't be too long."

The manager shook her head with a smile and ushered Rade into a chair.

She glanced at her face in the wall-hung mirror of the waiting room and cringed in embarrassment. She was now certain the man at the supermarket had definitely been amused by her appearance; her oily nose stuck out of her face like a sore thumb, it was dearly in need of a wipe. Wisps of her usually tidy hair were all over the place, and tired eyes stared back at her. She had chewed her lipstick off a long time ago, and the leftover residue clung to the skin of her dry lips in little lumps. She needed to drink more water she thought.

She shrugged and picked up a recent copy of the UK Vogue magazine on the chair beside her and flipped through, thinking to herself that she was missing out on a lot of former little pleasures.

Her favourite stylist, whom Rade called "*girl smiley*" because she could smile through the worst storms, came over to tell her that she was ready for her. She held on to the magazine absentmindedly as she walked over to the wash section. Her tense muscles relaxed as she felt the warm water and capable hands of *girl smiley* rub and massage her scalp.

"Ahhhhh," she whispered, but almost jumped out of her skin, when she heard a screech from a corner in the room.

"This is certainly not the hairstyle I wanted! This is the same thing you did to my hair last time." The voice continued, "I'm sorry, but you're too much of an airhead to be working in a hair salon! This is what I get for allowing an apprentice's apprentice touch my hair."

Wow, that's harsh! Rade thought, feeling sorry for the person being reprimanded.

"You are going to refund the money for my hair extensions you've hacked off!" There was silence, then the voice continued, "And please where is my magazine; can you get me my magazine?!" There was a flurry of movement as they searched for the magazine.

The tirade continued tirelessly as the lady mentioned it was quite convenient the magazine had disappeared. The lady had brought it as a pictorial reference for the stylist to copy, but it hadn't gone as planned from the sound of things. Rade had forgotten about the magazine in her hands till she heard footsteps in her direction, then stopped right in front of her.

"Madam," a voice said shakily, "please the owner wants her magazine; I can get you another that belongs to us."

Rade's hair had been washed and was being towel dried.

"Oh no! I'm so sorry," Rade apologised and handed her the magazine.

"It's okay," the girl replied collecting the magazine gratefully and hurrying away.

"Where did you find it?" The voice asked.

"A customer of ours had it," the hairstylist replied.

"Oh! So she or he didn't hear me screaming my head off? The person either needs a hearing aid or has sticky fingers."

There was a mixture of raised voices then hushed tones, Rade grimaced and was brimming with ire as she walked briskly into the styling room, and judging from the angry expression on her face she walked directly to the lady whom she guessed was causing the uproar.

She apologised and explained she thought the

magazine belonged to the salon. She wouldn't have taken it without permission if she had known it was someone's and had held on to it absent-mindedly while going to the hair wash section.

"It's alright," the lady said with a dismissive wave of her hand before she finished, and the Manager hurried over to Rade's side to intervene. She apologised to Rade adding that the customer, Miss Simi was just upset because Tina had been getting on her nerves all evening, it had nothing to do with her.

"A bit much in my opinion but understandable I guess; the sticky fingers bit was completely unnecessary though..." Her voice was rising, and as she made to continue, she glanced at the person walking into the styling section, and her heart gave a thump.

Was the man stalking her? "Don't be silly," Rade chided herself. It was the same man from the supermarket. She watched as he went over to the lady's chair, and Rade heaved a sigh of relief.

"Look, it's okay," the lady responded, "just calm down."

Rade's eyes widened as she bristled in disbelief, "Is this some kind of reverse psychology? I should be the one doling out that advice, I wasn't the one going into a hysterical frenzy over a magazine, and being awfully rude," she retorted.

"Yeah!" The lady said, "Maybe if your mind had been a little on the present…" She didn't finish her sentence before the man put out arestraining hand on her shoulder.

"Now that's enough, Simi; stop it!"

"No; please don't ask her to stop, let her go right ahead!" Rade exclaimed, her blood was boiling, and she was now spoiling for a fight. She was aching to go in, lips barred.

The other girl looked like she was going to charge up again, but the expression on the man's face kept her quiet; she knew the look well.

Rade saw the look that passed between the two and resentfully thought that they deserved each other. She noticed the drops of water around her shoes from her dripping hair and told girl smiley to get on with it.

All the spectators gradually moved on to other things, and the other two were conversing now, the lady mostly grumbling about her hair. The stalker, as Rade had nicknamed him in her mind, plied her with reassurances, and to Rade's amazement, the girl lit up at the compliment, turning her head left and right as if seeing the hair with new eyes. He smoothened the hair with a brush and turned her face to the mirror. She smiled and continued preening at herself in front of the mirror.

"It's not bad," he said.

The girl chuckled happily and smacked him on the shoulder playfully with a grateful smile.

Good God! The guy must really have a hold over this spitfire; she couldn't believe it was the same person almost popping a vein a few minutes ago.

The hassled salon girl gave the man a grateful look he returned with a slight headshake.

"I finally got the nail polish you wanted," he said, "but this colour wasn't easy to find; I was by the counter for a while, plodding through the nail polish baskets like an idiot."

"You're the best," the girl replied.

Rade shook herself angrily and realised she was gawking.

The Stylist was drying her hair when Lateef walked in with a shout, "Aunty Rade!"

"Stop yelling! I'm over here."

He hurried over and detoured briefly to say hello to the stalker, immediately he came over, she reprimanded him again about shouting her name in public.

Girl smiley commented as usual that Rade's beautiful hair didn't cease to amaze her, it was quite long, full, and healthy.

Lateef laughed proudly and said to the girl, "*You know Aunty na Americana, so her hair be like doz Oyinbo people.*"

The duo was looking at her hair in amazement through the mirror. Lateef seemed to have a fixation on Americans, Rade thought wryly.

"Please don't make conversation over my head," she cut in, "I have hair because it's genetic; my mother has such a full head of hair, she doesn't even know what to do with it, so it hasn't got anything to do with *Oyinbo*. Lateef do me a favour; wait for me at the reception. Did you pick up the stuff?"

"Yes," he replied, grinning as he headed to the reception, oblivious to Rade's foul mood. He was content with being sent on errands and being around her.

Rade asked for her scissors, and the girl replied she didn't require a trim.

"You don't have any split or weak ends!" She announced triumphantly, as she ran a wide-toothed comb through Rade's hair happily.

She acted like she didn't hear her the first time until Rade repeated that she wanted to cut her hair. "What?! The girl looked around at the other hairdressers who were trying hard not to gape.

"But, you didn't come for a hair cut! Are you

still upset? Please don't be," she massaged Rade's shoulders quickly with expert hands.

Rade sighed deeply and insisted she wanted a haircut.

The girl stood motionless behind Rade for a few minutes then came to stand in front of her.

Rade's expression brooked no argument, and she made the sign of scissors with her fingers as the stylist shook her head in return.

Rade wondered how bad a person's day could get; now even the hairdresser was refusing to cut her hair. How could everything go downhill from just oversleeping? People woke up late all the time.

The girl started snipping at the hair after a stare down match Rade won, and the Manager hurried over.

"What is the matter, Miss Doherty? I thought you just wanted a trim."

"I want everything off, and I don't mind you helping out because Lola seems to have hang-ups about doing it, even though it isn't her hair."

The other stylists watched in amazement; they didn't understand why Rade who took such great care of her hair was chopping it off.

The manager took the scissors reluctantly, Lola retrieved it from her, sighed dramatically and started snipping away, when she got halfway, she looked imploringly at Rade.

Rade shook her head and pointed to the model with closely cropped hair in the framed picture hanging on the salon wall. The Simi girl looked like she was going to say something, but seeing the expression on Rade's face, she swallowed her comments.

The snip, snap, snip sound of the scissors made Rade feel better. "That's the best I can do, that type of short hair requires constant grooming. Please leave it this way; it's easier to manage."

The rest of the styling was done in silence, and when it was over, she looked at herself in the mirror, her heart-shaped face looked very young and bare; she had forgotten her ears stuck out a bit. The manager came over, "I am so sorry about this evening; we aim to have all our clients relaxed and happy when they exit our doors not the opposite."

"It's okay;" Rade replied, "it's not your fault some people are so rude and without thought for other people's feelings."

She saw the man smile through the corner of her eyes and went over to the cashier to pay where she got more riled up seeing her bill, even after a generous discount. She was reminded of the added charge for the hair cut. The stares she was getting made her uncomfortable, and she quickly made her way out to the streets onto the office parking lot with Lateef following closely at her heels.

She almost chuckled out as Lateef stared at her hair in amazement and unconcealed disapproval.

She stared in horror at the mounting traffic; she was terrified of driving herself, and her stomach had been in knots when she drove herself to work that morning. Driving in Lagos required special skills; it was the motorcyclists that did it for her, zigzagging between cars like crazies, and cursing you out when you came close to them, even when they were at fault. What she didn't understand was the passiveness of the passenger; sometimes two passengers perched precariously at the edge of the seat, holding on to their helmets with eyes wide open, some encouraging the rider like people on a suicide mission. Her driver, Mr. Udoh, could never control his amusement whenever she started shrieking and exclaiming. "Please stay away from the motorcycles, please, please!" She'd often warned if he came less than a meter behind them.

"Madam, we can't leave the road for them; they are very stubborn people. I don't know why the government lifted the ban on them," he'd reply, chuckling and closing in on the *Okada* as they were popularly called, riling up Rade some more and almost drowning in his laughter, as she threatened to fire him, or get out of the moving vehicle, all in the same sentence.

They acted out the same scene every day.

She imagined the bridge that led out of Victoria Island to her home in Ikoyi; all the impatient drivers, the *Okadas,* the quick formation of a three-lane road to five lanes and back to two as the bridge thinned out. The disregard for indicators, her throbbing head, it wasn't a good mix; she could see herself running down at least three *Okadas* in terror.

"I don't feel comfortable driving, Lateef, but here we are your license is expired, so you can't drive me."

He looked at her in disbelief, "*Aunty Rade, please bring key make we dey go.*"

"But how; what if we get pulled over and arrested because of your expired license?"

He rifled through his pockets and brought out a ragged wallet from which he carefully extracted his driver's license and handed it to Rade; she scrutinised it closely noting it had expired six months before and groaned.

She touched the handle to unlock the car, and he got over his surprise on time to open the back seat door, motioning for her to get in. "*License na license; nobody go stop us.*"

She got into the back seat without an argument as he followed suit at the driver's and gawked at the dashboard in amazement.

"You never give me di key, Aunty Rade."

"Push that button," she instructed, motioning to the power button as he searched in vain for the ignition. "By all means, take your time," she muttered as he continued to stare at the dashboard, fiddling with knobs, the radio came on with a deafening start, and he apologised profusely.

He eventually got the hang of it, and Rade hoped they would make it home in one piece as they finally drove by the security man who had asked for the umpteenth time if she had authorized Lateef to drive the car. She explained yet again that she had asked him to drive her home; hence her being in the car. Perhaps he thought she was being kidnapped. She reassured him as best as she could and thanked him for being thorough. She was still craning her neck to catch a glimpse at the suspicious security man, as the traffic enveloped them. She knew immediately they hit the road, Lateef was indeed a truck driver. He drove her car like a toy; disdainfully.

They were crawling at snail speed, but soon after, he was weaving and inserting himself between every possible opening he could find. Rade felt sick; her phone had rung about five times before she was able to dig it out of her bag. She couldn't believe how many missed calls she had and it was ringing again as she answered to the panicked voice of her driver, Udoh, inquiring if she had asked some strange person to drive her car. The security man had obviously called him, and as she hadn't picked his previous calls, he'd decided to try for the last time before alerting her father. Rade was too tired to be angry as he rang off telling her to be careful and not be so trusting of strangers let alone allowing them to drive her car and even worse take her home. Her reply that Lateef wasn't really a stranger fell on deaf ears. After the call, she kept on staring at her phone and asking herself if her driver had really just called to tell her off as one would a five-year-old.

"*No mind that security o, him know me well well, all of dem fo dat una building know me. Na jealousi and bad belle dey worry am.*"

She didn't have the appropriate words to respond to his statement that the security knew him but was just jealous, as he looked at her through the rear view mirror. So, she took a bite of her vegetable spring rolls instead; it tasted bland, and it seemed even her taste buds were tired. She didn't bother with the food she usually enjoyed. It probably wasn't right to be eating so late anyway, she thought. She had scarcely eaten anything all day, and though she was slim, she was continually counting calories much to her Aunt's annoyance. She had a full bust line and a dimpled derriere, and that meant as she usually told people, she had tendencies to be fat, and she wasn't having any of that.

She was squirming around to find a comfortable spot in the car's plush leather seat and was making herself queasier in the process. Maybe she was cracking under all the stress, as she had been told she would, in not so many words, while absentmindedly noting that Lagos looked so beautiful at night; but she missed London. She appreciated things more now that she was away, even London's sometimes dreary weather seemed welcome in the face of the heat she had experienced earlier that day. She'd had a properly planned out life that had suited her.

The remaining drive home was a chase as Lateef went after two motorcyclists who had squeezed past the car and lightly grazed the side mirror. Her weary appeal to let it go fell on deaf ears as luckily the traffic eased and he went for the kill, almost bumping one off the road as the other sped away victoriously. Rade watched in horror as they cursed one another. The bike man had his eyes off the road, his neck craned at a 90-degree angle, one palm out with fingers splayed out in Lateef's direction, and in a split second narrowly missed a sharply instinctive man trying to cross the road with a pile of pillows tied with a single rope on his head. The bike man skidded to a halt looking confused as she yelled at Lateef to stop and find out if he was okay. The man with the pillows looked harried but just gave the bike man a disapproving angry stare as the latter apologised profusely pointing to the "culprit" Rade's car. He steadied his pillows and went about crossing the road again as the bike rider, relieved to be off the hook called out laughingly after him, asking if he wanted a ride.

Rade went off on Lateef, asking him what he thought would have happened if the man with the pillows had been hit, and they were arrested, and his expired license discovered; his answer irritated her further.

"*Anti Rade, you too dey fear o! E fo carry di pillo man go huspitul, and police go arrest am, becos dia time to operate don expaya, dem get cofu na, and afta everytin I fo beat am join, we no get any fault.*"

She was glad to hear the commercial bike riders had a curfew, at least, like that was a consolation.

She wondered out loud where the man with the pillows was headed, and he regaled her with pillow stories. He shrugged when she asked if the pillows were comfortable and what they were filled with, and he explained they could be quite lumpy but that if you pummeled them hard enough, you could get your money's worth.

"More like a broken neck," she thought to herself.

She was grateful when he pulled into the road leading to the close where she lived; she sighed in relief as he drove down the lane and horned at the gate. She made a mental note not to hassle her driver any longer; clearly, there were worse drivers than him. She could still see the pillow man's expression in her mind's eye. It took a while before the old gateman opened the gate.

She hoped her mother wasn't around as all she wanted to do was just curl up anywhere and sleep. She had suggested her father install an electric gate, but he refused, saying that the old gate man who had manned the gate for the past twenty-five years and was part of the family would be out of work. Then he launched into the story of how the neighbour with an electric gate was always getting stuck when there was power failure and other excuses Rade didn't think made sense.

Rade directed him to the side of the house where

she stayed, and he drove there and parked the car. It was a wide expanse of land and sitting right in the middle of it was a sprawling seven-bedroom house. The guest chalet at the backside of the house she occupied had been built alongside the main house and staff quarters where the domestic helps stayed. It had only been lived in for a brief period by a relative. It had two huge bedrooms, a generously sized living room, a fully fitted kitchen, and a spare room she was converting into a library. Her father, knowing how overbearing her mother could be, had suggested she move in there much to her delight and her mother's dismay. She felt Rade had been away too long, so she needed to see her, morning, noon and night if possible.

Rade reassured her she'd be coming over to the main house.

"But it won't be like having you in the room few doors away," her mother had wailed, "whenever I want to see you, I'd have to walk all the way over here."

"Well, that is no problem; you always were and still are a fitness enthusiast, walking should be enjoyable for you," Mr. Doherty had said to his wife, winking at Rade over her mother's shoulder, who eyed him angrily and continued her whining. Rade and her father had a good laugh.

She dismissed Lateef with some money for his transport back home, and he thanked her profusely. "*Wot of your food?*" He asked after she had retrieved her bag and briefcase from the car. Her tummy grumbled in protest at the mention of food. "You can have that if you want, I am not hungry anymore."

He smiled gratefully at her and thanked her for the food.

Rade managed to unlock and lock her door when she entered before carrying herself to her bedroom. She slipped off her clothes and couldn't recall the next day how she was still able to take a quick shower, but by the time she was done, her mind and body seemed detached from one another, and she took two pain relievers with a glass of mango juice for her throbbing head and got into her bed.

It was already 10.00pm. She woke up at some point during the night remembering she hadn't taken out her contact lenses. She went to the bathroom to do so and got back into bed.

She thought briefly of the man with the pillows that the motorcycle man had almost hit and hugged her feather-filled pillows tightly and snuggled deeper under her goose down duvet thinking things weren't so bad after all.

Chapter Three

Rade woke up with a stretch and felt very refreshed. Her stomach grumbled in hunger, and she smiled; a smile that gradually worked it's way to a scream when she ran her hands through her hair. She raced over to the dressing mirror and stared at herself, stupefied. She had dreamed she cut her hair, but this was real enough. The memory of all that had happened the previous evening came flooding back, and she shrieked with laughter. She couldn't believe she actually cut her hair as she showered, towelled herself dry and donned a red and black silk caftan her mom had given her.

After her morning devotion and while exhaling as she did her yoga stretches, she felt the remaining tension ebb out of her body and felt way much better than the previous day. She took another peek at herself in the mirror and suddenly wished she had her hair back. The thought of her mother's reaction drew an inward groan and she thought of ways to avoid going to the main house but had to, there were issues she needed to discuss with her father.

She walked over to the main house, inhaling the mid-morning air into her lungs as she strode through her mother's award-winning garden, stopping ever slightly to admire the lush greenery and kaleidoscope of colours of several budding flowers, then past the weather-beaten set of swings she had swung in as a child and into the ground floor living room. The room was impressive: high ceilinged from which hung two over scaled 17th century masterpiece chandeliers. The early morning sun streamed through the sparkling panes of the huge bay windows framed by drawn silk drapes. Masterworks hung proudly on the walls, plush centre carpets adorned the floor, and every piece of furniture and ornament in the room told a story.

The air was filled with a heady smell of fresh flowers. She soon heard her mom approaching the living room and had a sudden urge to hide; this must be how Adam and Eve felt when they heard

God approaching the garden after they had eaten the forbidden fruit, she thought. She stood her ground instead and plastered a silly grin on her face, which her mom returned with a genuine one, then a horrified stare when she noticed her hair; Rade walked over to her mom and gave her a hug and lip smack to the cheeks.

"Good morning, mom!"

"Oh my goodness, Moradeyo! Is this a wig?" She asked, and proceeded to run her hands through her daughter's hair invasively without warning.

Rade yelped and backed off from her as she started with a barrage of questions.

"What have you done to yourself? How could you scrape off all that lovely hair; don't you realise how lucky you are? The hair is your beauty; it's a woman's crowning glory. This short hair is all wrong, look at you now, more frail looking than before..."

Her response was the same. It was her hair, she had decided on a different look; it was just hair, and it would grow back. Mrs. Doherty snorted and shook her head. She grumbled out loud why Rade was so headstrong and added that she got the attribute from her father. She hadn't concluded her loud musings before Mr. Doherty asked from the door what he had done this time.

Rade greeted her father, and the two women

chorused that he had done nothing. He complimented her on her lovely dress and his wife corrected him and told him what Rade was wearing was a Kaftan. He nodded, and Rade shook her head in amazement at her mom before thanking her dad.

"Breakfast is ready to be served," Mrs. Doherty said. "Then let's go eat," her husband replied, entwining his fingers with his wife's as they walked over to the dining room.

Rade asked if she could be excused to make a quick phone call and her mom promptly protested. She suggested Rade eat first then make her calls, as she knew it would eventually turn out to be.

"Let her be, Ju," Mr. Doherty said.

Mrs. Doherty protested and asked if she didn't have a right to talk anymore as all her husband did these days was take sides with Rade. She went on to try and pressure her husband into admitting that their daughter hardly came to the house except she was in dire need of something she couldn't ask for over the intercom. Rade and her father shook their heads in unison, as her mother continued to list all the likely events that could bring Rade to the main house.

Rade reassured her mom she loved being with

her and explained her workload was heavy and that when she got back from work, sometimes really late, all she wanted to do was sleep.

She understood; it was just strange seeing that she had missed having her daughter around all these years and now that she was finally home, they hardly got to see. She admitted that she occasionally felt guilty about roping her into a job she hadn't really wanted, but they knew she was capable.

"Don't we?" Mrs. Doherty said looking over at her husband, who in turn smiled and gave a reluctant nod. She knew her mom trusted her wholly and had much faith in her but her father was another matter, he was still skeptical, and quick to ask if she was making any headway.

Mrs. Doherty passed a comment on her non-existent social life and asked after her only friend, Maimuna.

"She travelled to Jos; I was going to make a quick call to find out if she is back. But you don't allow calls on the dining table."

Her father excused her, and her mom fell in line.

"Run along then and come over to the table immediately you're through."

"Yes ma'am," Rade replied giving a mock salute and hurrying over to the patio to make her call. As she punched the numbers to her friend's house phone, her thoughts were on Maimuna, her childhood friend. They had been inseparable all through crèche, kindergarten, preparatory and half term of the first year of primary school before Rade left for England. They had both retained memories of each other, and she was the only friend Rade had reconnected with via a social network group. Maimuna dazzled Rade who was rarely dazzled. She was quite bright and had the most exquisite features Rade had ever seen in another human being. She was a beautiful woman; it was almost painful to look at her. She was also very restless but with an endearing nature that attracted people to her as if her beauty wasn't enough.

At the fourth ring, Aunt Asabe, Maimuna's aunt answered the phone, and they exchanged pleasantries. The aunt told Rade she had been happy to see Maimuna go out a little while ago, as she would never get what she wanted to do done with Maimuna around. Ironically, now she couldn't wait for her to return home because she had forgotten her mobile phone behind and called her from another line, asking her to answer all her calls, which she had been doing all afternoon.

Aunty Asabe ended their conversation saying, "You know, Maimuna is what you can call a necessary evil when she's around and tiring you out with her antics, you just want some respite, but when she's away, the whole place is quiet, and you're missing her."

Rade agreed and was still smiling to herself as she made her way back to the breakfast table with her parents.

Aunty Asabe reminded Rade of her Aunt Jo. She missed her terribly, for the years they'd lived together; they had never been apart for more than a few weeks.

Joan's husband, a diplomat, had died leaving her with three children. It had been quite difficult losing a husband who had sheltered her and provided for all the family's needs. Rade had been certain her aunty would send her back to Nigeria or have her parents enrol her in a boarding school. Having to cater for three children in a middle class environ in London where she hardly knew anyone was difficult enough and the added responsibility of a ward wasn't an easy one even though her parents had always sent money for her upkeep.

Aunty Jo, as Rade fondly called her, had been determined to have her stay. She had a very close relationship with her cousins, and her aunt regarded her as her youngest daughter. She and her female cousin were closer than she and her own sister could ever hope to be. Aunty Jo's eldest daughter left for America with her husband after their marriage, and her eldest son was also married.

She had always asked her aunt why she wouldn't remarry, but no man could hold a torch to her late husband it seemed. The last time she spoke with her aunt, she had tried her best to sound happy, but Rade knew she was very lonely; her children, Rade inclusive, whom she had given her life for had all left the nest to live their own lives. Her eldest son lived in North London with his Italian wife and two sons whom Aunt Jo adored. Aunt Jo's daughter-in-law liked her and wouldn't have minded a closer relationship, but Aunt Jo liked to think of herself as being independent and hardly went to visit except when she wanted to see her grandchildren or when they came over to visit with her.

Now with Rade gone, she didn't know how to bridge the gap she had created without it being too obvious she was lonely and would appreciate a more cordial relationship with her daughter-in-law after all.

Maimuna's aunty was widowed too; her mom was Aunt Asabe's younger sister. Maimuna's parents were divorced and both remarried. Her mother hadn't wanted interference in her new life with her new husband. Her father had been willing to have her stay with him since his new wife didn't mind, but Maimuna had decided against it. She had asked if her aunt whom she had always admired as a child, would have her, Asabe took her in with open arms.

"How is Maimuna?" Her father asked as she came into view.

"She's alright, I've been on the phone with Aunty Asabe all this time though." She helped herself to one sausage and scrambled eggs.

"This is nice," Rade said.

"I knew you'd like it; we're having proper English breakfast because of you; here have some baked beans." Mrs. Doherty said, passing her the dish.

"Is that all you are having?" She asked after her daughter had helped herself to a small portion.

"Yes," she replied, ignoring the toast bread.

"Don't tell me you're still on this weight loss thing; you're obsessed with your figure; you're almost skinny except for your bust."

"Oh, mom!" Rade said, "I'm not skinny by any standards except yours; I am a size six, and I'm very fit and healthy, though I do agree with you about my bust, no matter how much weight I lose, nothing gives in around that upper region."

Mrs. Doherty looked over at her husband, and asked if he was listening to his daughter; she reminded Rade that her generous bosom was an asset, and asked her how she thought she had managed to keep her father happy and satisfied all these years.

Rade grimaced and covered her ears, asking her mom to spare her the details and pleaded with her dad to rescue her.

"This is bordering on harassment; dad help me!"

He chuckled and settled his cutlery gently on the plate and listened to the interesting conversation between his wife and daughter. Now his daughter could encounter first hand what he had been enjoying by himself all these years.

He loved it and couldn't keep the smirk off his face until his wife asked him to intervene. He had to tell Rade she should be grateful she was a beautiful woman. He patted his daughter's hand and told his wife he was quite sure Rade was well aware of the obvious fact. Rade chuckled at her mom's expression.

Mrs. Doherty didn't understand her daughter's favourite mantra which was "I have the tendency to be fat."

"I don't understand this present generation's

obsession with body image. What is so bad about being fat; is it a crime? What happened to character and inner beauty?"

"Mom, fat people are usually unhealthy, and that's the problem I have with it. If you can show me a fat, healthy person, then no problem. I, personally, do not like fat and it's my prerogative to choose how I look; to each her own."

"You sound so ignorant and pompous! Is this why you starve yourself? I sincerely hope you don't get anorexia. I never had any issues with my weight as a young girl; I was plump but very comfortable with my appearance, and I had quite a number of admirers," she added, glancing coyly at her husband who stared back at her trying very much to keep a straight face to no avail. "It doesn't mean I was overweight. You, my dear, can never be overweight; it's even the other way round with you; your body weight isn't even proportional to your height."

Rade admitted defeat and reassured her mother she wasn't starving herself, that there was no chance she could ever be anorexic. So for full effect, she added another sausage and baked beans to her plate.

"Good," her mom said triumphantly, smiling at her daughter and buttering a piece of toast for her.

"So how's it going at Doherty's?" Her father asked.

"Not too stressful I hope?"

She hesitated before replying that everything was going well and gave him a brief update on the progress they were making and promised he'd get a full report at the end of the month.

Her mother winked at her when he said he was sure she was on top of everything and that he was just expressing concern.

She decided to take the plunge and mentioned to him that they were in the process of advertising for some new positions. She mentioned some of the open positions and left the most sensitive one for last. "Designs and Production."

Her father leaned forward in his chair. He asked her to tread with caution, reminding her that the head of that vital department was one of their oldest staff.

She explained why they would have to let him go or transfer him to another department better suited for him, such as Administration. Their fabric designs in recent years were boring and outdated. They seemed almost caught up in time as they churned out the same old designs season after season. She explained to her father that they needed to be more ingenious and creative to stay in business. They had already lost a few key wholesale customers, and a recent market survey had revealed what they lacked: newer, fresher designs. She reiterated an obvious fact, the partial ban on the importation of textile into the country and how it had created a huge market for them; a market which they sadly weren't impacting. They should, ideally be controlling a significant share of the textile market in Nigeria.

Mr. Doherty responded that running a business like theirs wasn't easy. They had faced many challenges over the years, some of which included getting raw materials. The cost of transportation from the cotton mills in the north, the wear and tear on the trucks due to bad roads, the years of poor electrical power supply, a surge in their overhead costs as they relied on generators, and the running costs of maintaining their equipment which led to the shutting down of some mills. It was a miracle they were still in business. He was hopeful that the new government would initiate a lot of change in the industry and create an enabling environment, but it had been a long journey to where they were.

She assured him she was not criticising in any way, Doherty Textile was a reputable brand, and there were reasons for that. The challenges they faced were evident, but if they were in business to be in business and not just to be a monument, they had to give it their best shot. She also pointed out that he had an emotional attachment to DT but that he couldn't keep milking his other investments to keep her afloat; Doherty Textile has to be able to stand for herself. She reemphasised the need for a good pattern designer to replace Mr. Akintoye and head that critical department. It was the core of everything they did, adding that if Mr. Akintoye couldn't come to terms with a transfer to another department, they'd have to let him go. Most of the staff employed emotional blackmail because they had been with the company for long; it almost seemed like they thought it was their birthright and could get away with being incompetent. Shortly after she came on board, one of the first things Rade had done was to research the salary structure in the industry and was pleased to discover they paid their staff quite well and even after the embezzlement, no one had been laid off, and also that the salary cut proposal was never adopted. They were overstaffed. They had some exceptionally competent people, but the lazy ones were just as extreme. She was convinced a few key people were aware of the previous Managing Director's shenanigans, but they had a resilient allegiance to one another, especially the older staff. It was a hard coterie to break, but she was learning quickly.

She had decided to hire an auditing firm after deliberations with her key team members who were for and against the proposition. She dismissed the previous firm her father had hired because they hadn't come up with any findings she wouldn't have deduced herself. They had been auditing the company's account for years and had become part of the system in her opinion. They required unbiased Accountants to get to the bottom of all the rut, give them a realistic position of their current financial status and future forecast. Mr. Doherty nodded his head in affirmation. "Excellent Rade! Please keep up the good work my dear."

"Thanks, dad," she replied with a smile.

"Now that's enough!" Rade's mom interjected, "it's a weekend, and we are having breakfast; please let us take a break from any further business discussions." Rade and her father consented.

Her father looked at her intensely and asked, "What happened to your hair or are you wearing a wig?"

"I'm surprised you noticed," Rade replied, "it's my hair, I just had it cut yesterday."

"Why?" He asked, and Rade smiled at the expression on her mother's face and filled them in on the edited version of what had transpired at the salon the previous day.

"Rade, you really should come over and eat with us at the weekends; it is so refreshing to have you on the table."

"I will, mom, I promise, it'll give you the opportunity to feed me well and fatten me up."

She went back to her apartment to do some work, ate a salad for lunch and took a siesta a couple of hours later. The rest of the evening was spent discussing with her mom about her flower business and general chitchat, which her mom enjoyed. Maimuna called at dinnertime.

"Was Jos cold or what? The weather in this country is the very definition of unpredictable."

Rade smiled, "weather aside, did you get up to anything interesting, and did you go shopping?"

"Ah! Yes; I got you a lovely leather purse and my kind of slippers you like."

The girls chatted until Rade mentioned she had a surprise for her.

"What is it; did you meet someone?"

"No!" Rade said, "I'll come and see you after Church tomorrow," she chuckled when she heard her friend's sigh of disappointment. Maimuna hated suspense.

"It's not anything big," she reassured her and hung up before Maimuna started pressuring her for more information.

She had dinner with her parents; then listened to music in her chalet until she drifted off into a restful sleep.

Rade left for Church with her parents the following morning. The Church service was different from what she was used to in a good way, but too long in her opinion and after the service, Rade was introduced to many people, as it had been since her arrival; many of the names she forgot right in the middle of the introduction.

"He is such a handsome young man, don't you think so Rade?"

"What?" She replied when she realised her mother had been talking to her? "Who is?"

"Mrs. Olaniyan's son, the one who just returned home from England like you."

"Oh him! He's alright." Rade replied, and quickly changed the subject before her mother pursued her new interest in matchmaking. She reminded her father she was stopping by at Maimuna's place and assured him she would find her way back home.

They waved good-bye as she alighted at Maimuna's and shook her head in amazement as her mother blew kisses at her, and her father drove off. Her mom was a trip! Rade had to laugh, thinking ironically that she couldn't recall her parents dropping her off anywhere as a child but are doing so now that she was an adult. Her mom loved driving with her dad on Sundays to and from Church as she imagined they were young again and cruising through the city streets.

As she entered through the gates, Maimuna's tall figure appeared in the doorway.

"Rade!" Maimuna exclaimed. "What happened to your hair?"

"Surprise, surprise," Rade answered.

She craned her neck to give her friend a peck on the cheek, and her nostrils filled with the familiar scent of Maimuna's blend of Arabian oud oils. Her hair had been released from its usual ponytail, and it fell in silky waves down her shoulders.

"What got into you? Though I must say, it does suit you; it's just that you look so different," she stated in her slightly accented English.

They walked into the house as Rade gave a detailed version of Friday's happenings at the hairdresser's.

"That girl sounds like a real piece of work."

"Goodness! He was all over her like a bad rash, and you know Maimuna, I've seen the guy before, but I can't figure out where for the life of me but I remember that face."

"Don't tell me you are eyeing someone else's man.

It's unlike you girl."

"You bet it is, and as you know, I like my men very dark, this one's fair skinned and obviously into badly behaved girls."

Maimuna guffawed, "Is he good looking?"

"He's alright I guess, but moving on, tell me all about your trip, and where's Aunt Asabe?"

Maimuna knew the former subject was off for discussion for the meantime and started to fill her friend in on her trip.

"You have to come with me to Jos on my next trip; we can go mountain climbing, the rock formation there is amazing. I just love it there."

Maimuna continued to regale her with beautiful stories of Jos for the rest of the visit.

Rade returned home, thinking it would be nice to visit Jos if she could ever find the time. After a bath and while applying her night cream, she remembered she had to call Phil.

Phil was Rade's best friend in London and just thinking about him made her happy. Her friends didn't understand her aversion to fair skinned men; a few didn't realise Africans had different skin tones until they compared hers with others and realised she was several hues paler than most. It was silly and quite shallow they said, and she agreed with them. She always joked that perhaps, a fair skinned person had broken her heart in her former life, which may be why she liked really dark men. She had never considered dating a Caucasian even though her few female friends and most of her many acquaintances were white. She wasn't flattered when Phil started asking her out.

He was her boss' friend, and from the day he met her, he was determined to get through to her. The fact that Phil had a reputation as a womaniser made Rade more determined to keep him at arm's length.

Phil loved a challenge; he persisted in his sending flowers and humorous messages for several months before Rade went out on a date with him. Phil always teased that it was the biggest mistake she ever made. That evening of their first date saw her laughing until her sides ached. For an English man, Phil had a wicked sense of humour.

He entertained her with one outrageous story after the other, few of which she was convinced were untrue; plied her with food and the best wine the Blue Elephant Restaurant reserved for special guests; then he took her home and bid her good night with flourish. The next six months they had dated was like a roller coaster ride much to a few people's shock because Phil who couldn't commit himself to a woman was actually seeing someone steadily, and Rade who was such a "nice girl" was dating a crazy womaniser.

They painted the town red, went on impromptu weekend trips to attend Paris fashion week and its likes, and actually had a great time together until Rade broke it off. She liked Phil a lot and had enjoyed being with him, but it was all too much; he left her feeling drained, and it had been extremely difficult to explain in few or many words how she felt. He freaked her out further by asking her to marry him soon after they broke up.

Phil came from an Aristocratic English family with old money, and he was naturally the black sheep. All the girls he dated or had flings with were mostly weird ones that would shock his family. He drove the latest model Porsche Cayenne and lived in the penthouse of an ultramodern apartment building, which he had decided on a whim to have decorated baroque style.

"You just choose anyone that fits a certain profile to help you destroy the thin ice between you and your family, and I refuse to be used for something so petty," Rade told him severally. But Phil would just shrug his shoulders and act like he didn't know what she was talking about.

The first time she had gone with him to his

parent's house for dinner, she was quite surprised to discover that they were more uptight than she had heard, and it was quite difficult to believe Phil came from that family. She sort of understood why he wanted to be different, albeit in an over the top manner. They all acted freakishly alike and did things in synchrony; Phil had held her hand almost all through the evening to the disapproval of his mother and sister.

A hot argument ensued between him and his parents when his mother casually asked if he was in a serious relationship and when he was going to settle down. He asked her not to ask such questions at the dinner table in front of a guest, and his sister had retorted, "what better time to ask; we never see you anyway, besides she can't be a guest since you've been holding her hand since you arrived."

Rade was squirming uncomfortably. The tightlipped argument heated up and they'd stormed out of the house soon after, dinner ruined for everyone especially Rade who hated scenes and had wished she could be teleported from the dinner table.

The two argued, like other times, over inter-racial relationships and marriages, his parents and everything possible that night.

They remained close, and people still found it hard to believe they had become just friends, but it was hard not to be friends with Phil, he was a genuinely nice person, a reliable friend, and more so it was hard to resist his charm. He was dating a Japanese girl before Rade left for Nigeria.

She would never forget how amazed he was when she told him she was leaving for Lagos; he looked as though she had said she was travelling to Mars.

"So what happens to me when you leave?" He asked clutching at his heart and falling to a heap on the floor.

She kicked him playfully in the ribs.

"Mr. theatrical," she replied and enveloped him in a hug.

A day before she left, Phil threw her a send-off party in his infamous South Kensington flat. It was a lovely party even though all the girls had ended up crying. She missed him and her colleagues at work terribly. Phil contacted her every other day, and during their last conversation, he had expressed his displeasure at her lack of communication. She pledged to do better, and he let her off with a warning.

She went to bed thinking of the wonderful life she had in London.

The week was a very busy one for Rade, she settled with her staff with smiles, and the tension of the previous week had disappeared with the weekend. By mid-day Rade told herself it would be a beautiful week, her workload was heavy, but she was making headway.

She was just getting in from her lunch break when Maimuna called to inform her about her cousin's party coming up that Wednesday which was two days away.

"Really; who throws a party on a weekday,' Rade asked.

"Many people I assure you, but this isn't exactly a party; it's his birthday, so everyone's just coming over after work to eat free dinner, catch up and go home."

"Are you catering?" Rade asked.

Maimuna was a good cook so she sometimes catered at small gatherings for family and friends when she could find the time. Maimuna said she wasn't and added that she couldn't hold a torch to Simi, the girl that would be. Rade had to ask her friend if she was supposed to automatically know who this Simi that outshined her in the culinary department was.

Maimuna chuckled and said she had been meaning to tell Rade something important. "You know the couple you told me about, the one you met at the hairdresser's?"

"I didn't meet them," Rade injected.

"Whatever," Maimuna answered dismissively. "From the description you gave, I may be wrong, but I have a hunch it's Zachary and Simi. It just occurred to me that's where she makes her hair. I've been wanting to introduce you; she's a great Chef, an amazing menu designer and event planner; as a matter of fact, we are second cousins."

"Good for you," Rade butted in, and the two girls burst into laughter.

"Those two are inseparable," Maimuna added.

"So, basically it means that bad-tempered lady will be there, hopefully, she doesn't spread her attitude through the food."

"Tut tut Rade! Simi isn't like that at all; your story is actually surprising because she's the sweetest person I know, but maybe like you, she woke up on the wrong side of the bed."

Rade was amazed at how Maimuna was able to maintain a close relationship with her extended family; she kept tabs on everyone and somehow knew what was going on with one distant cousin, nephew or niece.

They chatted for a while, and she asked what she could get Buba whom she had only met once, and chatted with briefly.

Maimuna told her not to bother her pretty head but if she liked she could bring a bottle of wine or whatever she thought appropriate.

Chapter Four

As Rade got ready for work on Wednesday, she had a niggling feeling she was forgetting something but the harder she tried to jostle her memory, the more elusive it became; there were no reminders on her phone, so she let it be.

She wore a pristine waist shirt with big crystal buttons under her pinstriped jacket; her feet were encased in a high-heel patent, leather court shoes and the skirt which ended above her knees showed off her well-toned legs.

After office hours, she headed to Church for a mid-week service her mom had been hounding her to attend. As the vicar, in his closing speech, mentioned an incident that happened at his friend's 60th birthday, Rade remembered Buba's party!

That was what she had been trying to remember

all morning. It was almost 8.30pm by the time she got into her car and headed to the neighbourhood wine shop. They stocked an impressive collection. She was happy with her purchase and reached for her phone to discover she had two missed calls from Maimuna. It was well after nine o'clock by the time she turned into the street that led to her destination.

She groaned in dismay as she drove towards Buba's house which wasn't too far from Maimuna's, there were cars double parked from the gate's entrance down to the end of the road, so she had to drive a little distance before she found a space for hers. She wished she had asked the driver to at least drop her off; he would have been the one to deal with parking.

She switched on the inner lights and ran a comb lightly through her hair, powdered her nose and applied fresh lipstick. She dabbed a little perfume oil behind her ears, laid her jacket neatly on the back seat of the car, then unbuttoned the top buttons of her shirt.

She checked to make sure the car was locked, and as she set out and round the car, she came in contact with an enormous Alsatian dog.

"Good God!" Rade muttered, staring in dismay that soon turned to alarm when she noticed another two approaching. She was terrified of dogs and wondered who owned such ferocious looking dogs and allowed them to roam freely. She was confused and frightened as the dog glowered and growled at her but soon after, eyed her disinterestedly and walked away.

"Show no fear," she recited in her heart, clenching her sweaty palms as she straightened up and tried to walk as nonchalantly as she could as the other two trotted past her hurrying after their obvious leader in the opposite direction.

Her shoes didn't help matters, as they made tapping noises on the cobblestone floor of the quiet street and she felt their presence more than anything else as she hurried towards Buba's gate, and took a glance over her shoulder to confirm her suspicion that the dogs had decided to follow her. It must be the tapping sound of her heels that had aroused their interest in her again, she thought. The dogs were obviously enjoying themselves, tongues lolling out, and eyes gleaming with excitement as they took a leisurely pace after Rade. She was done pretending she was unafraid and took to her heels, her heart pounding heavily in her chest, and as she dashed in to the half-opened gate, she collided painfully into someone.

She felt something cold spill on her as her brain

partly registered the pain in her chest from the painful collision, but it didn't deter her from running behind the person whom she had bumped into. She peered anxiously over the shoulder of the man whom she had made a human shield and watched as the dogs arrived one after the other and halted in front of the man.

The man's puzzled expression turned to understanding when he saw the dogs, and he gently nudged the gate close after man and beast had engaged in a brief staredown, and the dogs undecided on what to do barked in protest at him for interrupting their game. Just then a sharp whistle rent the air and the dogs turned and ran leisurely back in its direction.

"It's all right now," the man said to the terrified Rade over his shoulder.

"Thank you," Rade said breathlessly, and looked down at her damp shirt in irritation; a mixture of the cold liquid that had spilt on her and her sweat. "Sorry about that. Are you okay?" He asked, pulling her arm gently and moving her away from the shards of glass on the ground that had once been a whole glass in his hand.

"It's all right," Rade replied, "I should be the one apologising, and I'll be okay in a minute," she looked up and met the amused expression on the man's face and groaned.

"Not him again!" She said to herself, "what did Maimuna say his name was? It began with a 'Z', her stalker."

"You seem to get into trouble a lot," he said This brought Rade up angrily.

"I beg your pardon? Just because we've encountered each other twice in not very flattering circumstances doesn't mean you know the story of my life."

"That's true," he replied with a smile, which annoyed Rade even more. "Well, I know your name is Rade, and you work at Doherty's, and I've seen you once before the time at the hairdresser's."

Her eyebrows shot up inquiringly.

"At the bank," he continued. "I think you came to cash a personal cheque because you lost your bank debit card but you forgot your cheque book, and you were making a little fuss about the long process..."

"I remember quite well," Rade cut in as he made to continue.

Rade remembered the bank day in question well; she hadn't envisaged any delays and was in a hurry to do some shopping with her aunt who was still around at the time but was flying back to London later that evening. She wondered why the man kept seeing her at her worse.

He introduced himself as Zachary Bello and stretched out his hand. Rade placed her much smaller one in his reluctantly for a handshake and retrieved it quickly.

He told her she was a bit late and that Maimuna had been expecting her, and so had everyone else. She wondered out loud who everyone else was and he responded that everyone seemed to have heard about her one way or the other from Maimuna and they were dying to meet her.

Rade looked down at her blouse again and felt like stamping her feet. She couldn't go in like that.

"Don't worry," he said reading her expression, "it will dry very soon; you're lucky it's water. I'll go get Maimuna for you."

"I'll be grateful," Rade replied and felt embarrassed at her dependence on him.

She rubbed her temples wincing a little, and saw the dogs in her mind's eye again and took a deep breath.

"Oh dear!" Maimuna said smiling, and Rade knew Zachary had filled her in about what happened.

She eyed him accusingly, and he raised his hands in defence.

"I had to explain to her why you are outside and why you bumped into me."

Maimuna went over to her friend and pecked her

on both cheeks.

"I'm sorry about the chase, girl. Who leaves three big dogs unattended; hope you are okay though?" She asked.

She knew Rade was terrified of dogs. Rade affirmed she was and apologised for being late, and explained to her friend that she actually forgot about the party.

She remembered she had left the bottle of wine in the car which was probably a good thing as she would have definitely dropped it in fright with all the drama that had ensued.

Maimuna assured her they would get it later and slipped off the scarf she had over her shoulders and draped it over Rade's shirt. She entwined their arms and pulled her through the doors excitedly. Maimuna's familiar heady scent filled Rade's nostrils, and she felt herself begin to relax as Zachary followed behind, while admiring Rade's legs.

The introductions began immediately; the first two she was introduced to were people she had gone to nursery school with before she left Nigeria, and she was still trying unsuccessfully to remember their faces as children, and though she was doubtful, they reassured her they remembered her well.

Maimuna got Rade some food, and as she salivated, she remembered she hadn't eaten all day, and for once she didn't think of calories but tucked heartily into the meal.

She felt eyes on her and looked up to meet Zachary's dark eyes; he nodded his head in greeting from across the room, and she gave a stiff smile in return. She returned to her food with less gusto and wondered why he made her feel so self-conscious. She circled round, paying very little attention to the conversations but smiled and nodded when necessary; she wished Buba a happy birthday and for the first time got into a lengthy conversation with him, and while he was laughing over something she said, Zachary appeared beside him. "Sorry, Buba, I have to break your obviously interesting conversation; I have to borrow you for a few seconds."

Buba excused himself reluctantly and went with Zachary. Rade had a feeling he had done it deliberately as he returned by himself to explain there was something Buba needed to attend to. Rade made to walk away, but he placed a restraining hand on her arm. He asked why she was leaving and if she thought he wasn't good enough company. She was at a loss for words, and he took her silence for consent and went on to reassure her that he'd often been told he was a great company, so she was in safe hands until Buba returned.

She replied that all the people who had told him this were liars as she was bored already.

He grinned broadly and stared at her in appreciation. Rade was used to scrutiny, but this one made her feel like a little girl.

"What's the real colour of your eyes?" He asked, and she was once again at a loss for words. "You're obviously wearing contact lenses; aren't you?"

She shook her head in bewilderment. "You're so…" She spluttered to the end.

"Nosy, forward," he added, with a smile.

"That would be putting it mildly," she replied, "impudent would be more apt. How does the colour of my eyes matter to your wellbeing?"

"I'm just trying to make conversation," he replied, "the hazel suit you but I'm assuming they are not real and trying to imagine if you'd still look as interesting without them."

She was stunned. She advised that he try and keep his opinions to himself, adding that not every random thought that came to his head should be verbalised, but if he were so pressed to speak, perhaps his lady friend would humour him. He replied that he didn't have a lady friend, as Rade excused herself and brushed past him, wondering how a person could be so impossible. Buba met her halfway and thanked her for the impressive bottle of wine. Maimuna had obviously gone to get it from the car.

"What's the matter?" He asked noticing her set expression, "don't tell me Zach's annoyed you."

"I'm sorry, but your cousin is a pain in the neck."

Buba chuckled, "I apologise on his behalf, but Zachis really cool; he's a good conservationist and greatcompany, perhaps he's just trying to be mischievous."

That was all the excuse Buba could come up with.

"It's alright," she said smiling at him, "you're obviously part of the fan club he mentioned."

Buba responded with a hearty laugh, and she excused herself to go return a phone call, explaining it was an international call when Buba suggested she use his fixed line in the other living room. He assured her it was even cheaper and brushed aside all her excuses, and as he steered her toward the living room, someone beckoned to him, and she assured him she would find her way.

She opened the connecting door and found her way into the living room. Rade was immediately drawn to the paintings that lined the wall; she studied them and after having her fill picked up the receiver and dialled Phil's number. His voice always lifted her spirits. "How is my best girl?" She heard something in his voice and asked why he sounded dreary. He replied that his poor heart was still bleeding since she left him.

"You crazy boy," she replied laughing and filling him in after he asked what was news with her.

"Have you met any Nigerian man you like? You're so picky, it's irritating."

"Don't be mean, Phil! But you can rest assured I haven't. I'm here for work, and I have no intentions of getting involved with anyone; the men here are not my type anyway, too egotistical."

"Hmmmn; I don't have any first-hand experience to concur or disagree with your latter statement, but I do agree that I don't see you settling with a Nigerian man. You're a strange one, somewhat spoilt and you do need someone who can indulge you and let you have your way occasionally. I'll be thrilled when you meet someone who'll sweep you off your feet seeing I couldn't do it my self."

"Phil is this what you really think of me; a spoilt woman that needs to be indulged. I guess this is the price a woman pays for knowing what she wants. When a man is aggressive and egotistical, he's called self-assured; when he's a relationship-phobic, such as you, he is a charming playboy; this double standard infuriates me."

"Ah! There you go Rade. I've missed you! These arguments, the whole mental stimulation I get from our verbal sparring," he replied as they both laughed. "And by the way, I've broken up with Susana."

"Oh, not again, Phil! At least have the decency to sound remorseful," Rade said, remembering Phil's Japanese girlfriend. They hadn't really gotten along because the girl didn't understand Phil and Rade's closeness. She knew their story but still didn't believe they had gone on to be just good friends and were possessive about each other as good friends would be.

She was silent for a little while, and he asked if she was still there. Talking with Phil made her miss her usual routine.

"I'm with this gorgeous Kenyan girl; she's fascinating to look at, and not to sound at all like I'm stereotyping, she is a true African beauty, long gazelle-like limbs, slim neck, polished dark skin and brilliant white teeth. I've told her all about you, and she's dying to meet you."

She asked rhetorically if he thought the description he just gave was that of true African beauty and asked when he would stop doing crazy things just to irk his family. Who next; an Arab? It was obvious he was determined to date a woman from every race. She added that he needed to grow up.

"Do I sense a tinge of jealousy there?" He responded good-humoredly. "And I'm surprised you don't know I've gone out with a Lebanese girl before; it was great! Her parents just hated my guts," he said with an amused chuckle, and she couldn't help the reluctant chuckle that escaped her.

"What's her name? Your new girlfriend."

"Kenyatta," he said, "nice name and from Kenya too," their chuckles morphed into laughter, and Rade wiped a tear that had escaped from one eye, imagining the smirk on her friend's face; he was full of it!

Rade enquired if he had been going to Church.

"Oh, not again," Phil groaned. He still couldn't fathom how Rade could be such a believer. They both recalled how much stress she would go through during the week begging him to come to Church with her, on Sunday mornings she would go over to his flat and leave her finger on the buzzer before he opened the door.

While dressing, he would grumble and call her names, yet after the service he would tell her it wasn't so bad after all. The following week the ordeal of dragging him to Church would start all over; even the doorman of his apartment building had come to know their routine.

"I go occasionally, but it's not fun without you."

"That's nice," Rade replied, thinking it was a good thing he still remembered to go.

She reminded him it was important to go to Church because he would hear God's word, build his faith and grow spiritually, and of course, fellowship with other believers...

As she made to continue, Phil cut in and begged her not to get started and assured her he still had the Post-It by his dresser where she had written **"Forsake not the gathering of one another. Phil go to Church,"** with a big smiley for added effect.

Rade smiled and decided to let him be.

He promised he would look into his schedule and see how soon he could come to visit her. Rade shrieked, that would be wonderful, and the thought of him in Lagos was putting her in a darn good mood already; he would be a much-needed breath of fresh air, she thought.

Rade felt the door to the living room open as the mingled sounds of voices, music and clinking glasses wafted in from the other room, but there was silence again as the door shut, so she didn't bother checking if anyone had come in.

He asked where she was as he had called her a few minutes before their conversation.

"I'm out at a friends party, which is why I didn't

video call you."

"What! And you've been making me feel sorry for you, telling me you've been working hard and all. Isn't it rude that you're making a long phone call when you're out; where are your manners girl?"

Rade concurred and said her goodbye.

"I miss you, sweet pea."

"I miss you too, darling; I'll talk to you soon," Rade replied.

She was still smiling as she replaced the receiver. Just talking to Phil made her happy, even though he was a handful. As she made to get up, she realised she wasn't alone.

"Are you stalking me?" She asked Zach matter of factly.

"I came in here to have some peace and quiet; I didn't expect to find anybody in here. I was surprised to hear your voice, albeit in more pleasant tones," he answered, "besides I didn't want to startle you which is why I was quiet," he added.

She stared at him for a few minutes and got up to go. "Buba said it was okay to come in here and make a phone call."

Zach shrugged his shoulders and smiled.

"Why would you think I'm stalking you?"

"I don't know; you tell me." She responded with a questioning smile and walked out, the music and noise hitting her as she entered the other room.

After seeking Maimuna out who reprimanded her for being anti-social, she mingled for a while until she was ready to leave. She slipped off the scarf from her shoulders and handed it back to Maimuna with a "thank you." Her shirt had long dried.

Rade waited for Maimuna by the door, and it was then she noticed the girl; she had scarcely seen her all evening. She was standing in between Zach and Buba, and Rade noted that she was really pretty. She was wearing brown pants and a matching top with impossibly high spindle heeled shoes; it brought her closer to Zach's height.

Rade wondered how she could have catered in such shoes. Her mom always teased her about her heels; she wished she was here to see Zach's girlfriend's shoes. She was talking, and both men were listening with rapt attention. She wondered how tall Zachary was, realising he wasn't as tall as she first imagined, maybe an inch below six feet or six feet at the most. But he was quite self-assured, well built without the ripping muscles of the heroes in some romance novels Rade hated. He was easy on the eyes, a smart dresser if she could judge by two encounters. Someone you would see and immediately want to meet, she noted, observing him through her lashes.

Rade caught herself mid-way and chided her self for even thinking about him; he wasn't her type anyway, too smug and his buttercream complexion wasn't for her. His complexion and the texture of his hair gave a hint to the fact that he was probably of mixed race. She remembered now that if he was related to Maimuna, then he was Fulani, which explained his features. She noticed that he and his girlfriend looked alike. She knew men like him, ones that would date only women that looked a certain way and fit a certain profile. How disappointing. She wondered if she was a hypocrite. Wasn't it a fact that she had in the past and was currently dismissing someone because of the shade of their skin colour; some sort of profiling on her part too.

Zach was aware of the appraisal he and Simi were getting and hoped he met up to her approval. She probably thought he was a jerk.

She had a good figure, slim and well toned, though he liked tall girls, he knew he was interested in getting to know this one.

Simi jabbed her elbow into his side.

"Zach you haven't been listening to a word I have been saying. What are you looking at?" Her eyes scanned the room quickly until her eyes met Rade's, both girls looked away immediately, and Simi muttered, "Oh, Zachary!"

"What?" He replied with a snicker, "looking isn't a crime?"

Buba left the two and went over to meet Rade to see her out, and Maimuna joined them outside. The cousins were trying to persuade Rade to wait a few more minutes for a couple of friends who were heading her way so they could drive in convoy. Rade checked her timepiece and noticed it was almost midnight. She was quite surprised her mother who always checked her side of the house to ensure her car was in the driveway before she went to bed hadn't rung her.

"I have to go home now, I honestly didn't know it was this late; don't worry guys I'll be alright, it's a seven-minute drive home at the most, and the streets are well lit."

Buba shrugged admitting defeat and Rade smiled. The cousins escorted her to her car, as Maimuna teased her about being "a true Lagos girl," not only was she driving herself now, she was driving late at night. Her car had all of Buba's attention. She sped off with several promises to call when she got home.

Rade was half way when she noticed the headlights of a car behind her. It had been on her tail since she left Buba's house. She told herself it was nothing but as she went up the bridge the car followed and didn't take the chances given to overtake her. Rade stepped on the accelerator, and her Lexus leapt in delight, happy to oblige her, she kept track through her rearview mirror until she noticed that the car had pulled back.

She sped home, and as she turned into the gates that led home after taking a detour to throw whomever it was off her back, she heaved a sigh of relief but couldn't shake off the feeling that the car had been following her. She decided then she would have her driver full time and pay him overtime if she had anywhere to go late evenings. He would be glad to anyway; any opportunity to keep spying on her to feed his curiosity, and of course, office gossip. The culture of having drivers, full-time maids, nannies, etc, in Nigeria was alien to her as she had mentioned to her Assistant the previous day, but she now understood that in Lagos it wasn't necessarily a luxury; even their domestic staff had their own domestic staff. The only family that she knew closely that would beat anyone in Lagos hands down in terms of the size of their domestic staff was Phil's family. They had help for even the most minor chores.

While taking off her contact lenses, she stared at

her eyes in the mirror and wondered if Zach would still find her interesting. They were dark brown; she couldn't believe herself and shook her head to ward off the annoying thought. She remembered what he had said about not having a lady friend. "Imagine having such a beautiful girlfriend, albeit with an attitude, and denying her outrightly."

Chapter Five

The remaining week was a good one for Rade; she was excited over the fresh ideas she had for the company. Some were quite drastic; her conventional father would probably have a fit if she told him some of the unedited ideas that jumped to mind. She picked up her pen and started writing down plans in her organiser. Her former boss had always told her she was one of the best business developers he had met so now was the time to put it to test. She made a few phone calls to set up some appointments and started preparing for the meeting with her team and the other heads of department. Her mind was still in a whirlpool when Maimuna called asking what she was doing that evening; Rade told her she would just stay home and relax.

"Simisola just left the clinic," Maimuna said.

Maimuna is a Dentist. Aside from being one of the best, well-known Dentists in one of the major government hospitals, she also practises in a private Clinic.

"Who is Simisola?" Rade asked.

"Zach's sister," Maimuna replied.

"Zach has a sister also; how come I'm just hearing about her?"

"I didn't have to tell you," Maimuna said, her tone filled with amusement, "you had already met."

"You mean that girl… Is she Simi? I thought you referred to her as Amina once. That's beside the point; is she Zach's sister?" Rade rambled.

"Of course!" Maimuna replied, "why Rade; what did you think?" Maimuna burst into laughter as what Rade had assumed dawned on her.

Rade replied that nobody told her they were family and she had naturally just assumed they were a pair. She vaguely remembered Maimuna referring to them as an inseparable couple, and Maimuna responded that she meant they were quite close and always together, not inseparable in terms of a romantic relationship. She wondered why Rade couldn't see how alike they were; no one had ever missed the resemblance. Well, clearly she had.

"Simi is the female version of Zach literally," Maimuna added and admitted that sometimes she used both her names interchangeably. To close family, she was Amina but popularly called Simi. Rade rolled her eyes at her telephone.

"I didn't look at them closely enough to know if they looked alike or not," Rade replied feeling foolish.

After they hung up, Rade pondered on the clarification she had received on Zach's status, and she was nonplussed that she felt a huge relief knowing Simi was Zachary's sister.

The evening found Rade at home baking a chocolate cake she knew her mother would love. She was restless. She was having a conversation with her father in her head over the business proposal she wanted to broach to him over the weekend when the timer on her oven broke into her thoughts. She contemplated going over to her father's library to look for a book. African literature was her new thing; she never knew there were such prolific underground, African writers, not just the popular ones known internationally. She was blown away by his vast collection, which included all the genres of Nigerian literature. She had immediately started binging; reading till the early hours of the morning many times. She didn't feel like leaving her space and so decided against it.

She was lying very comfortably on her favourite chair and listening to Berna Ceppas' composition in a Cirque du Soleil compilation album, a glass of white wine in hand and complimentary blue cheese when her door buzzer went off; she groaned in protest. She ignored it and continued savouring the moment when the door buzzer went off again. She got up, thoroughly irritated and without finding out who it was on the intercom, she opened the door impatiently. The expression on her face would have looked good in a movie.

The last two people she expected to see on her doorstep were standing right there. How on earth did they get to her doorstep without anyone alerting her; she was shocked, to say the least. The three of them stared at one another until Simi took the initiative.

"Hello Rade, we know it's rude to barge in on you like this, but I would very much like to speak with you. This is as weird as it feels, and we apologise for barging in on you."

Rade was at a loss on what to do or say; she could stand there and have Simi say whatever it is she wanted to say, but instead, she ushered them in with an uncomfortable smile.

"You've got a nice place," Zachary commented.

"Thanks," she replied motioning for them to take their seats.

Her good manners went into drive, and she asked

what they would like to drink after a recital of all the drinks available; they answered in unison with Zachary stating what he wanted and Simi declining. Rade smiled inwardly as Simi eyeballed her brother.

Simi cleared her throat and started as soon as Rade returned with Zach's drink, and he excused himself to look at a sculpture on her mantlepiece after gaining her permission.

"My name is Simi; I know you are Rade. It was hard deciding if to get your number and call or text you or get your address and come over to apologise about what happened the other day at the hairdressers. I decided on the latter obviously. So the thing is, I was in a foul mood that day; granted, the stylist was inexperienced and was messing up even before you arrived, but I took it out on everybody. I apologise for my poor behaviour, and more so for making you cut your hair. It's a really small world, to think that you're good friends with our cousin."

Rade felt chastened by the apology remembering she hadn't been too quiet herself that day; she definitely wouldn't have gone out of her way to apologise if the shoe had been on the other foot. "I do apologise for the whole incident myself; everything was blown out of proportion. As for my hair, my anger, not you, made me cut it; it will grow back… in the next century, hopefully," Rade added.

The girls laughed and settled into a comfortable silence. Having them there made her nervous especially Zach, and she kept fiddling with everything her fingers came in contact with. Rade asked how they got her address and how much they had paid Maimuna for selling her out. Zach laughed, telling her Maimuna had no hand in it except innocently giving Buba her address after he enquired as casually as he could not to rouse her suspicion, and he, in turn, passed the information on to Zach.

"An extended family of organised crime; interesting!"

Simi and Zach chuckled and took a liking to Rade immediately for her sense of humour.

"We met your mom on her way out; she assured us you were in and allowed the Baba at the gate let us in before he buzzed you on the intercom. She's quite warm and very beautiful; telling her we are Maimuna's cousins helped a lot, of course."

She could definitely see her mom ushering Zach and Simi in, and would have equipped them with a map if necessary to get to her faster.

"I'll convey your compliments," Rade said with

a smile.

By the time they were leaving, she knew Simi was a Chef, and she managed a catering service company and was also a partner at a fast growing event planning company. Rade promised to get in touch with her if, by some off chance, she decided to get married in Nigeria, as she would definitely love to have an outdoor wedding provided the weather was right; she said it so seriously Zach asked when the wedding was to be, his eyes searching hers questioningly.

Rade looked away and said to Simi, "I don't know because I haven't even met the groom."

As she walked them outside, she noticed their car; it was the latest model of the E350 Mercedes. Rade was convinced without asking it was the one that had tailed her the night of Buba's party. She glanced at Zach, and their eyes met; as if reading her thoughts, he nodded his head, and she asked why with her eyes.

"I followed you home just to make sure you were okay because Maimuna was worried, though the streets are relatively safe. I could see you were getting nervous at my tail when you started speeding like someone competing at the Grand Prix, and taking detours when Maimuna had given me an idea where you lived, so I decided to pull back."

Rade had to smile at the Grande Prix dig; he definitely had a mouth on him on this one.

Simi kept asking what they were talking about when Rade thanked him for his thoughtfulness, and they said their goodbyes after promising to stay in touch.

Maimuna was right about Simi; Rade had taken a liking to her already. Zach was another issue altogether; she didn't know where to place him.

****

Two months later, Rade was in her sitting room, with crumbled pieces of paper strewn around, and her fast-growing hair was in disarray. Her pen was flying over a new sheet of paper every minute until she heard a chirp and stopped to identify the culprit. Her house phone was ringing; she allowed it ring some more hoping that the caller would give up but no such luck; at the fifth ring, she picked it up.

"Yeah!" She said, but there was no reply from the other end. "Zach is that you?" She asked. She heard the familiar chuckle and smiled. "Zach, what is it? She asked, relaxing a bit; "I'm in no mood for you now."

"What? I'm crushed," he responded.

Over the weeks, Rade, Simi and Zachary were fast becoming good friends. At their spare time, they got together at each other's, went to the movies or any other activity that caught anyone's fancy. Zachary and Simi lived together and were quite close. Simi adored her brother and told anyone who cared to listen. Their mother died while they were young. She had been a very frail Fulani woman; her husband, in turn, a tough man who didn't have much patience for his delicate wife, and the other wives he'd married didn't help matters. After their mother died, Zach's protectiveness over his younger sister amplified by several notches, and it wasn't easy living amongst wives who disliked them and half brothers and sisters who didn't care much for them either. Their father couldn't be bothered.

After secondary school, Zach had spent a year working in a friend's father's construction company much to his father's disapproval and then gone on to the university to study Architecture. Simi said that looking back and seeing how alienated they were from the family still fascinated her, but Zach was a man from the womb; he just took care of her, and still did like it was his lot in life to do so.

After she completed her secondary education, the six years as a boarding student and a close watch from Zach, who ensured she got good grades, she gained admission into the University immediately to study Food Science and Technology. Zach graduated while Simi was in her second year. Thankfully he got a job quickly, and things progressed from there, as he was determined to take care of his sister. Simi reminiscing on the days from school, told Rade that all her friends had fallen for Zach.

"He was quite a pain then," Simi said, "he was so serious you wouldn't believe he's the same person you know now; he's eased up quite a bit."

Rade smiled thinking of Zach and the fact that he was still pretty serious.

"He is quite dependable and good company too," Rade said.

"Ah! Then he wasn't," Simi replied, "I find it hard to believe he is just a few years older than me. Zach travelled to America for an extended period, and things were a bit difficult without him around to baby me, then voila, I met Dimka," she said, referring to her fiancé.

"After Zach's return, he decided to start his own

firm and asked his friend to join him later as a partner. He is a father, brother, friend all rolled in one. He can be quite annoying as expected, but I'm proud of him and will do anything for him as he has for me. Can you believe he still gives me a monthly allowance? It's ridiculous! A few people have expressed how uncanny they think our relationship is."

Simi smiled, and Rade blinked back the tears that filled her eyes.

"I've made you teary," Simi cried, and got up quickly to hug Rade.

"It's just so nice to see how close you two are."

"But you do know how bossy Zach can be, Rade? Sometimes he drives me nuts, and he says I do the same to him with my stubbornness."

"I concur with both of you," Rade said, and Simi laughed.

By the time Zach returned from America, Simi had started dating Dimka and had been waiting anxiously for Zach to meet him, but the first meeting was a disaster. He didn't like Dimka at first glance and vice-versa. Simi thought it was because Dimka, unlike many of her previous male friends, hadn't tried to patronise Zach and go all lengths to befriend him, and she told Zach that much, but he had rebuffed her allegations and didn't mince words telling her why he didn't like her boyfriend. Their feelings for each other hadn't changed much, but they attempted to be civil to one another for Simi's sake. It made her sad that her two favourite men didn't get along; she had never thought she would be with someone Zach didn't like. It was hard.

Simi told Rade that most people in their circle had said her previous relationships before Dimka had ended badly because she was always comparing her suitors to her brother. Zach's female friends weren't any better as they saw her as a threat and she always tried to distance herself from him if he was seeing someone to reassure that person that she was no trouble. Until she decided: no more! She would stay out of his business as he did hers but make it clear she was still protective of him as her brother and also as a man with a good heart whom people tend to want to take advantage of. It didn't help that Zach liked beautiful women and they usually came with baggage.

"I am hungry; do you have any food in your house?" Zach asked breaking into her thoughts.

"Zach, how can you even ask me such a question?" She asked mortified. "You live with a Chef! Besides, you're not so bad in the cooking department."

"Neither of us did any grocery shopping at the weekend. Simi is out somewhere and suggested I call you or Maimuna who unfortunately is on call and still at the hospital. So, you're my saving grace."

"Really! Tough luck, Zach; my name isn't 'Grace' and I'm certainly not in a saving mode."

He grumbled at their heartlessness and lack of empathy for a hungry man who just wanted a home cooked meal; adding that she dare not suggest he order takeout because he could have come up with that idea on his own.

Rade chuckled and told him she couldn't remember when last she had cooked a meal. She had scarcely eaten a thing in the past few days as she was up to her neck in work and wouldn't have minded someone cooking for her. Perhaps she would ask her mom to send something over; she'd like that.

"Alright then," he replied, "I'll come over and cook for both of us."

Rade smiled, "I won't get any work done with you around Zach."

"I won't disturb you," he said, "I need food, not a company."

"Touché, I guess I deserved that, though you could have fooled me," she replied.

She hadn't quite replaced the receiver on its

cradle when the doorbell rang, and she almost yelled out in protest; Zach alone was a handful, her mom on top of that made her groan. She opened the door to the smiling face of Zach.

"What's the name of the game you're playing?"

He replied with a grin. "I just saw '*My Best Friend's Wedding*' again, so I decided to try out my favourite scene at the end," he replied holding out his mobile phone.

Rade gave him a withering look as she let him in and he smiled good-naturedly back at her.

"You know that scene, don't you? The party scene at the end when Rupert Everet was speaking to Julia Roberts on the phone, but he was just around the corner …"

Rade raised her hands as he made to continue. "Zachary, I have seen '*My Best Friends Wedding*' many times, but unlike Julia Roberts, I am not amused; didn't even realise you are into chic flicks."

"Wow! We are in a prissy mood aren't we?" He commented.

"Yeah," Rade replied, "so no disturbances whatsoever, otherwise my invincible bouncers will escort you out in a flash."

"I'll get to work," he replied, striding purposefully to the kitchen after ruffling her dishevelled hair to her irritation.

She got back to her work, and there was blissful silence to her surprise until she heard the sound of pots and crockery clattering to the floor.

"Apologies!" He yelled from the kitchen, "just a minor disaster."

Rade continued her work until she heard a loud yelp; she hurried over to the kitchen and found Zach at the sink with his finger under the running tap. He had scalded himself with hot water. She cooed over him with a half smile on her lips.

"You can smile all you want, but it's not funny, make yourself useful and set the table."

She gave a mock salute and hurried to do as he bided, her stomach rumbling in hunger. She returned to pass him the mushrooms and watched in silence as he grated the cheese that would go with the perfectly done Bolognaise sauce and pasta they were having.

"You are so sweet Zachary," Rade said from the doorway.

"I know," he replied, boring into her with dark eyes.

"Conceited would be an understatement to qualify you," she said as they both laughed.

The meal was eaten in silence with an occasional sigh of contentment from Rade. She cleaned up afterwards as he made himself comfortable on her chaise lounge.

He observed the sheaf of papers strewn about and pointed out that she was overworking herself and had to learn when to take a break before she burnt herself out.

She explained that as he knew, drawing up a business plan could be difficult, and since she had too many ideas running through her head, sieving through them was becoming an arduous task as each idea was competing for attention.

When she accepted the offer to run Doherty Textiles, she had demanded they send her comprehensive status report on the business, and it wasn't pretty. Things had progressed a lot since then; there had been a lot of internal restructuring, and they were currently in the process of producing new designs, rebranding and gearing up to get back into the market. Two weeks ago, her dad had asked that she visit their electronics retail store and give him recommendations on how they could revive that arm of the family business. She had been in shock at the obsolete gadgets on display and was certain some of the televisions came without remote controls. Her first thought was that perhaps they could turn the place into an electronics museum. She wagged a warning finger at him when a laugh escaped him. So, now she had an added responsibility even though her initial instinct was to say no.

She went on to tell Zach that her father ran his businesses like charity. Maybe he'd made too much money and couldn't care less, but there was no such thing, because the rich people she knew made money, wanted to keep the money and make some more money. He seemed content with employing labour and paying them for doing nothing, and now she was the "wicked witch" who had come to ruin the free for all party. She also already had plans she was carefully considering once DT was in a good place and her contract expired. It meant that she was contemplating staying back in Nigeria, which had never been an option in the beginning. She stared back at him expectantly, and Zach said he realised her long-winded narrative was the background to what she really wanted to tell him, which was this grand plan of hers, and so she should spill. She eyeballed him but went on anyway.

"Zach, I love shopping malls; there's just something about having so many options in one location that thrills me. My friends get angry when we go shopping because no matter how big the mall is, I comb through the whole area and can be there for hours. Several weeks ago, I just got this idea of building a world-class shopping mall; one that will house the most exclusive brands and vendors, and it has stuck. I'm now trying to draw up a business plan to that effect."

"Little wonder your hair is in the state it is."

He had to go there, she thought.

"How about taking it one step at a time. I think you should complete your original obligations first, or see it to a considerable phase; then you can start thinking of doing your own thing. You have a two-year renewable contract if I'm correct?"

"Yes. But my business plan involves my father."

"Rade, I'm sure your idea is a great one but don't underestimate it. A few people have had the same idea but couldn't pull it off as there are many factors to consider which I'm sure you well know. Financing, location, property, amongst other things."

She sat up excitedly and barraged him with one thought after the other and the information that the landed property beside the one that housed the DT offices belonged to her father, and her grand plan was to show her father the business plan, gut out the building and convert it to a shopping mall.

"Sounds easy," he replied tongue in cheek.

She chided him not to be mean and had to laugh

at his comment when she thought of her father. She suspected he would not like the idea, but one could never tell; she would find the courage to broach it to him, and that was why she had to be armed with an airtight business plan.

They spent the whole evening bouncing back ideas; quite a few coming from Zach that Rade liked, and some of hers he told her to totally ditch because it won't work in this business terrain, seeing he knew the terrain better. He left promising to do some research and get back to her.

After he left, Rade went to bed feeling a lot better; it had felt good talking to Zach. She wasn't blind to the fact that she was beginning to like him a bit too much. Her body was tired, but her mind was crowded with thoughts, a blend of Zach, work and her dream shopping mall. It kept her awake till 3.00am. Then she heard the still voice in her heart, *"Thou will keep him in perfect peace, he whose mind is stayed on Him."*

The week proved to be hectic for Rade; she barely finished one meeting before it was time for another. Zach called her later in the week to give her an update.

He was recommending a brilliant Business

Developer. He claimed this person had a genius mind, drawing up bank loan proposals; his proposals got investors smacking their lips in anticipation of returns they may not be getting years to come, and of course, parting with their monies. Zach advised she set up a meeting with him as soon as she could.

"Okay, you seem to be missing something here; you do know I worked as a business developer, don't you Zach?"

"I know that, and from what I've read, you're pretty good, but you need to remove yourself from this. Let's meet up and discuss over lunch."

"Zach, I can do without lunch; I'm on something right now and don't want to leave, it will break my chain of thought."

"Stop it!" He chided, "Do you know how busy I am? Life's about finding balance."

"Please Zach, don't push, I most certainly do not have the strength for your bullying today."

"Good," he replied.

He announced that he would give her some time to round up what she was doing and meet him at a cafe close to her office. Rade's cry of protest was met with a click of the receiver.

Thirty minutes later, Zach and Rade were arguing

over what she would have for lunch. She ordered a Greek salad with no dressing.

"This is not food," he said disapprovingly.

"Typical African man," she replied.

"Whatever! Who eats a salad without dressing, at least have a vinaigrette dressing." He scrutinised her closely, "maybe you do have an eating disorder," he added.

"Please Zach, you're beginning to sound like my mom, just let me be."

"No," he replied, "someone obviously has to take care of you; you're so slim, thin now actually," he said for more emphasis, "if you continue like this, your bust is going to look awkward and too heavy for you to carry because you're losing weight everywhere except up there…" The embarrassment on Rade's face made him stop.

"You can be really mean when you want to be, Zach, but you've made your point, Mr. bossy. Why don't you order something appropriate for the underfed girl."

"That's my girl!" He said as Rade glared back at him. Their discussion ranged from the business plan to personal matters. Rade smiled inwardly at the frown on Zach's face whenever she mentioned Phil. Both men had developed wariness for one another though they had never met. The last time she had spoken to

Phil all he kept repeating was that Zach was almost taking over her life. The remaining part of the lunch date was spent with Rade cajoling Zach to take on the contract if her father agreed to her proposal.

"You are counting your chicks before the eggs have hatched. I can recommend a reputable construction firm, if it comes to that; mine doesn't have to do it."

"Why not?" She asked, "you don't like to do business with your friends?"

He just shrugged, but she pressed on, "It's either you don't believe this idea will see the light of day or you think I can't afford your services."

"I always knew you were smart," he replied with his lips twitching.

"Why? You…" She spluttered to an end and swatted him with a newspaper.

Later that evening, Rade kept smiling to herself when she remembered their conversation. That night, she added another request to her long line of supplications to God.

Chapter Six

Rade's sitting room was filled with the sound of plates, clinking glasses, music and chatter. She was impressed with her friends. She had invited them for her Church's annual three-day music fest, and they hadn't missed a day. It didn't matter that curiosity was the major propelling factor; they were having dinner at hers after the last day of the event. "I really enjoyed myself despite my initial skepticism; so many talented gospel musicians performing at the same place," Buba's friend from the office commented; she had a reputation for not mincing words.

"Rade I think your Pastor is really gorgeous but what's it with that stony-faced wife of his? She was looking suspiciously at every girl like a Pastor is part of an average girl's dream."

"Helen!" Maimuna chided, as Buba burst into laughter.

"And you know what?"

"What?" Everyone chorused and Helen smiled achieving what she enjoyed most, being the centre of attraction.

"That pious looking, music director of yours that kept running to the Pastor like he's God manifest in the flesh looks very familiar. He looks like the "predator" I saw at the nightclub last week. He was so desperate; he made a pass at almost every girl in there including me. Everyone could smell his desperation; it was pitiful!"

They all shook their heads, and Helen cried, "Why do you all shake your heads like it's impossible; why would I make up such a story? Anyway, he left with one of them dirty prostitutes that hang outside the club. The more I think about it; the more positive I am he's the one."

Buba asked if she had followed him outside and how she knew he had left with a prostitute, which drew a chuckle from Zach and protests from Helen. Rade said she didn't understand how anyone could live a double life; the pressure of trying to keep up appearances would kill her. No matter how much a person pretended, it would all unravel eventually. The People that felt the need to judge others were another matter entirely; she believed that role was reserved for God only and He is the only one that knows the heart.

"That is true," Maimuna replied, "the Bible itself says it that *there is no creature that is not manifest in his sight and that all things are naked and open before the eyes of him whom we have to do.*"

"What? Maimuna, you are becoming more and more scriptural, should we be worried?" Helen asked, and didn't agree with Rade, arguing that she disliked fake people, and thus, had the right to judge anyone who lived a double life, like the music director. She also was at the receiving end of people's judgment every day of her life.

"Judge not that you may not be judged. It's written somewhere," Simi said, and asked Helen if she was even sure he was the one and went on to tell her that she could disapprove of a person's actions, but she was in no position to judge.

Helen protested at the gang up and was sure everyone was going crazy except Zach and herself. She asked that they cut out the preaching session since they all just got back from the Church.

Buba agreed with Helen, and they all agreed to move on after Simi had decided Helen's name would now come with the preceding title "Judge Helen" to which she responded that Simi was now the one judging her and they all agreed to let her be. Judge Helen said she didn't know Rade was so good with children, "fancy our hard-nosed business executive being a Sunday school teacher."

She asked where Rade found the time, and also mentioned how she couldn't stand children after a certain period but was quite impressed by the children from Rade's class who had sung exceptionally. Rade smiled proudly and explained to Helen how easy it had been to volunteer seeing she loved children.

As if she suddenly received an epiphany, Helen looked at Zach and asked why he had been standing out in front. They had been asked to close their eyes when the pastor made the altar call, but Helen had taken a peak and saw Zach standing out in front looking very subdued.

"I think I am interested in hearing what you were doing out in front," Buba added smiling at Zach.

"I went to rededicate my life to God," said Zach.

Rade smiled at the expression on Helen's face.

Helen asked why, after brushing off Buba's question as to why she had opened her eyes when the whole Church had been instructed to shut them.

"At one point in my life I got born again, but I disconnected from the Spirit and stopped the fellowship. I was filled with questions and angry at some Church people, so, I went off track; in more popular terms, I backslid."

Helen burst into laughter.

"I like that one," she said, "backslid," she repeated out loud, "like Michael Jackson's moonwalk. But can someone explain to me what that has to do with being a Christian? That's one of the things that frustrates me about the religion; too much jargon, especially the Pentecostals in Nigeria; there's a terminology for everything. I offered a colleague a piece of cake during lunchtime last week because she was looking quite miserable and she said, 'No thank you, I'm on the mountain.'"

"What does that mean?" Rade inquired looking perplexed.

"There you go madam children's church teacher; me and you both. She refused to tell me, and I was going to google it before another colleague put me out of my misery and told me it meant she was on a hunger strike, sorry, fasting and wouldn't be eating till much later. Why couldn't she just say that?"

Rade still looked perplexed, and they all laughed in spite of themselves, and she told herself Helen would beat Phil hands down in being the "most impossible" person on earth.

Simi said that every religion just like some professions had their jargon or unique lingo. She explained to Helen that when a person got born again, which simply meant a spiritual rebirth; you had to believe in your heart by faith and confess with your mouth that Jesus is the Son of God, that He died and was raised on the third day. After this, the Christian walk begins, and the Christian faith is a relationship with God, accessible only through Jesus Christ and energised by the Holy Spirit. However, if you start to disconnect in your fellowship with God as Zach had said and your commitment level is waning steadily, it is termed backsliding because there is no progression or growth in your spiritual walk instead you were seemingly going back to where you started."

Helen had been listening with rapt attention and asked how Simi knew so much after converting from the religion of her birth.

"So it can be termed a relapse then, instead of backsliding?" Helen argued.

"I thought you had something against jargons; I guess it's Christian jargon you have a problem with then," Buba said as he refilled his glass with some juice.

Helen looked really ticked off, and everyone

started laughing again.

"So tell us why you relapsed, Zach."

Zachary smiled, "I truly believed and even more so now to have converted from my family's religion to my Christian faith, but my Church lifestyle definitely started because of a girl; a very beautiful one!"

"These girls! They can make a man do all kinds of things," Buba said to Zach who nodded in affirmative.

Rade could feel her heart racing; it was the first time she had heard Zach talk about a woman like that. Was this jealousy she was feeling in the pit of her stomach?

Everyone except Rade chorused he spill the juicy details as they settled into more gossip-friendly positions.

"I met Oge at a friend's place, and it was her '*don't touch me; I am too much*' attitude that attracted me to her, aside from the fact that she's just the way I like my women, tall, slim and extremely beautiful. I chased her because she was a challenge and I love challenges. We eventually started dating after a little ado, and by then I knew she was religious, though it didn't quite explain how off she could be; there was something very closed up about her."

"Almost cold," Simi chipped in.

"Oge means money in Ibo language, right?" Rade asked and raised her hands in defence as everyone looked at her in irritation, wondering how this bore any relation to the story Zach was telling.

"No Rade, I think you mean *Ego*," Zach said. "Her full name is Ogechi but everyone called her Oge, and yes Simi, she was definitely cold. She had a quiet demeanour, but when she opened her mouth, it wasn't all sweet and peachy like you would expect; she had a caustic tongue and could make whoever crossed her feel like the lowest ebb in the world, yet in the same vein, be quite sweet too. We got serious, and I got religious; I started going to Church with her, I joined one of the groups because of her, joined the fundraising committee for the proposed new Church site and I was grateful she had brought me closer to Jesus," he added the latter with sarcasm. All this while, nothing physical happened between us; she was some kind of a prude, and she didn't like talking about sex even when I brought it up on a light note except I insisted and cautioned her to stop being so uptight. She was adamant if I loved her then it shouldn't be so important."

"How frustrating," Helen chipped in. You mean you weren't having sex?" How is that?"

"I thought it odd as it didn't seem like she was trying to resist me or anything, almost as if she

131

wasn't physically attracted to me, though she claimed otherwise. I then concluded that perhaps women are better at controlling their desires, unlike men, but I told myself, I could wait until she was ready; besides I wanted to please her, I was smitten."

"Yes, you were," Simi and Maimuna chorused.

He smiled and continued that things progressed between them and somehow they knew they were going to get married. He couldn't remember proposing to her, but she had already started planning what part of town they would live in, how many kids they should have, and so forth. The role of good wife suited her; beautiful, well composed and well spoken but underneath all that was merely ice. They were the most enviable couple in town, and people just loved seeing them together.

After a long silence he said, he must have been crazy to think he wanted to spend the rest of his life with someone so out of touch with him. Things started to unravel after this particular day when he had gone to see her to take her laundry to the dry cleaners, and when he entered her bedroom, she was sorting out her things and throwing clothes all over the place.

Helen raised her hands to interrupt and confirm he had indeed said he had gone over to pick her things to take to the dry cleaners. Zach repeated that whenever he was taking his dress shirts to the dry cleaners, he would stop over to pick hers, which he did every week, as Oge wore the most expensive designer labels, most of which bore the "*dry clean only*" caution.

Helen said that she had always known that fancying Zach wasn't a mistake and she was ready to start dating whenever he was; she added that any man who could do her laundry had her already.

Maimuna rolled her eyes heavenwards and asked if she could ever be serious?"

"I am," she replied, "it's an open secret that I like Zach."

He replied he was flattered as they all giggled except Rade who was trying unsuccessfully to hide her irritation; she wished Helen would quit interrupting.

Zach continued that one of her tops had gone across the room and landed in her wastepaper basket; he went over to pick it and for no reason peered into the basket and inside it were two used condoms.

"What!" Everyone in the room chorused.

"I was surprised! It looked like something from another planet. I mean it was just condoms, but in "saint Oge's" room; it was damn odd," he laughed.

133

"Wow! Zach how come you never told me this?" Simi asked sounding hurt.

He asked what the condoms were doing in her wastebasket, and she kept asking what he was talking about; he even told himself she probably didn't even know what a condom was until he chided himself not to be stupid. He repeated the question, and the expression on her face was one of shock and many other things he hadn't understood at the time. Her hands started to tremble after which she sat down abruptly on her bed and remained immobile until he went over to her. She told Zach that she suspected it was probably her younger brother who had used it and dropped it in her wastebasket to wind her up."

The groans that went through the room were dramatic.

"Her brother! And you believed her?" Maimuna said in dismay.

Zach looked at Maimuna and said she would have if he had not already hinted them some deception on Oge's part had partly caused their break up.

Oge had always complained about her brother and expressed her wish that he was more like Zach. He asked her why he would drop it in her own wastebasket since they didn't share a room. It didn't make sense, but he couldn't and didn't want to believe Oge was having sex with someone else. She promised she was going to have it out with him; she was appalled at how easily he could have ruined their relationship if Zach didn't trust her. So, he affirmed that he trusted her, and went on to reassure her that she should be glad her brother was at least responsible enough to be protecting himself if he was having sex, which sent her into another fit. They resolved it with Zach making her promise she wouldn't be too hard on her younger brother, and that she would not broach the subject to her father as she was determined to do. On his way home, her immediate reaction to the question stayed on his mind, but he had pushed the thought away, thinking how embarrassed she must have felt.

Buba had his head in his hands and was shaking it in disbelief as Helen tried to keep a straight face. Her expression was killing them.

Everything seemed okay until the Pastor and two heads of the Church summoned him to an important meeting; it was like facing a grand jury. They went on about how he had sinned and had led one of their "wonderful sisters" into sin with him and rebuked him for not having the decency to look repentant. The bashing went on; they employed all the Church jargons Helen would frown at, and he got even more nonplussed. He finally got a break when they all ran out of steam, and he asked them what point they were trying to make as he was really confused. His Head of Group put him out of his misery by telling him he was suspended from attending group meetings until he set the wedding date.

"You have set a bad example for the young people here who have always admired you as a couple; now they'll assume it's okay to have babies before wedlock. How do you think Oge's father, a respectable Deacon in this Church feels; you think he's happy his beloved first daughter is pregnant outside of wedlock?" Zach said, quoting the Head of Group.

Everyone in the room gasped.

"I guess I still looked bewildered because they asked why I was playing dumb and started to look confused themselves."

"Oge was pregnant!" The friend's in the room all chorused.

"I didn't wait to hear the rest; I almost killed myself rushing out of the Church to her house. I met her parents, and the look they gave me could have melted iron. Her mother was really upset and breathing fire; she made so much fuss. Oge came out, and it was then she dropped the bombshell;

she informed them the baby she was expecting wasn't mine. I knew that for a fact but the rest were in shock; we hadn't done anything more than hold hands, kiss, and a little necking. Her parents almost went mad; her mom just kept gaping at her in amazement, and so did I. I couldn't believe who this mysterious person was."

"What a con!" Helen retorted. "You can never trust all these Christians; they are all hypocrites."

"Stop the name calling, Helen," Maimuna answered, wagging a finger at her.

Zach felt sorry for the parents, especially her mom who looked as if her world had collapsed and her brother, in turn, looked at him with pity. He couldn't believe how deceitful she had been. He knew her family could be a bit pretentious, with their exaggerated airs and pride cloaked with religious piety but he saw them for who they were. Oge wasn't one of the warmest people because of her upbringing, but she seemed forthright enough. He had even started to make up excuses afterwards that perhaps she might have been raped but then reprimanded himself not to be silly.

Her father came to see Zach the following day. He was a severe, wealthy, well-respected man in the society and Church, and also a complete snob. He came to plead with Zach to accept the baby and marry his daughter immediately. He said it was one thing for her to be pregnant, but the fact that her fiancé wasn't even the father of her baby was another thing entirely. Zach remembered how irritated he had been when he saw an announcement of their engagement in the papers and their Church newsletter placed by Ogechi's father without their permission; at least, so she had said after apologising profusely. The tabloids would have a field day.

"He said my future was secure as his son-in-law and things were going to get better for me."

"I hope you punched him in the face?" Buba asked.

"I was tempted to, but this is someone I thought was going to be my father-in-law a day before. I just asked him to leave."

A couple of days later, Oge came to Zach to apologise. She explained that she loved the mystery guy but was quite sure she loved him too in a different way. She knew Zach was better for her and would be a better husband, but she couldn't help the way she felt about the other man. He asked why she could claim to love him yet have sex with another man and led him to believe she would never have sex before marriage. She shrugged and said she had told the other man the same thing, but unlike Zach, he wasn't a gentleman and had worn her down with his demand for sex, and they had been quite careful, like the used condoms Zach found in her wastebasket after the man snuck into the house the night before. She said she had almost broken up with him because of his recklessness after that incident, but the sneaking around was an aphrodisiac, and things just got out of hand. That was her second pregnancy as the first one was terminated and she had planned on having another abortion, but he had refused and threatened to tell her parents; from that point everything had spiralled out of control. Zach said it was surreal; he had never felt so many crazy emotions go through his head at the same time.

Oge added that she knew Zach was a strong man and he would be fine, even though his heart was breaking into two. She said other ridiculous things, and he managed to convince himself she was not quite right in the head, though he imagined that it must have been quite a difficult position for her to be. "That must have been the last day she was at ours; I remember bumping into her in her rush to leave," Simi said, and Zach nodded.

"She relocated to the US but kept calling and sending text messages for a long time asking me to forgive her and thanking me for taking care of her throughout the time we were together. Since then, I've been off women in terms of serious relationships, and I held a misdirected grudge against the Church, blaming it for the burden it placed on Christians to be what they are not. I heard she got married to the guy against her parent's wishes, but they'd rather she was married to a frog than be a single parent; so they got on board eventually."

Simi said she had never heard the full details until this day because though Zach was crushed, she could never get him to talk about it. He would just skim over the obvious fact that he and Oge had broken up, contradicting the different versions of the story whirring around.

"I am sorry Simi, I wanted to but I was too angry and hurt; there's nothing as painful as the feeling of being used and deceived by the one you care about."

"Why didn't she just break up with you instead of carrying on with two men?" Maimuna asked.

"Come on Maimuna! Zach treated her like a queen, and she liked that so she had to keep leading him on and using him. It is called eating your cake and having it; just another self-centred daughter of Eve," Buba answered angrily.

"Wow! To think you were saving the seemingly special gourmet meal for a special occasion, meanwhile someone else had been snacking on it for breakfast, lunch and dinner," Helen said raising her eyebrow leeringly.

Buba swatted her lightly on the knee reprovingly. They thanked him for the story and asked if he was really okay. He reassured them he was fine and had gotten over it and forgiven Oge whom he added shouldn't be judged, saying he'd only shared the experience because Helen asked why he backslid.

"Relapsed," she interjected and ran for cover behind Buba as Simi made a mock attempt to strangle her.

It was quite late by the time Rade ushered them out of her place. Her mind preoccupied with Zach's story as she laid under her duvet, imagining how hurt he must have been, his male pride bruised from the rejection as most men would be and his heart broken, as he had obviously been smitten by her or whom he thought she was.

Weeks passed with no response from Rade's father on the business proposal for the shopping mall she'd given to him. Mr. Doherty was impressed with his daughter's proposal. She had the drive, and he had to admit she was quite good at her job. Her total commitment suited him just fine, as all he wanted to do was work from behind the scenes and stay home with his loving wife.

The parents were discussing their daughter in the garden. Apart from her family and Church work, Mrs. Doherty's time was spent in her garden. She had been in the flower business for over three decades, employing many hands and setting up several people on their own, but the orders still got bigger by the day. She was a seasoned florist tending to her plants and flowers lovingly and showering the overbearing affection her family sometimes rebuffed on the helpless plants. She was squinting at the leaves of a potted plant she was sending to Rade's office while her husband helped arrange an array of Cactus in preparation for delivery. He enjoyed helping his wife whenever she gave her staff the day off; it allowed her the opportunity to boss him around.

"He's a nice man; I don't know why they are wasting so much time, young people waste too much time on unnecessary things."

"Yes; he is," her husband replied, knowing his wife was referring to Zach, "but it's better they take things easy than rush into anything. That's what I would expect you to say to her. Their upbringing is quite different, we don't know anything about the extended family except the sister, Maimuna and her Aunt, but there is no doubt he's a fine man. Tell her to take her time to know him."

"I did! I told her to take her time but not waste too much time either. She told me to stop pushing, as usual. I'm just scared she's getting sucked into her job; I see the glint in her eyes on her way to work, then the tiredness in them on her return. I don't want her to become one of those workaholic ladies we see these days with no husbands or children who pretend they are content and actually have a life. Yinka you have to do something, our baby mustn't end up a tired old spinster."

"You are going a bit overboard; she's still young. And why do you judge women who don't have husbands or children? It's deplorable coming from a woman with your understanding; it may well be a matter of personal choice," he smiled as she snorted in disbelief.

"Moreover, you recommended her for the job, now you're complaining she's spending too much time at it. She's an adult Ju, and a good businesswoman, let her use her talent. She sent me a business proposal for a shopping mall." He gave his wife a brief synopsis of the proposal.

"She wants to lease the Goldmine property," he continued, as his wife raised her brows surprised, "the business plan is quite convincing, almost too good to be true. But I've read between the lines and unearthed a few holes; so I've proposed in my mind what I'll do, but I will test her resolve and see how much tenacity she's got."

"And in your bid to play God, what if she fails the test? I think Rade still observes things through rose-tinted lenses; things are not as straight forward here as they are where she's coming from, and I hope she's not looking at this as some kind of pet project."

"You should give her more credit; I don't think you understand how good she is when you kept pushing for her to come. She's faced many challenges, dealing with the staff, meeting timelines, and all else, but she has quickly overcome her initial shock and is quite integrated or integrating well into the system. And I am not playing God; everyone gets tested before they can move to the next level or phase at every point in their lives. Do you know how many tests you've faced but were not aware? Rade is using her personal relationship with me to her own advantage. I told her I am not willing to sell the property when she requested the asking price like she can beat the dozen offers we have already, so she proposed a long lease and I plan to schedule another meeting with her next week to discuss further. She's also asked for the value of her shares at Doherty's; she's probably thinking of selling."

"Wow! So much has been going on behind my back. Darling, do you remember a shopping mall was what we had in mind when we acquired that land but everyone dissuaded us, killed our dream literally; now thirty years later our daughter has the same idea."

He entwined his hands with his wife's pulling her to him.

"She's going to be very busy," Joanne Doherty cried, "what time will she have to get married?"

Mr. Doherty shook his head. His wife was like a pit bull when she picked on a subject, she would jaw lock, and it was almost impossible for her to let go. "Joanne, she's not even engaged yet, and you're talking about marriage. Here you are complaining about her overworking; you are over sixty, my dear girl and your flower orders are getting bigger by the day; you're looking for more land for more gardens and employing new staff; you are looking at the speck in your daughter's eye when you have a beam in yours."

"You are the wisest man on earth, and I am glad you are my husband," she replied with a curtsy which evoked a chuckle from her husband.

At the same time, Rade was on the phone with Zach; they were deciding where to go for business dinner. She dropped the receiver and turned around to find her friends watching her; she puckered her face at the expression on her friends' faces. Maimuna winked at her, and Simi's knowing smile made Rade giggle happily.

"Zach's taking you out for dinner, and we're definitely not invited."

"Spot on, girl; this is a business dinner, and we don't want any distractions and stop giving me that knowing look Simi."

"What look! It must be your conscience eating at you Rade, 'cause I'm not giving you any look," Simi replied winking at Maimuna who was peering through the windows at the city below and pretending not to listen.

As both girls left Rade's office, she whispered a silent prayer of gratitude for the good friends that had formed a tight circle of support around her and hoped she was to them what they were to her. She couldn't wait to see Zach later that evening and was ready when he called to say he was outside.

Ten minutes later, they were seated at a hidden spot in a waterfront restaurant in Victoria Island. At the peaceful calm of the water, the heady smell of the incense and the soft music, Rade took off her shoes under the table, and thought how she loved the metropolis at night; it was a far cry from the hustle, bustle, blaring horns, and traffic hold-ups of the day. She loved the fact that he had picked an outdoor place for them to discuss; the hours on end enclosure in her office was beginning to stifle her.

She gave him an update on the first meeting with her father; then proceeded with her proposal to Zach to join her as a partner.

"I went to have a look at the property today, and I was sensing some funny vibes; this proposal is between a tight circle of people, so maybe it was just my imagination."

"The walls have ears my dear, and siblings of Landlords get the same treatment meted to the Landlords around here - hateful respect, so please let's hear back from your father first before you go and start inspecting property Miss busy-body. I'm already looking at other options just in case he says no."

"Zach! There's nothing wrong with me going there to have a look. I just needed to refresh my memory, and didn't realise the place is that huge! Besides being there inspired my faith; I just know in my gut that place is mine, well ours, if you decide to accept my proposal. I need you on board, Zach."

He couldn't help but smile at her; her enthusiasm

was infectious.

She prattled on for a while as he listened to her in silence, then she caught herself with a start.

"Let's have dinner," they both chorused simultaneously.

Chapter Seven

As time went by, Rade was quite convinced she knew the whole of Lagos, though everyone she encountered told her otherwise. She had never quite known a city with many faces and different perspectives as the persons who forwarded it. She was dragged everywhere her friends could think of: the private beaches where the sand and water was clean and a select rich group came to show off their boats, girlfriends and drinking prowess. The public beaches were not quite the same, but there she ate the tastiest fresh grilled fish with her hands and was sure she was high on second-hand marijuana smoke. Art exhibitions, where she saw the most thrilling arts and book fairs, and the cultural centres where they went to watch plays and concerts. The burgeoning underground music private sessions where budding musicians performed non-mainstream music. The State library, theatre and museum. Buba took her to the old railway station where she saw coaches she didn't think still existed, then the markets where she lost Simi a couple of times; a veteran who knew her way around every nook and cranny of the market. They attended posh dinner parties where everyone spoke with a foreign accent and laughed at each other behind their backs. Then the bukas, the tiny, not very clean sheds where Simi said she had eaten at one time or the other much to Zach's disapproval; there Rade learnt to eat steaming hot Amala with her hands, firewood cooked Jollof Rice and Moin-moin cooked in leaves which became her favourite.

Maimuna still found it hard to believe Rade hadn't grown up eating Nigerian food living with her Aunt and had never visited any Nigerian restaurants in London; they watched with pity as she sweated and complained the food was too spicy until they bullied her and advised her to "suck it up."

"Nothing as bad as a Yoruba girl complaining food is too spicy; it's a big shame," Simi added.

She was indeed experiencing the Lagos culture and living the Lagos life, and she loved it.

She spoke with Phil as often as possible, and it just

made her miss him more. She didn't understand what was going on between her and Zach, but she knew they were playing a silent game with each other, she didn't know who was winning. She was quite sure on most days she was falling in love with him, and she saw the way he looked at her, his protectiveness whenever they went out, and the heat in his eyes when she was chatted up by men, yet they never spoke about their feelings for each other. Her mother was constantly pestering her about him, and it was beginning to get on her nerves.

Renovations at the electronic store were under way; they'd sold all the old gadgets, and gotten sole franchise with the upscale Bang & Olufsen and another popular electronic manufacturer. Much money had gone out on rebranding and advertising, and things were looking up. They had employed key new staff at Doherty Textiles, and some of their new designs were anticipated in the market after the relaunch that had reputable distributors, fashion designers from all over the world interested in African textile in attendance. Rade's ears were full of commendations from every quarter, and she was being praised as the newest "beauty and brains" silver spoon kid on the block by a few tabloids to her friends' amusement. She was in a mode she hadn't thought was possible; she had in such a short period become savvier and very diplomatic, learning patience as she talked shop while smiling and coaxing wary customers.

On the other hand, the shopping mall proposal seemed to be going nowhere; the major bank she had approached through recommendations and assurances from close sources that had claimed they were loan friendly turned her down, citing loopholes in the plan. The interest on the loan and the collateral another bank had demanded made her head spin. She was still smarting from the rejection.

Months later, Rade was calculating figures in her head; she could reel out the numbers needed at every stage of the project, including the miscellaneous, at the drop of a hat yet everything was in limbo. She frowned unconsciously and chewed on a fingernail; it was unbelievable she had formed a habit she greatly detested. Her eating habit had gone to the pits over time, and her saving grace was Zach who had become her self-appointed dietician, constantly quizzing her on when and what she ate whenever he got the chance, which was always. As happy as she was about the great feat she and her team had achieved at her father's business, the pressure was still high, her two-year contract was unbelievably almost over. She had just received the offer letter of a permanent position at the expiration of her contract with an impressive salary and allowances by industry standards. She had been quite sure at the beginning she would run back to London as soon as her contract expired, but a lot had changed since then, especially her relationship with her parents. She knew they loved having her around, she liked her job, had a business plan of her own that she wanted to see materialise, and she had met a man; yet everything seemed loose ended to her. She was feeling bad after barely listening to Lateef when he dropped by to pay her a visit in her office. He was now employed as a truck driver at DT. He enjoyed the commute from the factory located in the outskirts of the city into town. He got a thrill operating big vehicles and loved his driving job, and would do anything for Rade to express his gratitude. He thanked her for the umpteenth time for the job opportunity, saying prayers and promising to repay her one way or the other. At his exit, her mind kept wandering, then halted on Zach, and she sighed. She missed him, even though she'd spoken with him only the day before. How was that even possible? Missing someone you saw and spoke to frequently. She walked over to her window and opened it, picking up a habit she had dropped four years before as she felt disappointment wash over her.

Rade was still in a pensive mood when the familiar scent of Maimuna's Oud perfume filled her office. The girls sat across each other in silence for several minutes until Maimuna broke the silence.

"The problem with you is that when things get difficult, you bottle everything up and shut everyone out. These days it's either you don't speak at all or when you do you're almost biting heads off; please ease off. If we could wave a wand and present you your shopping mall, I swear we would, if it would just bring a smile to your face. But these things take time, so you should see all the roadblocks as mere challenges; if it's meant to be everything will eventually fall into place. It would help if you learned to take things one step at a time and stop being so impatient. You should be savouring this moment; just think of all the hard work you've put into Doherty's, you've done a fantastic job, and that was your primary assignment here. Be grateful Rade, and please stop being a spoilsport, you're blessed! I'm in no way undermining your challenges, but there are people with bigger issues in life, and they're going at it like troopers.

Frankly, I miss my friend and don't care much for this churlish attitude. Do you know how many people would give anything to be in your shoes? I know you are a perfectionist, but life can't always be arranged in the way you want it. How can you be so discouraged at such minor setbacks? It's only been just a year; some people have been waiting years for their business plans and dreams to materialise."

Rade stared back at her and sniffled back a tear, which came in torrents as they burst into laughter. She had to laugh at her own silliness.

Maimuna had a few hours off and coaxed her into leaving the office earlier than usual, and that evening a more relaxed Rade sat at the edge of the swimming pool in the private residence of one of Zach's acquaintances. The friend was hosting a small pool party for an American business partner who was in Nigeria and in business with another group of Nigerian partners to bid for an oil block. Simi smiled noting that Rade looked much better than she had in a long time.

"The size of this house is ludicrous for someone who lives alone," Rade said in awe, staring at the impeccably dressed stewards that came out bearing bottles of expensive champagne, red and white wine and setting the table for an array of grilled seafood, roast lamb, pork chop and salads.

Simi and Buba nodded, it was a fifteen roomed mansion with an indoor gymnasium, a wine cellar that housed the oldest and most exquisite liquor, a private movie theatre, squash court, indoor heated swimming pool with a popular logo engraved at the bottom. The furniture in the living room and bedrooms were ones you only saw at private viewings or on the pages of magazines, but you never thought anyone actually bought; the house reeked of money.

"What's with that?" Simi asked pointing at the bunny at the bottom of the pool, "Zach regaled me with all sorts of stories about the guy and his crazy concepts when he was designing this house. I hear some crazy things go on in those bedrooms behind closed doors."

"Really? I didn't realise Zach designed this place. And what do you mean crazy things?"

She verbalised what Simi mouthed to her, "'they have orgies in Nigeria!' I was wondering what a single man needs fifteen bedrooms for; this place should be a boutique hotel. I hear a lot of rich Nigerian men have a lot of those where they host their mistresses and girlfriends. What does this guy do anyway, not drugs I hope, and how do you and Zach know him?" Rade asked Buba.

"Wow! A dozen questions at the same time,

madam. Aside him being Zach's client, and that they play tennis together mostly at his insistence, that's it I guess. But he is known for being one of the finest polo players in the country; you should see the horses in his stable. His father is loaded with a capital L, all old money, and he is an only son. There have been rumours of shady deals but no proof. The guy has his finger in every pie and is now going into the oil sector. He's currently separated from his wife, and they have one daughter. He is an okay enough chap."

"I hope he doesn't think we are into his nonsense; though since he knows Zach, he should know better," Rade whispered, and the trio giggled, and hushed as the person in question left Zach's side where they had been discussing with the American business partner and his wife.

"We haven't met formally, my name is Zacheus," he introduced himself to Rade and stretched out a hand which she took as he helped her up from her cramping crouched position.

"Rade Doherty, thank you for having us in your house," she replied shaking her head as Buba and Simi started giggling.

"You know what? Just call me Ugo," he added, beaming at Rade. "I always get that reaction when I introduce myself to people. They just expect you to be as short as the man in the Bible when you answer that name."

She lost his attention before he barely finished his sentence, as his eyes widened in appreciation at whatever he was looking at. She had to turn and sigh in understanding as Maimuna and Helen walked into the swimming pool area; they went on a tour of the house first and had been in the changing room for a short while.

Ugo was openly gaping as he exclaimed, "Maimuna!" He ogled her one piece clad form some more, "you should be a model; you're a stunner!"

"I know, right; if I ever get tired of the medical profession that will be my next resort; I've got the right figure, skin and good bone structure."

"Gosh Maimuna, a 'thank you, Ugo' would have sufficed."

"The girl knows what she's got," Simi injected.

"God has been very kind to me, thanks to my parents and their perfect genes."

"Maimuna! We get the message!" Everyone chorused, as Maimuna dissolved into peals of laughter giving Ugo a playful dig on the shoulder.

"Ugo, what are you doing to my people over there," asked Zach who was still conversing with the American couple.

"Ugo?" Rade repeated the name quizzically.

"Ugo, not Ego," Helen replied, shrugging off the towelling robe that had been provided for everyone. Bathrobes and towels of the softest cotton, they were gentle on the skin and smelled of indulgent fabric softener.

"How do you know what I was thinking, Helen?"

"You seem to have a thing for that name. Is there a reason why? The other day Zach mentioned Oge that's the same name you mentioned."

Everyone slipped into the warmth of the water and Rade told them about a Nigerian girl she met in London who just came from New York on a business trip with her husband and just hated London, and told anyone that cared to listen how dreary it was.

"She's from the Igbo tribe, I know; she wore the most expensive items, fur coats, minks, etc, and spent thousands of pounds buying random stuff to stop herself from being bored to death, as she claimed, and would always pay in cash. A friend's younger sister who works in one of the Louis Vuitton shops got friendly with her and invited her to one of our get-togethers, and everyone was dying to meet her because she's Nigerian, but a far cry from me, they said. I finally did, and boy... she was something."

An all American girl with the pride of an Ibo princess"

is how she described herself. I don't even know what she meant by that, but everyone just nodded when she introduced herself. Somehow we got talking about names and their meanings and how some celebrities in Hollywood have ridiculous names for their children, and then someone suggested we mention our names and what they meant, some didn't even know what their names meant. When it got to her turn, she just said, *My name is Ego, it means money*."

The room literally went quiet, and then the boys just started clapping in awe; it was like a scene from a movie, everyone was quite dazzled by her, it almost seemed she cast a spell on all of us, and we addressed her that way till she returned to the United States.

It's the way she said it, with deliberateness. The name has stuck in my mind since."

Everyone immediately started using the line with their own names. After the water dip, they decided to have dinner and Paula, the American business partner's wife, complained of her weakness for red meat, which she was trying unsuccessfully to eliminate from her diet. Rade confessed to everyone she had smoked a cigarette earlier that day, a habit she quit almost four years ago.

"I didn't know you smoked?" Zach said frowning at her.

"There are quite a few things you don't know about me," she replied as silence fell around the table, and they held each other's gaze.

"Well I used to; I just picked it up somehow and then one day I just knew I had to quit; I did and never looked back."

"Until today apparently," he replied.

"Give her a break, Zach. That's one thing that puzzles me, how some people can quit smoking just like that; it took me years and it was gradual, I kept falling and getting back up," Buba answered.

"I took a few drags, and it didn't do anything for me, I felt so guilty and silly afterwards; it's one habit I don't want to pick up ever again."

"I've never been a cigarette person; I prefer marijuana; it's healthier," said Helen.

"I agree," Brian replied.

"Please Helen, don't even start with your propaganda; I don't care much for any kind of leisure drug, none of it is good for you; I don't care what anyone says, you can never do a little, there is always the tendency to overuse?" Simi rebutted.

"Shame on you, Simi, you're a chef and do not know the nutritional value of cannabis. One of your pastry chef colleagues is popular for her *Happy Cookies*." It relaxes me; I don't classify weed as a hard drug, you can't compare it with cocaine or heroin; in fact, I think we should be having some right now."

"That's a fallacy! Weed having nutritional value, that has sure piqued my interest, and you don't think weed is a hard drug, tell that to the authorities if they ever find some on you."

"Don't be so stuck up, Simi! Is it the legal status that makes it bad? If so, it's legal in many places, and the whole world is catching up" she replied.

Rade asked what the difference between weed and pot was and the answers were the same, it was all semantics. She cracked up when they started listing the local names, igbo, hemp, ganja, etc.

"I've done all the types of drugs that have ever existed, and I can tell you from experience that drugs literally destroy you; I'm happy I'm not on that path anymore, but I still have friends that are still totally sucked in. It's an expensive habit, but that's no deterrent for them as they are so rich, maintaining the habit isn't a big deal at all; still, it takes its toll. They make it seem harmless and cool at first but it's a vortex, it sucks you in, its an evil spirit, even more so than alcohol," Ugo said with much emotion.

Maimuna mentioned it wasn't an exclusive habit for the rich as everyone was "doing" it; the urchins, bus drivers, underage children, prostitutes had their own improvised drugs which didn't cost too much, like cough medicines that had codeine, a combination of cheap over the counter medicines, petrol, glue, horse tranquilizers…

Brian interrupted in amazement and asked if Maimuna was exaggerating a little bit, if not a lot for that matter, and she promised to send him a report on an independent research she and another colleague had just conducted on the kind of drugs the people on the streets were taking. People would do anything to be in an altered state of mind, and a cheap high is the answer.

The group was split into two; one group who had done some kind of drugs at some point and the other who never had. Then Buba decided to tell them his story.

"I've taken weed a couple of times but the last time was the final straw for me," Buba said.

"What happened?" Maimuna asked.

'I'll tell the story!" Helen said, and everyone nodded, not surprised she had something to do with it.

"Weed makes Buba hungry, it does different things to different people, it's also an aphrodisiac, but that's another story for another time. Anyway, I decided to make some soup with the leaves, which he ate; this is after he had smoked a couple of wraps already and by the time Buba was done, I saw another side of him I didn't think was possible. He started singing loudly then proceeded to belly dance for me without music. I laughed so much, then started crying in my stoned state, but after a while, it became scary as he just wouldn't calm down; I had to get two guys to hold him down for hours. Then on his way home, he was convinced his car was a space ship," Helen shook her head, recalling the incident.

Everyone laughed! It was just so hard picturing gentle Buba any other way. Simi added that Helen should be arrested for even suggesting weed was harmless, and Buba's story only confirmed it.

She also mentioned two men she knew who had gone insane from abusing marijuana and another acquaintance she knew got depressed when he took it, which sparked a new session of arguments between herself and Helen.

Helen advised Simi to study the different species of cannabis; there's the one used for medicinal purposes, people with cancer were getting help, and there she was casting judgment. For her, it was a relaxant. Another species could make some individuals pensive and strung up.

Simi told her she had nothing against it, it was

herbs and created by God but that any drug that altered your normal state could give room for demon possession.

Rade had to stop the laughter that attempted to escape her lips when she saw Helen's expression at Simi's comment.

"I think this weed and drug talk is already making us high," Zach said, and they all broke into laughter again.

"Rade you should try some on your hair since you're trying to grow it back, it promotes hair growth," Helen suggested.

This piqued Paula's interest, and she wanted to know more and Helen was happy to fill her in on the ridiculous things one could do with it, and the interest on the woman's face at her 'over the top' recommended cannabis usage left the group gasping with laughter.

Rade complained she had a headache from laughing too much, and really wondered if Helen was well in the head.

Simi and Maimuna told her she was banned henceforth from seeing their cousin, Buba because she really is a bad influence on him and everyone else for that matter. And she promised them she was trying to be a better person, which was why she was always inviting herself to their gatherings because she knew they were good people and could, maybe one day, rub off on her.

"Rade you need to let me mix something for you to grow back your hair quickly."

"Let her be, Helen; the things Nigerian women apply to their hair, all them greasy pomades and hair oils are gross enough, don't add weed to the mix please."

Zach was still shaking with silent laughter.

"What on earth do you mean by that? Nigerian women aren't the only ones who apply things to their hair; Caucasian, African, Asian women apply all sorts to their hair. Do you know how much hair sprays, holds and gels white celebrities and models put in their hair?" Maimuna asked Buba.

"I kind of agree with Buba," Rade injected, "I notice many women around here use a lot of hair pomades, really unpleasant smelling ones, and they apply them on their extensions too. But all it does is attract dirt, and with the weather here, it's crazy. The African hair really doesn't need all that grease, neither do the extensions. Good shampoo, leave-in conditioner and minimal hair oil for the scalp will do so that the scalp can breathe. I'm sure they wash their pillowcases every day."

"Please let's not get into the hair extensions topic; I have gotten into much trouble for it, so I plead the fifth," Zach continued still shaking with laughter as Paula continued to stare at Helen in open admiration.

"Yeah, yeah, let's not; we are beautiful African women, we have kinky, full hair, we decide we like hair extensions, we pay good money to buy them, fix them and tend to them. Why does the world have a problem with that? White women wear extension too; enough already."

"Why are you looking in my direction, Maimuna? I don't have issues with hair extensions. Actually, I do a little bit with certain types, some are just nasty," Zach replied, "besides I don't think you wear extensions Maimuna; so why are you so on the defensive?"

"I thought you were pleading the fifth, even though you are no American, and you still managed to squeeze in your opinion. I detest it when men put down the very thing that attracts them to a woman. I see how you men ogle women with flowing locks, and then, on the other hand, start castigating them; just leave the weave wearing women alone please, it's their prerogative. They are no less women."

The discussion became heated, everyone with a different opinion. Helen gave Zach a lecture on how African women had been wearing their own unique type of hair extensions before the

Europeans showed up.

Paula ended the conversation with flourish when she pulled up her hair and showed the group the line where the lighter shade of her blonde extensions and her thinning hair met. Helen pumped her fist in the air and did a victory dance in front of Zach. The girls gave a round of applause, while the men stared quizzically until Helen, matter of fact, promised her she would personally deliver a cannabis concoction that would grow her hair back before she returned to the US. Even Brian who had snoozed off in the middle of the discussions chuckled in his sleep.

Everyone was still giggling as they got into their different beds.

****

A few months on, Rade was wondering what her birthday without her old friends would be like, especially Phil, who always planned something special for her.

"Rade! Did you hear what I said?" Rade snapped out of her reverie and realised Zach had been talking to her.

"I said the amount here is reasonable enough to get us in the preliminary stage of our project. With what you have, we can start some groundwork. We need to hear from your father in regards to the property ASAP."

Rade kept smiling at him as he proceeded to tell her what she already knew had to be done but in the Zach way; very detailed and thorough. The figure on the draft was impressive enough to make her gasp.

"Where did you get this money, Zach?"

He smiled, "I stole it."

"I'm quite sure you did. Seriously, you don't have to tell me but you never really made any financial commitment; I thought at some point you were only trying to humour me."

"Humour you! I'm a businessman, darling; if I didn't see potential, I would have told you straight up. I was just playing an advisory role when you first mentioned it to me. This money is from different legitimate sources, have no fear."

"This is great, Zach! You're one person anyone would love to have on their team; I'm glad we are partners, this is definitely another step forward; it's time we gave the lawyer another call."

"Feeling's mutual," he replied, placing a kiss on her forehead, and she lingered beside him before stepping back quickly as the air between them started to thicken.

On her birthday, the girls organised a party. She received an exceptionally designed model house from Zach, and Simi was convinced it was one of his best designs so far. The only problem with it, Mrs. Doherty commented, was that the beautiful girl that was placed on the terrace of the house looked lonely and needed someone by her.

"It is a gift with a hidden message," she stated, looking slyly at Zach.

Rade shook her head and paid her mother no mind. Then, to say she was shocked was putting it lightly when her parents handed over their present to her. A letter stating that the Goldmine property's signed deeds would be handed over to her in two years if she could fulfil certain minor step by step obligations in her opinion! It was unbelievable; she had imagined a lot of things but not this. After the conversation with Maimuna, she had asked for forgiveness for her bad attitude and decided to channel her energy towards keeping her faith strong and enjoying the peace that followed.

That night, while preparing to sleep, she still found it hard to believe her father had even considered giving her the Goldmine. She wasn't the oldest child, and she knew he still wanted her to head Doherty Textile; she didn't deserve this.

Phil called a little after midnight and was shocked to hear that his uncle whom he had sent to deliver a message to her hadn't contacted her, and he sounded a bit worried. Very early the next day, Rade received a special delivery from her friends in London. A shoebox containing a pair of limited edition courts from one of her favourite designers, Alexander McQueen. She was gawking at the shoes and with her spare hand trying to open the box from Phil when her intercom rang; it was her mom. "There's someone here for you."

Rade knew it had to be a person of interest from the tone of her voice. Rade waited a few minutes and decided to step outside when she didn't hear her buzzer, and she stood there gaping; the man approaching her was almost seven feet tall and thick-set, and he totally dwarfed Rade.

"Good morning, Ms. Doherty? He asked, and she nodded. "I'm Mark, Phillip's uncle," his expression showing he was used to such open appraisal.

"I am so sorry," she said, putting out her hand which he engulfed in his, "and that is my mother," she added, looking past him at the approaching footsteps she knew was her mom's. He turned and exchanged pleasantries with Mrs. Doherty who wasn't trying to hide her curiosity.

He gave his apologies for not bringing Phil's message on time; he had been in the Port Harcourt since he arrived in Nigeria.

"So you are the famous Uncle Mark?" Rade said, remembering her conversation with Phil about his uncle whom he said was totally Americanized, one would never believe he was English. Phil adored him; he was the only member of his close or extended family he got along with, except his aged Nan, in whose eyes Phil could never do wrong.

"The very one, babe," he replied, and Rade laughed at the expression on her mother's face.

Mrs. Doherty excused herself; it was then Uncle Mark gave her a properly sealed parcel with her name and address on it. She thanked him and wrote down his address, promising to call and check on him from time to time since he was now in Lagos.

For the first time since she started working, Rade got to the office very late; she wondered if she deserved all the good things happening to her, but the only answer that came was "grace."

Phil's parcel contained birthday cards and a draft, which she kept peering at; then she dialled his number. "Philip Tate!" She exclaimed.

"I love it when you call my full name; you sound just like my Nan, bless her soul."

He was coming on board as an Investor. All she had been doing was dumping on him about all the challenges she was facing. Rade was speechless until he asked if she liked the dress, only then she realised that she hadn't opened all the packages; it was an evening gown of the sheerest silk. She held it up to her face trying not to imagine how much it had cost, knowing Phil.

"Becca and Christine mentioned they'd bought you a pair of shoes so I got the dress, sent them with Uncle Phil and told him to post them so you could wear it for your birthday, but he totally ruined it. I hope that man you fancy yourself in love with can take you somewhere befitting of that dress. It's lovely!"

"And overpriced from the look of things. Phil, why do you keep splurging out on me like this? It's so licentious, it's criminal…"

"Nothing criminal about spoiling a beautiful woman who deserves it; I have the money and can buy whatever I like."

"Phil, do you know how many mouths this would feed? I've never known you to buy anything cheap. What is it with you and extravagance? With you, it seems the more expensive, the better."

"I don't look at price labels, sweet pea; if I see something I like and can afford, I get it; don't make me apologise for being able to afford my lifestyle, the poor don't apologise for theirs. Besides someone would say the same of you; Uncle Mark sent me a text to say you live in a bleeding mansion the minute he arrived at your parents, you earn a six-figure salary, and you just inherited a property called the Goldmine. Am I sensing a double standard here?"

"Touche," she smiled.

He told her he got the money from a few of the paintings he just sold.

Rade remembered the first time she had seen Phil's works; she was stunned. Her boss, who incidentally was Phil's friend, was a collector and he had groomed and honed her eye for Art, and Phil's had definitely caught her eye. His works had depth and intensity; obviously where he put all his emotions. He also spent a lot of money buying the best art materials; an expensive hobby, he called it. She cajoled and bullied him to have them exhibited to no avail; he was not ready. Even close associates had never really seen any of his paintings. The few he had hung on his wall were unsigned, and people would ask to no avail whose works they were. He said it was like asking people to read his diary. Rade finally booked an appointment with the Curator her boss used, much to Phil's irritation and the woman's delight.

The curator fell in love with both Phil and his paintings the minute she laid eyes on them. Subsequent meetings had led to private exhibitions; the latest was a huge success, and a few of his most expensive works were purchased by his father's friend for a ridiculous amount; incidentally, two out of them were Rade's favourite. He had worked on those paintings for a long time but had never thought anyone would actually pay that much money for them and told his enthralled Curator that much. It probably helped that Phil was from a wealthy family. He thanked her for encouraging, more like bullying, him into showing his work. His last words before she hung up was that she was a wonderful friend and he loved her to bits.

Rade was excited! She felt like taking the day off to relish all the goodness; then her intercom buzzed; it was her driver reminding her she was running late. His reprimanding voice brought her right back to earth, and she rolled her eyes at the receiver wondering out loud when he became her timekeeper.

During lunch break, Rade was brimming with

excitement, as she hurried over to Zach's office; the flight of stairs to Zach's office seemed longer to Rade since she had opted not to use the elevator and her brief wait in the reception wasn't one she welcomed.

"Guess what? We have more money!" She made her opening speech as she entered into the office; she didn't wait for his reply but launched into details. He was lying crossed-feet on his thinking leather chaise lounge and staring at the skyline above; his gaze followed her as she paced in front of him until she was done.

"Hello to you too."

She smiled back sheepishly and leaned over to kiss his cheek as they inhaled each other's scent.

"Pardon my manners. Zach, I'm excited!"

He was impressed and glad they were making progress but was personally tired of hearing about this great Phil. He watched with amusement as she danced to his ringer and he ignored the call and allowed it to play for her; he loved seeing her like this. She sighed and went over to examine the cactus plants her mother had sent to him after he excused himself to answer the subsequent call, and started whispering to the plants.

He reminded her afterwards of an old friend's wedding they all planned to attend over the weekend in Ibadan, which is an hour drive from Lagos. She exclaimed she would have to call Maimuna immediately, who had promised to organise something traditional for her to wear. He let her go, reminding her there was a bank holiday the following Monday so they would be there all weekend and return Monday afternoon.

That evening she was thinking of Zach and beginning to wonder why he hadn't articulated any feelings for her. Wasn't her green light visible enough? She had almost asked him a few times but thought against it. They held hands sometimes, he flirted with her, he was always calling and texting her, they went on dates, and he bought her small presents but nothing more. Or did he assume they were together already? She knew that wasn't the case.

Maybe he was seeing someone! The thought brought her up with a start; she didn't think so, but anything was possible with men. They had known each other for a year now. Phil considered Zach a weak man and didn't care much for him, especially as he hadn't declared his intentions. She had replied that not all men were as forward as he was, but she was beginning to lean a little bit towards his view.

Chapter Eight

Rade spent the rest of the week placing orders for Doherty electronics, and also later that week, she and Zach finally received the existing plans for the Goldmine property from her father's Architect.

At the weekend, Friday late afternoon, after close of work, she got on the road to Ibadan with Zach, Simi and Maimuna. There was a traditional wedding ceremony before the one in the Church the following day. Everyone was dressed up so elaborately in their native attires, Rade's eyes were widening at each turn. She had observed how extravagantly people dressed up to Church on Sundays, but she had never attended a traditional wedding ceremony.

Simi had given up on her when Rade mentioned she had never attended a traditional wedding ceremony as even she had travelled from Nigeria to attend a couple of traditional wedding ceremonies in London and they didn't disappoint. Nigerians never disappointed when it came to celebrating wherever they are. She thought her mother had gone overboard because soon after she mentioned the wedding they were attending in Ibadan, she had promptly called Maimuna ordering her to stop by however late in the evening and rescue her friend before she disgraced them all by wearing something inappropriate. Her protest that Maimuna had something planned out already fell on deaf ears. That evening Maimuna was pinching an exasperated Rade as Mrs. Doherty started bringing out a variety of expensive French laces and the new line of cotton wax fabrics from Doherty's and asked her daughter and Maimuna to choose. Her mother's dressmaker made several outfits and sent them over the next few days.

"Nigerian women are the vainest females on earth, gosh! Everyone here is so beautiful," Rade said, looking around in awe.

She was fascinated especially by the women with headgears perched at different angles, an open display of expensive jewellery and copies, a variety of local fabrics made into interesting outfits, embellished with beads, stones, fringes and anything sparkly for an added edge. They were all sizing each other up, discreetly and openly, and loving every minute of it.

Simi laughed, genuinely amused at Rade's reaction. "If you notice, Maimuna and I are probably the most simply dressed."

"No way! Why do you say that?"

"Because we are Northerners; your people are more flamboyant when it comes to dressing."

"What do you mean my people?" She asked irritably.

"Yoruba people are very elaborate dressers, is all I mean, the headgears, the wrappers, the *Aso-oke* on the waist and shoulder; it's all quite fascinating! Our dressing, hairstyle, make up can be too but in a totally different way."

Rade asked why Simi called herself a Northerner, even though her father was from Ilorin. There seemed to be no straight story to where she and Zach came from.

"No mystery there, Rade, my father is Fulani; he just settled in Ilorin. My maternal grandma has Yoruba roots, hence my name Simisola."

"Don't the Fulanis have Arab Ancestry?" Asked Rade, observing both Maimuna and Simi's features, she squinted closely at Maimuna's profile.

"Our history has various versions, my dear, and our

ancestry is still the subject of many debates. There's the Spanish side of the story and the Arab side, but Fulanis are a large culturally diversified tribe that have settled in some parts of West Africa. It is said that somewhere between the late eighteenth and early nineteenth century we brought Islam into Northern Nigeria through Jihads blazed by Shehu Uthman Danfodio, whose descendants we are purported to be, by the way. Fulani's have settled in various parts in Northern Nigeria and mixed with the Hausas, and that's why we are commonly called Hausa-Fulani. Zach, Maimuna and I are a far cry from what people imagine Fulani's should be in terms of our lifestyle. I guess it's because we schooled in the South/West and more so, we converted to Christianity. And by the way, not all Fulani's are prototype like Maimuna; just think of Buba and his colour like black marble. I need to give you a book on Fulani history; it'll be a good read."

"Simi, enough with the history lessons," Maimuna grumbled as Rade listened with keen interest. "Rade's missing all the interesting stuff."

"We must continue this later," Rade mouthed to Simi and burst into laughter as the groom and his friends, Zach included, were asked to lie prostrate in greeting before the bride's family, which they all did enthusiastically, chests hitting the floor simultaneously.

The next day, the skies were blue and the air crisp. The service was motivating, and the couple looked dizzy with happiness. As Zach mingled with the familiar crowd, he wondered what the man that had been making eyes at Rade from the previous day was saying to amuse her so much; he looked away in irritation and caught his sister's eyes, who wriggled her eyebrows at him. Trust Simi to notice everything.

After the reception, they drove back to the groom's house where they were staying. Zach's friends had refused to let them lodge in a hotel and insisted they stayed in his family house, which was big enough to contain them. It was an old house in the suburbs of the ancient city. That evening Zach and Rade were alone in the room that was assigned her. Maimuna and Simi had gone for an after party organised by a friend of the couple on the other side of town and Rade excused herself; she had experienced enough excitement for the day. Zach had offered to keep her company and promised to meet up with them later. He was doing neither as he adjusted himself to a more comfortable position on the chair where he had fallen asleep. He was tired; he had done much running around on the groom's behalf. He woke up with a start sometime after 8pm and met the smiling face of Rade who had been observing him. She shook her head and asked him to go get the much-needed rest. He heaved himself out of the chair tiredly and promised to check up on her later. She walked him to the door and on saying goodnight, Rade impulsively raised herself on her toes and touched his lips with hers. To say he was surprised was putting it lightly but it didn't last long, his male instincts took over, and the kiss which was meant to be a brief, impulsive one turned to one full of passion and purpose.

It went on endlessly; his kiss was long and delicious. He stopped for a moment to look into her eyes, they were dreamy and revealed words her mouth couldn't utter, and he gently caressed her ears with his lips as he whispered sweet nothings that made her wet with desire. He pulled her closer in a tight embrace, kissing the pulse beating wildly at the column of her neck, while gently walking her backward until they found themselves back in the middle of the room, urgent fingers groping and pawing at each other. Clothes rent the air; he released her bra and watched it slip away, as his lips continued to travel down and the sensation shot through her like scorch of fire. She knew he was undoing her slacks, but she was in a fog of desire and was shivering with the thrill. He slid her slacks down, and she willingly stepped out of them. His hands on her hips felt like fire, he moved them down, and she felt her underwear go down with his hands. The sound of his belt buckle hitting the floor with his jeans froze them apart for a few seconds as if to reconsider, and then they resumed as he touched her core and she moaned in pleasure. Rade felt the soft prickle of the carpet on her bottom as she was lowered onto her back and his mouth remained in possession of hers. His lips found the rigid tip of her soft breasts, and she trembled with pleasure, and his obvious bulge ignited a craving that consumed her. His eyes roved over her as he rose to push down his underwear; his waist was trim and lean, his thighs taut; she had no other thought in the world other than how much she wanted him. Lips and tongue followed where fingers had touched and stroked as he continued nibbling and suckling on her lust-filled body. He opened and stretched her, and the feeling of being filled and completely possessed overwhelmed her. He was slow and deliberate, and Rade felt herself clinging to Zach like her inside was hugging and grasping him. Then the roaring in her ears, like the sound of a thousand galloping horses, her feet forming a perfect arch a ballet dancer would have been proud of as the ripples coursed through her. The air was heavy and still, and an observer may have been oblivious to the activities in the room until she or he heard the urgent whispers, deep moans and unintelligible sounds of unbridled desire emanating from within. Zach noticed he was quivering, and his skin tingled and broke out in goose flesh as her nails dug into his back.

Rade gasped as the centuries-old unrhythmic dance of love continued, the tempo increasing with each stroke; there was no stopping the two until more ripples were shared between them as he emptied himself into her, replete.

A little while later, he eased himself off her and pulled her into his arms as their lips fastened. She allowed herself to stay there a while and started to feel her body begin to droop, giving in to sleep as he stroked her arm. Then she shook herself and stood up gingerly on legs that could hardly hold her up and felt his seed run down the inside of her thighs and embarrassment washed over her as he stared at it in wonder. She hurried over to the bathroom. Her back stung from the friction of the carpet and the icy blast of the shower woke her up. Zach stood unashamedly naked and watched, drinking in the sight of her.

"Rade, I imagine you are as shocked as I am right now, but please say something."

She just turned her back on him and let the water wash all over her and almost jumped out of her skin when he touched her arm.

"Please, give me some privacy."

He nodded and draped a towel around his form on his way out; she heard him lock the bedroom door, thinking it was kind of late for that now; imagine if someone had walked in on them. He went in the shower after her and returned wearing his now crumpled clothing; she was sitting impatiently on the edge of the bed and wanted him out so she could focus on her thoughts. He excused himself, saying he knew she wanted to be alone and promised to check on her later. She held her breath as he came close to her and gave her his usual peck on the forehead.

Rade locked the door and rushed to the bathroom, she stared, stupefied at herself in the mirror. What had just happened? She and Zach? It was unbelievable! She had never felt such pleasure. She cut herself short; her mind was in a whirlpool, this was all wrong. She refused to think any further, and by the time Maimuna and Simi returned, she was tucked into bed and pretending to be asleep. The two girls noticed immediately that something was wrong but couldn't place it. Rade refused to meet Zach's eyes let alone talk to him when he returned later to ask if she was up to a late dinner, which she declined. She just wanted to sleep, so he brought her a cup of hot chocolate and kissed her hand. She ignored the message he sent later at night asking if she was okay and if she wanted to talk.

The next morning they decided to show her a bit of the ancient city, and Rade was enthralled. They went to the Mapo town hall built on one of the seven hills of Ibadan and also where the Olu'Badan of Ibadan palace is situated. She liked the old Post Office, and driving through a street in the Beere area, Rade couldn't believe such old houses still existed; they were built so closely together. The houses with their rusty aluminium roofing sheets with very little patches of grey, almost hypnotised Rade as she kept closing and opening her eyes because the sunlight bouncing off their rusty edges made all the aluminum roofing sheets look like one plain sheet, but when she opened her eyes again, they took another form. She suddenly wished she had any artistic expression for this.

They took her to a tower named after the first president and commissioner of the old Yoruba land, Captain L. Bower, and looking up the labyrinth of stairs from the bottom it almost seemed impossible that one could ascend them until you did. Climbing the narrow winding steps up the tower left them panting and gasping for breath. They all gasped as the view of the whole city spread out before them when they got to the top.

"This tower has been here since 1936, and most people who live in this city have never been here to see Ibadan like this. Another good view is from Cocoa House, that's if you can get to the penthouse," said Maimuna.

Zach nodded in affirmative and pointed out Cocoa House to Rade, which was quite a distance away from where they were.

"You can also get a spectacular view like this on the top of the Mapo hall where we are just coming from."

Rade was peering through her binoculars while Maimuna was clicking on her camera.

"Now I can boast I've visited Bower's Tower in Ibadan; the largest and the oldest city in West Africa and the second largest in Africa; it pales in comparison with the Eifel Tower in Paris, and the other magnificent ones but who cares, it's a tower nonetheless," Rade continued to scan the area.

"You should see it at night when the whole town is lit up; it's nice!" Said Maimuna.

They made their descent down, and she promised them on their next visit to Ibadan, she would show Rade her alma mater, the premier University, the prestigious University of Ibadan. Zach and Simi sniggered. They hated it when Maimuna started her old university talk; she loved her alma mater.

The drive back to Lagos that evening was an uneventful one. They dropped Rade off at home first, and while helping her with her suitcase, she told Zach she didn't think they should see each other for a while.

"Now you're taking things a bit extreme," he replied, "we are adults, what happened was unexpected but beautiful. We are attracted to each other, but you choose to ignore that fact; you skirt around matters that concern us, and now this happens, and you start acting like a shrinking violet."

Rade gave him a withering look, which he returned with an apologetic stare.

"I'll have my suitcase now," she answered and retrieved her weekend case, which Zach was still holding; she said goodbye to her friends and walked away without a backward glance at Zach who was staring at her in anger and frustration. The screech of the tyres brought a grim smile to Rade's lips.

What a weekend she thought and sat down miserably in her favourite chair, what was the matter with her? The weekend had been fun regardless, but why did she feel this way? She felt vulnerable and a bit confused, and she didn't have an answer to her question.

By mid-week, Zach called Rade and was surprised at her cold reception.

"What on earth is the matter with you, Rade, are you going to keep malice with me forever; what do you want me to do; apologise for making love to you? Okay, I apologise, even though I remember you urging me on and I have scratches all over my back to prove that…," there was a brief pause, then he continued, "okay that was distasteful, and I apologise; please tell me what you want me to do."

"What do you think the matter is; all this is okay for you I presume? You are a man, and it's okay to wave things aside so casually. Don't you get it? It's just a bit much for me to take in. We had sex on the floor, without protection, in someone's house, with the door unlocked, anyone could have walked in, without warning. We are not dating, and it's not like we intended to have a one night stand, though I think we know how we feel about one another, but we have never verbalised those feelings, and we just jump at each other like animals, lust-filled animals, and you ask me what the problem is. Isn't it obvious?"

"What is obvious?" Zach asked.

She hung up, and Zach groaned. He understood a little bit; it was still kind of weird even to him, but why couldn't they just move past that awkward phase. He realised this was another part of her he didn't know. He always thought of Rade as level headed and cool but she was acting like a real drama queen, and he didn't know what to do.

They'd agreed to talk about business only, and Rade's frostiness towards him whenever he tried to broach that particular topic, reminded him of the first time they met. After two weeks, it seemed like she hated seeing him and everyone was equally as puzzled.

Weeks slipped by, and everyone was wondering how long the drama would last. Rade missed Zach terribly but anytime she wanted to call him, pride wouldn't let her; she was too pigheaded to finish a silly fight she had started. She missed his voice, his laughter, his presence and even his bullying. It was a month now, why couldn't he just call her, she thought. Wasn't a man meant to chase a woman; after all he claimed he cared about her. Whenever she saw Simi, her heart would skip hoping he would be with her. She knew it was her fault but how would she stretch out the Olive branch?

She hadn't told Maimuna what happened, every time she wanted to talk about it, she would just clamp up. She was also worried about Phil; her calls kept going to his already full voice mailbox and he hadn't replied any of her e-mails.

"This place is going to be something," Maimuna said, "I'm so happy for you Rade."

The two girls were taking a tour of the Goldmine premises. Rade smiled back at her friend, who was taking pictures as usual.

"Thank you, Maimuna, your support means a great deal to me, especially after you told me to stop fretting and start having faith."

Maimuna smiled, and Rade decided then to tell Maimuna about her and Zach. Maimuna's eyes kept getting wider and wider as she jumped up and down excitedly.

"Simi and I have racked our brains over what could cause your love fight, and after hearing this, she guessed right. Is that why you've put Zach through hell this past month? From what you are telling me, he didn't rape you. That's what happens when you bottle up your emotions; both of you are always together, and you talk about everything under the sun except each other, that was bound to happen. And if I may ask, was it good? Actually, don't bother answering that question."

"You are crazy, Maimuna, you don't just get it at all; but to answer your question, it was mind-blowing, and just thinking about it makes me hot and ashamed at how uncontrollably I behaved. The embarrassment and anger I feel is really at myself, and I've just taken it out on Zach; it was just so sudden! Then my period was eight days late, Maimuna, I freaked out! I asked God for forgiveness over and again as if He didn't hear me the first time I did. Do you know how many times I wanted to call you or him? I couldn't do the pregnancy test until three days after buying, not just a strip, but a whole pregnancy test kit; all the possibilities of what could be were running in my head. I was praying every minute, as I know I'm not ready for a baby neither is Zach. I am happy it was negative; then I felt guilty that I was so happy it was negative like it would have been such a terrible thing. It's been difficult for me even though I know I overreacted."

"I'm so sorry to hear that, I wish you had told me.

But please get over it, you don't need to carry such a burden. The worst thing ever is not being able to forgive yourself, gosh! Even God has moved on."

Maimuna started teasing her and tried to tickle Rade who wasn't having any of it. On their way out, she saw a familiar car and her heart skipped a beat. "Zachary is obviously in the premises," Maimuna commented looking around. He was nowhere within sight, but her eyes kept searching. Then Maimuna called out, "there he is."

Zach was approaching at a leisurely pace, stopping briefly twice and glancing over his shoulder as if waiting for someone.

The two drank in the sight of one another and exchanged slightly warm greetings; she was quite sure he could hear the pounding of her heart. Why was he having such an effect on her? How sex could change things; not that her heart didn't use to pound before. Zach had always made her very aware she was a woman and he a man she was attracted to.

He opened his arms for a hug and peck from Maimuna who was eyeing them openly. Rade wished he would say something to her, tease her or even meet her eyes, but he almost completely ignored her. She had half hoped he came to see her, but it didn't even look like he was pleased to see her.

She wondered why he hadn't shaved and caught herself. How was it now her business if Zach shaved or not. He looked good as always. She looked over his pale blue jeans, and her mind started to wander as she remembered his taut thighs and how they felt against her much softer skin. He looked at her in that minute, and she could swear he could read her thoughts. He addressed her and started giving her an update on another meeting he just had with the previous Architect to discuss the property and all the challenges he envisaged they would face looking at the drawings on the original plan when he was interrupted.

"Zach, how ungentlemanly for you to go on without me!"

She and Maimuna looked around puzzled, but Maimuna's expression turned to familiarity as she watched the tall, slim lady approaching.

Rade remembered Zach once saying "Tall and slim; the way I like them."

"This place is huge; I couldn't remember where you were parked."

"Mandy," Zach introduced them. Mandy is an interior designer, one of the best interior designers he'd ever worked with, he added for effect.

And if Rade had an object in her hands, she would have plunked him on the head with it without any remorse.

Mandy was pleased to meet Rade, oblivious to their partnership or the Goldmine project to Rade's relief. They were on their way to a site when he got a phone call from the Architect requesting a brief on-site meeting to review an updated drawing which Zach declined suggesting a café not far off because of Mandy. She and the Architect had engaged in a conversation after that and Zach left them to get his car parked in the Goldmine due to limited space at the Cafe. Rade wasn't sure if she liked her. The duo said their goodbyes to the girls, and Rade and Maimuna watched as he opened the passenger side of his Land Rover for her, and as they drove away she was still chatting, and Zach was smiling at whatever it was she was saying to him. They both sighed as Rade got into the passenger side of Maimuna's car.

"I don't like what I'm seeing, Maimuna."

"Well, stop blowing hot and cold, Rade, and decide what you want. You can't put a guy through hell for something you both did, then get jealous when you see him with someone else. Anyway, don't worry about Mandy, she and Zach were on and off for a while, but I don't think anything's happening there, not for Zach, at least. There are rumours she is hypersexual, but she does run one of the best interior design firms in the city; she's really good, and that's why Zach always works with her if the need arises. She's also very rich, and she introduced Zach to Ugo. Remember Ugo?" She continued, as Rade nodded. "She's been in Nigeria for so long you forget she's South African. I could see you were trying to place the accent."

"Goodness Maimuna, thanks for the reassurance, you do know how to make a girl feel great. And who says nothing's happening for him there? Men are so silly, they can hardly resist a woman who chases them; their egos won't allow it," Rade was angry just thinking of them driving away together.

"Sorry darling, you know I tell it as it is. I think you guys should get your act together and settle your lovers tiff. We all know Zach is over his head in love with you without any shadow of doubt," Maimuna replied with a wink at her friend who was tugging absentmindedly at her seat belt as Maimuna started giggling, expressing pity for the seat belt.

After yet another month of not talking to each other, Rade had given up hope of ever talking to Zach. She had scarcely seen him that month, and when they did, he was always so annoyingly polite, talking to her like someone he just met, she knew he was punishing her because she had made efforts at being friendly.

She rang the house after ringing Zach's mobile, which he didn't answer. Simi was out of town for a job and was taking extra time afterwards to spend some time with her fiancé.

Rade thought that with Simi away, Zach would call her but he didn't; she hung up in disappointment after many rings and promised herself she would never call him again until he called her.

Later that night, the insistent ring of her land phone woke her up, she scrambled for the receiver and tipped over everything on her dresser in the process.

Zach! She thought and hoped. It was Becca; she had been trying to reach her for a few days, she said, but her number was always busy whenever she tried. Then she gave her the most incredulous news that Phil had been missing for a few days, and a few people feared he had been kidnapped or maybe even dead as no one had contacted the family asking for ransom. As she launched into the details, Rade went numb with shock.

She rang off telling Rade she would keep her updated. Rade sat down immobile for a while. Phil, her own Phil, bubbly Phil could be dead or missing, a tiny voice in her head reminded her.

She had the same thought on her mind. She wondered if Uncle Mark had heard, but he would have called her; she tried his number severally, but it was unavailable. She was trying unsuccessfully to remember when last they had spoken. Her mind was in turmoil. She needed to talk to someone. She dialled Zach's number without hesitation, and after many rings, his sleepy voice came on the phone.

"Zach, Phil is missing!" She cried, with a sob she went on and on next to hysteria.

"Rade! Relax just a bit and tell me what's happening; I can't get the head and tail of what you are saying."

Rade replayed the phone call from Becca; Phil had been declared missing or probably dead. They had been looking for him for about nine days. It all seemed like a joke at first, knowing Phil who was fond of taking off without telling anyone. He went sailing with his girlfriend Kenyatta, and since then they haven't seen them or the yacht; a couple of hours has turned to nine days and still no word from either of them.

"I am sure he's okay," Zach reassured her, "he probably decided to elope with his girlfriend and go get married or do something crazy and will probably show up apologising to everyone."

"I hope so," Rade cried, "though I can feel it deep down that something's happened to him. I've been thinking about him a lot lately and wondering how he is because his phones have been off, his voicemail is full, and he hasn't returned any of my emails. And just yesterday, while I was praying, I kept seeing his face at the back of my mind; I've just had this constant urge to pray for him more than before. I didn't even realise it's being reported on Sky and BBC News, but I've not watched or listened to the news lately, I've been so caught up with other things."

"Me neither. Did you pray for him?"

"Yes."

"Then he'll be okay; that's all we can do for now." He reassured her for almost an hour and asked why she hadn't answered when he called her back thrice after seeing her missed calls from earlier. It was then she started looking for her mobile and realised it had slipped under her pillow and she had been lying on it. Rade hung up feeling much better than she had in a long time.

Talking to Zach, as usual, calmed her; he had a way of making everything seem okay, such positivity. She prayed and hoped that Phil was okay as she drifted into a peaceful sleep where she dreamt Phil was smiling and telling her not to bother her pretty head about him.

It is said that *when it rains, it pours*. And it appears the rain is only just getting started, as if the Phil situation is not enough trouble to deal with already. Three days later, Zach, Rade and Maimuna sat together in Rade's apartment, Rade had her arms around Maimuna, and Zach's face was set in a hard frown.

"We have to report this to the police; just let me know whenever you feel up to it."

Maimuna shook her head, "No Rade, it's embarrassing enough as it is, I don't want the Police involved, it'll just get blown out of proportion; then because of the person involved, it will go hush, hush."

"What do you mean? You can't let him get away with it," Rade said, shaking Maimuna's shoulders vigorously.

"I also don't want the little girl involved. It is not her fault her father is a jerk."

Zach shook his head and came over to Maimuna's side, peering at the bruises on her forehead and the red palm imprint on her cheek. He touched it, and she winced, flinching back from his touch. Rade was getting a salve to apply after the ice pack. Zach was seething inside and desperately wanted to get his hands on the man that hit his cousin, but she wasn't dropping names, and he needed a name. He had been terrified when Maimuna called crying over the phone. She asked him to come over to Rade's house because she didn't want to go home and alarm Aunty Asabe. Even in her distress, Maimuna was still thinking about others. It was Rade who narrated the story to him, Maimuna was still in shock.

She had a patient, Lola, a little girl she had come to regard as a friend; she was adorable and loved Maimuna and enjoyed her hospital visits. She usually came with her father who was divorced and dotted on her.

He was a rich, handsome man and every time he brought his daughter to the clinic he made subtle advances, which Maimuna turned down. He was always trying to buy her one expensive item or the other; he didn't just get that she wasn't interested.

After Lola's last appointment with Maimuna where she came to get braces for her teeth, she asked Maimuna when she could come over to visit her before she returned to the United States where she lived with her mother; she was persistent. Maimuna agreed very reluctantly, and they fixed a date for late lunch at 5:00pm in Lola's house the week after, which was the only time Maimuna could squeeze in.

She went for the late lunch date and was surprised Lola wasn't around, but the father was available and looked quite pleased with himself when he explained that she had gone to visit her grandmother and would be back very soon and that, in fact, he wasn't too pleased because she had stayed longer than agreed. Maimuna then had a drink at his insistence, and after an hour, Lola still hadn't returned. She announced she was leaving and he asked her to wait a little more; he kept on telling her how much he liked her and she brushed him aside telling him she was flattered but wasn't really interested in a relationship. It irked her the way he went on and on about them looking good together. She had had enough; it was time to leave, and as she got to the door he made his final move. He pulled her and kissed her fiercely on the lips. To say she was shocked was putting it lightly, and she shoved him away from her, then the struggle began, in spite of it, he kept trying to paw at her body; he obviously wanted to have her with or without her consent. Cold fear had settled at the pit of her stomach.

As she continued to ward him off, he got more excited, and Maimuna weaker. He was a strong athletic man, and even the targeted knee at his groin area was sidestepped. He ripped Maimuna's blouse. He slapped and hit her hard a couple of times on the face when she tried to scream; she scratched his face and headbutted him; he then grabbed her throat, pushing his weight on her stomach and forcing her legs apart after hitting her thighs really hard. She started to panic when she felt the air on her thighs as her skirt was pulled up and his groping fingers searched her out. She was going for a hard punch to his larynx when she heard the sound of the impressive gate to the house opening and a car driving into the compound. He still laid on top of her undecided, then she hit him on the neck and shoved him off her with all her might; he rolled away as she struggled with her things which were scattered all over the floor. He looked into her eyes with lust filled ones pleading with them.

Maimuna scrambled over, and sighting a door, which she guessed might be the guest bathroom; she made for it, her heart pounding wildly, her whole body feeling battered and her mind in shock. She wondered how the whole ordeal would have ended if not for the timely sound of the gate opening and the car driving in. She couldn't believe what had just ensued. Then she heard her little patient's excited voice and put her ears to the door. She was asking if her Doc had come because she noticed an unusual car in the driveway and why he told her that her grandmother wanted to see her when she had been surprised, albeit pleased by her visit.

Maimuna sagged on the door, and after listening for a few more minutes and hearing the voices disappear into another room, she opened the door and fled. The puzzled expression on the security man's face as she almost sped through the gates hadn't helped. She was shaking uncontrollably as she drove; her tears blinding her until she parked and called Zach, who asked her to stay put, but she couldn't and asked him to meet her at Rade's. She managed to drive to Rade's place who screamed when she saw her friend.

Zach paced about wondering what to do; how he could get the man's address from Maimuna. He stared at his cousin wondering what man in his right mind would want to hurt such a woman. She had put up a good fight, but the look in her eyes said something else, she was devastated, nearly raped and assaulted by someone she knew. He came up straight; there was more to this story; his gut told him.

"Maimuna, tell me who it is that did this to you, you know I'll find out sooner than later, you know me. Why are you protecting this bum?"

"Zach, please back off a bit," Rade pulled her

friend closer; she was still shaking uncontrollably, but she understood exactly how he felt, the same rage welled inside her. The room was quiet except for Zach's ragged breath. Then Rade's mobile phone, which had been ringing incessantly all the while without being picked up started ringing again, and he glared at it like the culprit.

"Answer it," Maimuna muttered, "someone is obviously trying to reach you desperately," she said, sipping a drink.

It was Becca telling her they'd just found the remains of Phil's girlfriend and the yacht, but there was still no sign of Phil's body. This was disheartening news for Rade who was determined to believe that somehow her friend would turn up, and everyday Zach kept telling her he believed Phil wasn't dead. They had been following the story on the news closely.

"What happened out there? Does anybody know?" She asked in a shrill voice as Zach and Maimuna listened with concern.

"Take it easy, girl. Phil took the boat out with his girlfriend who wanted some alone time with him; she had been complaining all week they weren't spending much time together as they were both so busy. She had just returned from a modelling job in Monaco. What we don't know is if he listened to the weather forecast that suggested there might be a sudden change in weather that day; a storm was brewing. It seems the wind and waves picked up, and they were obviously heading back for the shore when one of the stays on the mast broke. Phil didn't radio any message he was in danger or at least there was no indication he did. The conclusion is that the boat capsized and the couple drowned, probably after attempting to swim to the shore, but it was dark. The autopsy identified Kenyatta's battered body which had drifted to the shore, but there was still no sign of Phil. Becca hung up telling Rade that Phil's parents were going crazy, and Kenyatta's parents had flown in from Kenya; her burial was in two days.

Rade felt tears trickle down her face for the girl she had never met. What a terrible misfortune. She went over to Maimuna whose turn it was to hold her friend. Zach stared in resignation wondering what on earth to do about the girls.

Chapter Nine

The days after were sad ones for Rade. She got depressed anytime she thought about Phil. The memories of the great times they had together haunted her and Zach's shoulder had become the resting place for her head. Maimuna was still trying to get over her shock, but all the cocktail of emotions had been replaced with the most prominent one, anger. She had become further enraged after her little friend, Lola, called her a few days later telling her sorry about the Diarrhea she had developed that night and had to leave before she got back from her granny's place. Adding that she hoped Maimuna was feeling much better.

Maimuna was livid at the excuse the vile man had given for her hasty departure. He called several times a day after the incident despite her refusal to answer his calls, neither did she answer any calls from a withheld or unknown number. She was dealing with it her own way. She still hadn't told Zach or Rade who he was. Simi was still out of town on her much-deserved break.

Rade sighed contentedly, despite all the unfortunate incidences, it was great to be in love and be free to express it. Zach had asked her in the most formal way if she would be his girlfriend and Rade had laughed and answered she would love to be just that. He expressed his fears and asked if she could handle them being business partners and in a relationship at the same time.

"Why would you even ask such a question? I'm not a child; I already had feelings for you before I literally begged you to partner with me on the project."

"Well, your behaviour after we made love got me worried, Rade, I was confused. I knew it was unplanned but not altogether unheard of since we are attracted to each other. I never asked you out because I didn't want to pressure you, wasn't sure you had the time for a relationship, and timing is key to every purpose under the sun; you may be doing the rightest thing in the world, but at the wrong time; it may amount to nothing. Your behaviour was quite childish, and that's why as much as it killed me, I decided to give you some space and keep an eye on you from a distance."

"That is so unfair! I may have overreacted a bit." Zach raised his brows. "Well, a lot; I just panicked, though I do apologise for being mean, I was confused, we had sex, my period was more than a week late, and I freaked out even more. I didn't know how to make up with you without being silly, and by then you had started treating me with kid gloves, and then proceeded to rub in my face an interior designer that looks like a supermodel; that was annoying. And where do you get off presuming things? If I was spending all my time with you, what made you think I wasn't ready for a relationship? Nothing's changed now, I'm still busy and may even get busier. So what's the difference between then and now? Just admit you were frightened I would turn you down and bruise your ego; though thinking about it now, you're kind of right as usual."

"I'm so sorry; idiot that I am. It never even occurred to me you could have been pregnant after that night. Goodness, you must have been upset. Please forgive me."

She nodded.

"And as for turning me down, never such a chance;

you are hot for me. I know exactly when you started falling for me," he ducked as she swatted him with a newspaper, "and my ego would never have been bruised in the unlikely event of a refusal; I would have chased you and the story would still be the same. See how I made you get to like me; we've come a long way from that day you ran from the dogs right into my arms."

She was chasing him around the room now.

"And Mandy knew how I felt about you from your five minutes together; she teased me all the way to the site we were going. It's amazing how you women pick up on things."

"Yeah, she would; seeing you guys have been together before."

"Oh gosh; Maimuna and her mouth. There's honestly nothing between us anymore."

"There had better not be."

"Wow! Are you a jealous type? My feisty madam."

"You'll find out soon enough," she replied, which turned to a whoop as he lifted her on his shoulder and spun her around as she screamed and begged to be put down.

Zach didn't kid himself about being in love with Rade; it was hard to explain, but she had become the focal point of everything. He was in deeper with each passing day, and even though she was a handful, he did his best to be patient with her. She made him laugh, and he always seemed to be smiling at a private joke they'd shared with each turn. They were learning to understand each other. A month before Christmas, they were on their way to the sports club. Rade's tennis was rusty, and she had arm-twisted Zach into taking her with him. His mobile rang, she was flexing her arm in anticipation of the game but stared worriedly at the rigid expression on Zach's face as he listened to the conversation on the other end via bluetooth.

"Where are you?" He bellowed, then hung up in exasperation.

"It seems something dramatic has to happen in each one of our lives lately. It's Simi; she's been in town for two days now, she didn't want to say which hotel she's in, but I think I have an idea, somewhere closest to the Airport. I'm sorry baby, rain cheque on the Tennis if you don't mind. Let me drop you back home; we can meet up later."

She shook her head, "I'm coming with you. I want to see Simi. Are we driving to the mainland now?" She asked.

He nodded and made a swift turn and headed for the fourth mainland bridge.

"Why is Simi staying in a hotel?" She asked, getting more puzzled by the minute.

Zach didn't reply until a while later.

"She's broken up with Dimka."

"What!" Rade exclaimed, Simi and Dimka had already fixed their wedding date for February.

"What happened?" Her heart sank in her chest.

"I guess we'll find out when we see Simisola," he responded.

They drove in silence until Zach entered into the parking lot of the assumed hotel.

"You think she'll be here?"

Zach nodded his head, coming round to open the door for Rade. Fingers entwined, they made their way to the reception.

"She most likely got off the plane very upset and would think of the closest, most expensive hotel to come lodge and blow all the money she just made and cry her heart out, of course."

There was a little fuss at the reception; the front desk manager told them blankly he couldn't disclose any information as to whether Simi was there or not if they didn't know what room she was staying.

"My sister is distraught; she just called my fiancée and I moments ago, but we couldn't get the room number because my battery went dead," he stated, raising his mobile phone. "I wouldn't want her to do something foolish especially in a four-star hotel room," he added for effect.

213

The front desk man's eyes widened, and he excused himself, "I'll check if there is any Ms. Mohammed in any of our single rooms," he muttered, and browsing through the screen gave them the room number reluctantly.

"I'll call and let her know you're coming up."

"Don't worry," Zach said, "we'll just go up to her."

"You were right!" She said as they followed a concierge into the lift. Zach shrugged; if only the receptionist knew they had been bluffing.

The receptionist quickly called Simi's room; though she didn't answer because she was in the shower. It was the persistent knock on the door that brought Simi out of the bathroom; she couldn't remember ordering anything when she heard the voice outside the door say "room service." The sight of her brother and Rade made her sigh miserably and she let them in and walked over to the bed where she slumped and just started talking without any prompting. Her relationship of almost four years was over. The phone rang, it was the receptionist, and Simi assured him she was alright.

"You never liked him," she said to Zach.

He didn't say anything but just shook his head.

"When I arrived Jos on the first day, Dimka wasn't even around; he had travelled to Abuja, and his mom was acting very funny. We are not the best of friends, but she's been friendlier, so I decided to stay in a hotel.

"Wow!" Zach butted in angrily, "you seem to have a thing for hotels; you could have gone to Buba's family house."

"He came back the next day, he was livid because I lodged in a hotel, but I insisted I wanted to be there. Everything was fine, we were still making all the wedding plans, and if he's a jerk in some other ways, you can't fault him for being very loving and making a woman feel special. On the fifth day, we were supposed to go to his friend's place for lunch. I waited and waited for him. His mobile phone was off, so I called his house and was told he wasn't in. I was so upset I didn't go to check on him that evening, and he didn't bother calling me that night either. Then I started getting really worried.

So the next day, I decided to check on him since he wasn't at work either. I got to his house and went over to the side of the house where Dimka stayed and met his mother on her way out with the housekeeper who was carrying a tray loaded with dirty dishes. She said Dimka wasn't in and was trying to talk me into going to have tea with her in the kitchen, but I declined and walked right into his room because by now, I knew there was something wrong. He was in there with a girl, very intimate scene; the two just getting out of bed and being served breakfast.

"I wanted to die," Simi said with a sigh.

"You should have seen the expression on his face; he looked so stupid. I wanted to kill him and the girl, but I didn't have enough strength; I just walked out of the room, and my walk of shame out of that house was a long one. His mother and sister who had come to watch an envisaged scene just observed in silence as I walked away. I had to wait for a taxi outside the house, and it seemed, though I know it's impossible, that God had deserted me as my prayers to have a car whisk me away quickly went unanswered. So, I started walking, it was a long walk and with each step, my heart grew heavier. I've never known such pain and shame in my life."

Rade's chest was burning; Zach just stared at his sister in silence.

"He came to see me that night, blabbing all sorts of rubbish, slightly tipsy as always. He said he was sorry but it wasn't his fault, the girl was all over him; she is a family friend, and she wouldn't take no for an answer, and whined that I was never around anyway.

I listened to him in silence. I had cried so much, I just didn't have any energy left for anything else, and then he got nasty. Who was I to look at him that way, I was too full of myself anyway, and that pompous brother of mine didn't help matters.

I overlooked his many faults, all his whining and insane jealousy because of how I feel about him but there and then I knew I deserved more and it hurt so much. He's always wanted all my attention on him, and he resented anything that stood as a threat to him, and that included, my brother, my work, my friends, Lagos and anything he could imagine. I couldn't say anything; all I asked him was if he was truly going to go ahead with the marriage. That got to him, and he started pleading, and I couldn't help but cry. If he could cheat on me when I wasn't too far away, I was only staying a few more days, and he couldn't even respect that; then what could have been happening when we were miles apart? I've heard stories about his philandering ways, but I never dwelt on them not to upset myself. I know he cheats on me but thought, perhaps, marriage would change him; I don't know why I thought that. I do love him, maybe I was just too lazy, settling for less because of the hassle of meeting someone new who in time you'll find out is like the rest. The biggest problem was how he made me feel, and that's what should have helped me make a decision a long time ago; the choice has always been mine to make. He drains me, makes me listless and I'm always on the defensive; it was like he was sucking up all my energy and we weren't even married yet."

"After he left," Simi continued without missing a beat, "his mother called the next day, she was quite sorry she said, but I had to understand that it was hard for most men to stay with one woman; it was one of the things women have to live with."

Rade gasped and shook her head in disbelief.

"He came back pleading, and I must confess, I almost gave in, but something held me back. How could I decide to make the life God has given me a living hell? I told him it is over and he shouldn't call or try any manner of reconciliation. I mean we've gone so far with the wedding plans. I can't believe I'm no longer getting married. It's surreal! I miss him, but I'm equally appalled I put up with his rubbish for this long," she wailed, and Rade went over to her side.

"You've made a difficult decision; I know nothing's set in stone, but I support you. You know I want the best for you as you mean the world to me; anyone who hurts you has hurt me, Simisola."

Simi started bawling as she held on to her brother. "Let's take you home."

But Simi shook her head vigorously, "I don't want to go home yet, I'm not ready; I can spend whatever I want now, there is no wedding to save for anymore," she said with a fresh bout of tears.

Zach pacified her and asked what she wanted to do instead. She didn't know, but she knew she didn't want to go home; she didn't mind company though. So they called Maimuna who was surprised she was back, and she promised to join them on the mainland as soon as she could. A harried-looking Maimuna was in Simi's hotel room a few hours later asking for the umpteenth time what the matter was. Zach had gone out and returned at the same time Maimuna arrived. He watched in silence as Simi narrated the story to their cousin, whose mouth kept getting wider as she muttered expletives in Hausa and Fulfulde.

"Oh Simi; I'm so sorry. Why are men so wicked, why can't they realise that it is other people that usually suffer for their self-gratifying, self-centred acts?"

Zach sighed, and Rade glared at him, and he raised his hands in defence.

"You may not have heard Simi, but Ugo tried to rape me."

"What?!!!" Chorused the three in the room as Maimuna realised with dismay she'd just revealed the identity of her assailant.

Zach was out of the room in a flash; the girls hardly got a chance to stop him.

Several hours later, the girls were yawning tiredly as they left the Ikoyi Police Station where they had gone to pick Zach after a phone call from his partner and Buba. He had sought Ugo out expressing shock he dared to remain in town after what he did to his cousin, and punches followed after that, most of them thrown by Zach. Buba had been called to the scene and someone at the exclusive membership club Ugo went for drinks had called the Patrol Police in the area to report disorderly conduct. They arrived the scene soon after and picked them up wanting to know why such respectable gentlemen had degenerated so low as to have a public fight. Ugo didn't want the story out and insisted they would settle it, until the girls got there and everything went to the pits.

Maimuna had reported the incident at the same Police station, and they had a warrant out for Ugo's arrest but claimed he was out of town when two officers had gone to his house to bring him in. They were forced to arrest him there as he continued to plead with Maimuna.

The girls were reprimanding Zach as he sat unremorsefully in Buba's car, who in turn was complaining bitterly he hadn't gotten any chance to "knock off a few of Ugo's teeth" before the police arrived as he ferried Zack off to pick his car from the scene of the incident. The girls were still shocked especially Rade who had seen first hand what Ugo had done to Maimuna.

He was a friend, how could he have thought he would get away with it. No wonder Zach had felt there was more to the story than Maimuna was telling; the disappointment and hurt in her eyes had said it all. The betrayal of trust; it was someone she knew closely, someone whose house she had been comfortable enough to visit, not the father of a patient called Lola. Ugo's daughter's name was Adaeze, and they had all, except Rade, met her. Simi went on to give them the statistics of females that were raped not by strangers but by friends, family members and the people closest to them, yet they could never speak out from fear, causing a scene, stigma, being doubted, the list was long.

"You're right Simi, though he didn't penetrate, I still felt ashamed like I caused it somehow. I just wanted it to go away and didn't want to cause a scene, especially knowing Zach; Ugo is his client and they are closer than mere acquaintances. We go to his house occasionally for goodness sakes, and his daughter is my patient. He's always told me he likes me and everyone knows he's a charmer, but I would never have thought he would do that to me. I think the familiarity made me go easier on him initially; I kept thinking he would stop and all the awkwardness would be over. I was still responding with some respect. Why would he want to hurt me? Going to make the report was one of the hardest things I've had to do, and the Police officer taking my report didn't make it any easier; the innuendos he made as I was asked to narrate the incident over and again before writing my statement; almost as though it was my fault."

Rade was livid.

"Coincidentally, I recently heard he's back to his drug habit; he obviously relapsed after how passionately he spoke about quitting the other day. I kind of feel sorry for him, and it makes sense now, though inexcusable, and on the other hand, I want to hurt him deeply. Why should I feel pity for someone who assaulted me? I am the victim."

The girls were fagged out. No one wanted to drive back to Simi's hotel on the mainland; she still didn't want to go home, neither did Maimuna after all the commotion, nor Rade who had just seen another side to her boyfriend, and wasn't in the mood for another night of waiting for an update on Phil who was still missing. They opted for a small hotel after paying with Maimuna's card; she was the only one quick enough to grab her bag after the call from Buba.

Chapter Ten

Two days before Christmas, by the swimming pool at Zach and Simi's house, three ladies laid quiet on deck chairs, each lost in thought in her own world. The climate was undecided on what it wanted to do; a dull sun peeked behind the clouds, it was hot and dry during the day but a slight chill set in when nighttime fell.

Rade rushed in, beaming and screaming excitedly, startling the ladies out of their reverie.

"Guess what?" Rade exclaimed! Standing over the three ladies and peering down at them.

"He proposed! Zach asked me to marry him."

Simi and Maimuna got up excitedly; they had never seen Rade look like this; like she was going to burst with happiness. She pushed Maimuna's long legs away making space for herself at the edge of her friend's deck chair, and Maimuna, in turn, decided to sit up.

"I thought you went to church?" Helen asked curiously.

"Well, we did go to Church," Rade answered. "Zach proposed to me in the Church; talk about being original! There we were listening to the Christmas carols, and I was telling Zach how proud I am of my children: I work in the children's Church, remember. We were already getting funny glances as usual because we were whispering and chuckling, when he faces me and starts to give me that look! The one that makes my heart melt and start beating wildly, then he whispered: Will you marry me, Rade?"

The girls were following with rapt attention.

"And?" Maimuna prodded impatiently.

"A deep well of happiness bubbled up from inside me, and I said yes so loudly, we attracted a bigger audience than the ones seated around us who were already staring at us in amazement. It was an electric moment, completely unexpected."

"I hope you guys didn't kiss inside the Church?!" Maimuna inquired indecorously, "please tell me you didn't!"

"No we didn't, mommy Maimuna; we just held

hands, but it was really hard trying to concentrate after that."

"You two sound like something out of an old romance novel; imagine proposing in Church; how quaint," Helen chipped in, her voice slightly tinged with envy. She had always had eyes for Zach.

"Well," Rade answered, "it's a good thing you compare us to the romance novels because you know what? They always have happy endings."

Simi and Maimuna laughed, with Simi giving Rade the thumbs-up sign. She was really pleased with the news.

"So where is lover man?" Simi asked, and whistled to catch her brother's attention as they sighted him at the bar watching the replay of the goal scored in an ongoing soccer match. He turned at the sound of the whistle and taking a last glance at the television he headed towards the girls. Simi met him halfway; a towel draped around her with outstretched arms open for a hug, he returned the hug with a bigger one and a puzzled frown.

He inquired if something was the matter with grave concern on his face, and she asked why he would think something was wrong.

He said because whenever anything happened to any of them, he would be immediately summoned.

He had seen the outstretched arm scene many times, and it scared him silly.

The four girls laughed, and Maimuna said she couldn't blame him.

"Rade just told us she's making you the luckiest man in the world," Simi said.

Zach beamed, then frowned, "Did she actually put it that way?" He asked.

Zach pulled Rade to him, kissed her eyes and whispered that they get out of there.

"We're going to love and leave you ladies," Rade said blowing the girls an exaggerated kiss.

Her friends gave her an exasperated look she chuckled at.

"Where are you going and where is the ring?" Helen asked.

"Well the proposal wasn't planned, so my beautiful lady has told me she would like a chance to pick her own ring, and I have obliged her. As to where we are going, you ladies need to start minding your own business."

"Ouch!"

"Come over here," Simi motioned urgently, and Rade obliged her. She asked Rade to give her brother a run for his money and return with a befitting rock. Most women didn't usually get the opportunity to pick their engagement rings, the man usually just bought it, and the woman would have to pretend she liked it and gush over it even if it looked like crap.

Zach screamed in mock horror. "Simi, am I hearing correctly! My own sister is plotting to make me go bankrupt over an engagement ring; thank God I never sought your help in choosing one for Rade as that was the original plan."

"You bet," Simi replied, as he reached for Rade and with arms around one another, legs nearly crossing each other they wandered off whispering sweet nothings.

"Com'on guys, just in case you've forgotten; you can actually walk independently of one another as opposed to like conjoined twins," Maimuna said watching the two with a big grin on her face; they paid her no mind.

A month after their engagement, while on their way to check the progress on the Goldmine property, and discussing their wedding, Rade suddenly said, "when am I going to meet your father? We can't get married if I don't meet him."

"We can," Zach responded flatly. They were trying to pick a date for their wedding.

"We could, but we won't." She reminded him, he was the one always preaching about not bearing grudges and forgiveness; she understood it wasn't easy to forget how badly he had treated their mother, he and Simi but he had to try somehow. Acting like his father didn't exist didn't help matters; she knew he thought about him often. She hadn't always thought the world of her father, she was aware he wished she was a boy going by all the indications during her mother's pregnancy, and he'd never minced words about it while she was growing up. They had never had a post up father and daughter relationship, and living apart hadn't helped matters, but even she couldn't believe how much their relationship had evolved through deliberate nurturing; they were now so close, even her mother had started getting jealous.

"Zachary, are you listening to me?" She asked peering at his impassive face. "Please, don't shut me out; I don't like it when you do that."

"I am listening to you," he replied, meeting her eyes. "You have to forgive, to receive forgiveness; please let it go."

She asked that he work through the bitterness, open the door he had shut just a little bit and give room for reconciliation.

"I forgave him a long time ago Rade, but I really don't want anything to do with him, he's not going to add any value to Simi and my life at this point, he may well come and complicate it further. You don't know him; he's a proud, cold-hearted man; it's like he's carved from stone."

"Zachary! That's your father you're speaking about."

"But that's the truth and him being my father doesn't change that fact."

She reprimanded him for being obnoxious, and he apologised with a shrug of the shoulders and pulled her nose playfully.

He asked if she planned on being a naggy wife but admitted that he loved it when she got on his case. He was rewarded with a cheeky smile and a hug.

"How about this weekend?" She continued.

"What?" Zach asked puzzled.

She propositioned that they visit his father that weekend, all three of them. There was a long silence when she was done but she pressed on, promising to help convince Simi, who he was quite sure would disagree. That was one area he was sure his sister wouldn't listen to him.

Simi disagreed immediately and was taken through the same drill as Zach with Maimuna's assistance. Rade was convinced, despite all her business dealings that this was one of the toughest negotiations she had encountered, it required her best persuasive and negotiation skills. The duo was a hard nut to crack. She had to add that her parents needed to meet their father.

They initiated contact, and that weekend the four were in Ilorin, Kwara state to see Zachary and Simi's father.

Rade saw the joy on the father's face when he saw his children, which he tried almost successfully to hide.

Zachary was a replica of his father except for his skin, which was deep mahogany. Rade had to resist the urge to touch his skin; brown, leathery skin that somehow glowed at the same time. He ushered them in and hugged his daughter tightly to everyone's surprise. Rade was introduced, and his expressive eyes revealed approval; not that either of his children cared. He insisted they stayed for the night when they mentioned that they would be returning to Lagos that evening. Rade could see Zach was about to say no, so she pleaded with her eyes. He returned her bright smile with a scowl after confirming they would stay the night. He called out to his wife, a newly married one from the look of it and asked her to take them to the rooms that had been prepared for them.

Zach remarked that all his wives seemed to have deserted him and that the current one seemed even younger than his own daughter. He was stating the obvious, and no one had an answer to his quip. About thirty minutes after dinner, the girls retired to their rooms, one of which Simi said had belonged to her and one of her half-sisters. They left Zach and his father in the living room, after having sat there with them in uncomfortable silence; the room was designed like some sort of palace. The tension between them was unbearable; unspoken words hung thickly over them. Rade pitied the young wife who was trying all she could to make them comfortable but Zach wasn't making things easy for her; he declined everything she offered, but the girls had tried their best to make up for it.

That night, the girls couldn't help but hear the loud argument that ensued between father and son, and the loud bang of Zach's bedroom door a little while after. The three girls tiptoed to his room; there was no reply to the knock, so Simi opened the door slightly. Zach was pacing up and down the length of the room. She held her finger to her lips and motioned to the other two while she quietly closed back the door unnoticed, and they all filed back to their rooms. Zach was lying on the bed when they returned about an hour later.

He verbally attacked Rade the instance they walked in and accused her of talking him into coming to Ilorin when his life was perfect and just okay without his father. He was fuming at the fact that even after all the years of absence and silence their father still had nothing to say.

Rade insisted she hadn't made him come; she had only suggested something he had been thinking of doing, which pride and anger had prevented. His frustration was because he was hoping for something he probably would never get, an apology. Forgiveness doesn't require an apology from the one that had wronged you. She told Zach he needed to let go so he could find peace, as the grudge he held against his father would always have the power to hurt him. She reminded him of his copyrighted quote, *"life is short, so a tall grudge is unnecessary."*

She was convinced their father was genuinely happy to see them, though being there brought back a flood of memories for them.

He took a deep breath and admitted that he was fine for the most part when he didn't give much thought to his father, but on other days, the resentment was almost palpable and felt like a rodent that gnawed at his insides especially when he encountered the older man's lack of remorse and sense of entitlement.

He acted as if he hadn't wronged his children in any way. She reminded him, he once told her that he read somewhere that African parents never apologised. He scowled at her, and she went over to wrap her arms around him; he leaned into her as she began to stroke his hair and massaged his temples.

"We're still here," Simi chipped in.

"We know," they both replied.

Her touch relaxed him, and her fingers continued to work deftly at his temple and stroke his hair. He listened in silence to the girl's chatter until he started stifling and muffling yawns. The girls left him sleeping peacefully.

Later that night, Rade, who was restless and unable to sleep in an unfamiliar bed, found her way to the kitchen and was startled to see Alhaji Muhammad still awake.

"Are you okay sir?"

He replied with a curt nod.

She explained she had come down to get some water to drink but it was like talking to a brick wall, and after hurriedly gulping down a glass of water, she muttered goodnight, telling herself she now understood why his children called him cold.

"You remind me so much of their mother," he

said in his heavily accented English.

Rade was startled and turned to face him.

He continued without any encouragement, "she was such a gentle and breakable looking thing, but she had inner strength many didn't know about, even her own children; they always think of her as their fragile mother. Her father was a nomad, and she was quite young when I married her; she was given to me to foster goodwill between both families. She resented me immensely as I was much older than her and marrying a brash man like me wasn't any young girls dream. It wasn't unusual that when I saw her, I wanted her as mine. She was very beautiful. We lived like strangers, and my other wives didn't like her because she was quite detached and lived in her own world. She rarely spoke to anyone, but her delicateness brought out the protectiveness in me that angered me because it made me appear weak; men such as myself were not known for pampering their wives. The doctor said she wasn't strong enough for the rigours of childbirth. So you can imagine how ridiculed she became amidst the other wives who knew she was special to me. They called her 'kwalliya', a mere decoration in the house, but she held her head up high and would never give them the satisfaction of exchanging words or seeing her sad.

I was shocked and overjoyed when she found out she was pregnant; the people around didn't believe she would bear the child and the other wives tormented her endlessly.

"Why didn't you do anything about it?" Rade asked.

"I did; I was constantly reprimanding them to leave her be, but it just seemed to fuel the jealousy. I didn't understand her feelings towards me also; it was as though she hated me even more than she did before I married her. She would perform all her duties perfectly and take time off to go visit her family; she was determined to stay healthy, especially for the baby. She eventually gave birth to my son, Zachary, my replica, and he was the envy of all the wives, and I was a proud father. Mother and son simply adored each other, and it was apparent there was no room for any other person in their world. It was painful, and I felt excluded. I started treating Zachary harshly and made sure he was given chores that would keep him away from his mother; I wanted him to be a strong boy, not some mummy's pet. He knew what I was doing and resented me for keeping him away from his mother whom he was already so protective over at a tender age. A few years later, she got pregnant again to everyone's surprise and gave birth to Simi;

she almost lost her life in the process."

He continued that though, he would have wanted more children with Zach and Simi's mother, he was warned by the doctor that except he deliberately wanted to kill his wife, she shouldn't have any more children and they agreed. He had even accepted that they insert an IUD.

Simi had been more understanding as a child; it was as though she pitied her father and had this knowing look in her eyes, but she was just a little girl and couldn't do much. He said people had said it was because Zach was a replica of him that is why they didn't get along, but he cared for his son very much.

After a few years, she got pregnant yet again and had a miscarriage, and no one would have known about it if he hadn't caught her throwing away some blood-soaked towels. He was very upset. She confessed later she had gone to another clinic to have her birth control device removed because she wanted to have another child to please him and it was then he realised that she had grown to care about him. He said it was the nicest thing anybody had done for him, as all his life he had been taught to be tough, his father had been a very severe man; caring for his cattle and putting them before anyone else. It was the only way he knew to be.

Things changed between them, but perhaps because of the years of antagonism or because they were still too young, the children didn't notice, but the other wives definitely noticed things had changed.

A few months after, she took ill and didn't mention it to him that she had been feeling some pains and having fevers. Apparently, her womb was infected because of the lack of proper care at the clinic where her birth control had been removed and where she had subsequently gone back to for the evacuation after the miscarriage. She had also been drinking some concocted herbs given by a reputable herbalist to "cleanse" her system when she started noticing she was feeling unwell. He was angry and went all out to have the clinic shut down and beat up himself about not taking her to his original hospital for the evacuation. It seemed the infection opened a can of other sicknesses because she just kept getting sicker with little relief. She struggled to get well but the infection had taken its toll, and the initial lack of proper medical care didn't help matters. She eventually died in his arms leaving him with two bewildered children.

He was devastated and in his grief, shut out the children again and they, in turn, blamed him for their mother's death. The other wives made things worse; none of them tried to show the children any affection after the loss of their mother; instead, they blamed them and their dead mother for their husband's lack of interest. The gap yawned deeper over the years until they left the house. He felt bad that over the years, he hadn't taken any responsibility for his children like a father should, but he had endeavoured to keep abreast of everything they did. When Zachary travelled to the United States, he had attempted to contact Simi and hoped she would come home, but it was obvious Zach had taught her to be independent. He added that his children thought of their mother as a frail woman, but he remembered her as the strongest person he had ever known. He was really proud of them, and she would have been too. Rade was surprised at the turn of events with all she'd heard about Zach's father; she was quite shocked he had opened up to her without any prodding.

"I appreciate your telling me about Zach and Simi's mom, but your children don't know any of what you've told me, and they deserve to know."

He shrugged.

"When I saw you, I knew he had chosen well; you remind me of their mother; I'm sure Zach thinks the same."

"Well, he's never mentioned anything of the sort

to me," Rade replied with a smile.

"He probably doesn't realise it, but his subconscious may have when you met. Tell me how you met," he requested.

She narrated the hairdresser incident with Simi, and he laughed heartily much to Rade's delight.

"You should tell them about their mother," Rade said again.

"I don't know how to," he replied sadly.

"If you don't then I will."

They discussed the interesting architecture of the house, and Rade asked if the old house had in any way inspired Zach to be an Architect, and his father said he doubted it. Then he went into the history of Ilorin town and why his family had decided to settle there. The grandfather clock on the wall chimed and they both exclaimed! It was 4am in the morning. They exchanged goodnights and dissolved into laughter when they remembered it was already morning.

The shock on Zach's face when he entered into the kitchen for the same reason Rade had come a few hours before and saw Rade and his father laughing with each other was a comical one.

Rade hurried past him with a smile.

Chapter Eleven

A few hours later, Rade felt the pillow being tugged off from under her, she grumbled and turned over on her side, burrowing herself deeper under the duvet, ready to go back to sleep until she felt a drop of water on her cheek; she opened her eyes tentatively and met a pair of laughing eyes.

"Zach!" She screamed in protest, grabbing a pillow and throwing it at him, he dodged it easily.

"Sleepyhead, everyone's been waiting for you."

She checked her watch and saw it was 10:00am.

"Gosh," she muttered. "I am still very sleepy."

"What were you and the old man discussing into the wee hours of the morning?" Zack asked, "I shouldn't be, but I am jealous; I didn't know you are into old men."

Rade chuckled, "Well, now you know, your father

is such fun to talk with; he was telling me some wonderful stories," she winked at him enjoying herself.

"Him? What kind of wonderful stories could he possibly be telling?"

"W-e-l-l, I don't know if you'll be interested."

"Rade," he said threateningly.

She asked him to beg, and he added that he was even willing to kiss her feet and she replied that it would be much appreciated.

Simi burst into the room startling the two until they saw the breakfast tray she was carrying. She had decided to treat Rade to breakfast in bed. Rade was touched by her thoughtful gesture and told Zach he should be ashamed of himself. He replied that waking her up should earn him some points.

Maimuna walked into the room looking like she had been summoned to a town council meeting; she came over to the bed and ruffled her friend's hair. Rade was now certain they wanted something. She told them she appreciated all the pampering and attention, but it was getting a bit much, and she was becoming afraid. It then dawned on her that they were desperate to know what she had discussed with their dad. She had a good time making them wait, then told them what he had told her, and watched their expressions change from curious to surprise.

Simi was trying to find the right words, "all these years and we never even really knew how mommy died," she looked confused, and Maimuna didn't bother to say anything. Zach's face was unreadable.

"What are you thinking Zach?" Rade asked.

He shrugged like his father and smiled, "I just find it interesting that all these years we only knew so much about our parents' relationship, except the obvious, and our mother's death but you come into our lives, and suddenly, the whole story is unfolded. I guess it takes just one person to trigger change, either good or bad."

Rade nodded when Maimuna added that communication also helps; holding the gaze of a very solemn looking Zach, and he shrugged and broke into a smile.

"Go ahead; eat your breakfast before it gets too cold."

They watched her eat in thoughtful silence.

"Oh please, how large is Rade's head at the moment?! How does it feel being a heroine?" Maimuna asked as Rade attempted to keep a straight face until she joined the others in laughter.

When they came together for lunch, there was a

comfortable silence pregnant with questions on the table. Alhaji Muhammad glanced at Rade with questioning eyes, she nodded back at him, and her heart went out to him when she saw the look of joy and relief on his face.

Later that afternoon, he made an attempt at reconciliation, and his children met him halfway. Voices were raised and hushed. Questions asked by the children were met with satisfactory and not so satisfactory answers from the father, but there was no doubt, progress had been made. They promised to keep in touch.

It was touching to see the sadness in his eyes as he watched them leave.

Zach went over to his father and promised they'd try to check up on him soon again.

He said he was sure Zach wasn't planning on going to marry the beautiful woman all by himself without a father's support. He asked that they keep him updated on their wedding plans and if there was anything they needed him to do, he'd be happy to help.

His children glanced at one another and Rade broke the silence promising to keep him in the loop of things. Then he reluctantly advised them to be on their way before it got too late, and the young wife came out with bags of fruits for them and waved frantically as they were driven off to catch the last flight back to Lagos.

"Quite overzealous, isn't she?" Zach remarked.

"Zach," Simi said in expiration, "be nice." But they all agreed Zach was right.

He suggested that anyone who planned on eating the fruits should bless them first. Simi said that for such an enlightened man living in modern times, he was quite superstitious, like many people; she was surprised he could say something so banal.

"What has modernity got to do with believing people practice *juju*; it's a fact."

"What is *juju*?" Rade asked.

The three stared at her, and Maimuna said she still found it hard to believe how naïve and annoyingly ignorant Rade was about certain things; she wasn't worldly-wise on certain subject matters.

"Voodoo may be a more familiar word for you, as there is also a genre of African music called Juju."

"Oh, okay," Rade answered asking her friend to get off her case.

Simi said there were good deeds you could do through *juju*, and it was Zach's turn to glance at her in disbelief. Rade asked what the funny expression was for and said she agreed with Simi, as there was black and white magic, just like there were good witches and bad witches.

Zach said there was no such thing, as the Bible didn't say so and it was the code of conduct for believers. "God forbids witchcraft and doesn't recognise any good deeds through 'white magic.'"

He continued that he never used to believe anyone could be charmed or put under a spell until he became enlightened. The believer that activates the power in relevant scripture by faith is covered but to say that spells or charms don't exist is silly. You cannot be oblivious to the spiritual happenings in the world. There is a constant battle against principalities, powers, rulers of darkness of the world and spiritual wickedness in high places but the Bible states, "*that we are secure in Him, who is the head of all principality and power*".

He affirmed he'd met many people with real-life stories and that surprisingly, the most sophisticated and most unlikely people, who sometimes even scoffed at its existence, were the ones who dabbled into all forms of juju, spiritism, spells and charms.

The trio filled Rade with different stories, but the one that stayed with her was the one about a brilliant boy from an uneducated, poor family who was lucky to get a scholarship to study abroad. Everyone was so happy especially his aunty; she was ecstatic on her nephew's behalf and told anyone who cared to listen.

Years later, he became very successful, got married, and everyone knew how much he loved children but he was unable to have any and it began to put a strain on his marriage. He never considered adoption, and after years of seeking every medical treatment available and having special prayers offered on his behalf by several people, his beloved aunt died.

After her passing, they had to clean out her bedroom and in the process found a small pouch with his name written on it. In this little pouch, she had kept his "seed" all those years. Her envy and jealousy at her nephew for daring to get an education, develop himself and be more successful than her children made her seek punishment on him. He would never have children of his own.

The girls laughed hysterically, asking Zach how he could make up such a ridiculous story at such short notice until he convinced them he was telling the truth and actually knew the parties involved.

Rade kept exclaiming in disbelief. She thought it was a good excuse for men shooting blanks.

"How did she do it, did they actually see any semen in the pouch; how is that possible?"

"It's spiritual Rade, there might just be an object to represent his seed, or there probably wasn't anything in it, and the pouch was just symbolism. All the tokens they ask people to bring are just a demonstration of their faith. Faith is the key ingredient."

Rade continued to look at Zach with an amused expression. She then turned to Maimuna as if just remembering "As for you going on about how ignorant I am about certain things; I grew up in London, not in Venus, so I know about voodoo, don't get me started on stories I've heard albeit much different from the ones I heard today."

Maimuna made faces at her.

Zach added that his partner's former driver used to boast about some charm he'd put on his wife so if she ever cheated on him, she and the person she cheated on him with would die and it wasn't a joke. "It's called *magun*."

Maimuna and Simi laughed at the expression on Rade's face.

"That is so sick." Rade answered, "are there actually love charms like that; why would anyone want to wield such power over another human being, override another person's free will?"

"A few Nigerian women have been known to charm some foreigners, who end up not knowing how to even find their way to the Airport much less return to their homes," Maimuna said.

"Maimuna, that's a horrid thing to say!" Simi exclaimed.

Maimuna asked her to stop acting like she didn't know what she was talking about. It was an open secret, and some of them even boasted about it openly, like the driver Zach just mentioned. She reprimanded Zach on the notion that *juju* was African, stating that Brazil was renowned for voodoo practice. She nodded in affirmation when Rade added "New Orleans."

She shared that on her first visit to Lebanon, an eerily striking Lebanese woman had taken a look at her, asked her if she was married to a rich Sheik as she was so beautiful. When she replied "no," the woman had proceeded to ask her to her salon where she showed her an array of love potions and charms that would land her any man she wanted. She had never seen such a collection including the natural aphrodisiacs and herbs that made her native *kayan mata* look like child's play.

Zach agreed with Rade about people not knowing where to stop. "It's all about power; even God respects the free will He gave us but we can't do that with one another. No manipulation or spell lasts forever. Prayer is the recommended way to ask for whatever we want, and any kind of prayer should be done in faith. Jesus said that we should ask whatsoever we want in His name and that we should have faith in God. We know that faith works in love, and love is not selfish and self-seeking. When you pray, you are at peace because faith brings rest. To practice *juju*, voodoo whatever name you call it, you must exercise faith also, but that faith is not in God, they do not care about God's will; they want things done their way and will go to any length to get what they lust after."

"I had a plan on casting a spell on you, Zach, to ensure a lifetime of loving care, beautiful children, and all that good stuff, even you would be begging me not to set you free, but it's off the table with all this talk," Rade said tongue in cheek as Zach smiled back sheepishly.

"You don't need a spell for all that. Why cast a spell on what has been given you freely, my love?"

The other girls whooped and gave Zach a round of applause.

When they arrived Lagos, Zach picked up his car which he'd parked at the airport carpark overnight and drove everyone to Rade's house as they continued their chatter. Their voices and laughter filled the premises, and Rade went to the main house to check on her parents and was told they were out. Stepping out of the house, she drew in the scent of magnolias from her mother's garden and then exhaled, feeling grateful. The trip had gone perfectly; Zach's dad got a second chance with his children; the wind behaved on the flight back; Simi seemed to be doing great getting over her broken heart; Maimuna's flashbacks over the assault by Ugo had abated. The four of them stood in the middle of the lawn talking, teasing and laughing; none in a hurry to go into the house. The late afternoon sunlight glowed against Rade's cheekbones and glinted off the scatter of crystals sewn into the neckline of the kaftan she wore. After everything they had been through these past months, they all deserved this perfect day with one another; they were all taking great strides moving ahead.

Back in the office the next day, Zach and Rade got on a lengthy business discussion over the phone, and he frequently chuckled in between the conversation; his fiancée had a way with words. He informed her he was going out of town for a few days and she asked him what a few days meant.

"Three days," he responded and asked if anything was the matter when he heard the silence at the other end.

He was pleasantly surprised when she said, "nothing, but I will miss you."

He said the same and asked if she would like to come with him; it could be a working break for her. He added that they would have to make a deal that she would try not to be too much of a distraction. He was a certain way when he was working.

Her response wasn't kind, and it brought a guffaw from him. She asked him over for dinner and asked if there was anything he would especially like since he was going away and would most likely skip meals.

He commended her for being a good girl, and for finally taking mother-hen's tips on how to be a good wife.

Rade laughed; she was getting so dependent on Zach being around her, it was almost scary.

She admitted it was her fault he had become spoilt, pig-headed and quite cheeky too, and asked how he would defend himself if her mom discovered that he referred to her as mother-hen. He boasted that he and Mrs. Doherty were in an exclusive relationship no one understood and that she was his "girl" so he could handle her. Rade told him the dinner invitation was cancelled.

"Com'on Rade," he pleaded, "don't be so mean, I like the way you spoil me."

The verbal sparring continued as he tried to cajole

her into changing her mind over the retracted dinner invitation, but she was having none of it; he promised to behave himself and try not to be so pig-headed. She hung up with a smile on her face. Zach was easily the most interesting man she had ever dated; their relationship was deep and exciting. They were together most of the time, yet her heart still beat faster whenever she heard his voice and saw him, everything seemed better when he was around, he was rock solid dependable, and she knew he would never betray her. The thought of spending the rest of her life with him made her sigh in contentment; she tried to picture them in ten, fifteen years. The most interesting man she'd ever dated, she reminisced.

Then she thought about Phil! He was still missing, and everyone was left to imagine the worst. His family was distraught. Rade didn't know what to feel anymore, and Zach always had a reassuring word whenever she mentioned Phil. He would have been over the moon about her engagement to Zach. At least he's finally made up his mind, he would say.

Zach called back soon after and she teasingly asked if it was an hour yet as he was still on probation? Something in his voice made her sit up straight; he wasn't in a playful mood.

He said he wanted to confirm their dinner date, as he wants to discuss something important with her. She asked him to give her a preview as he sounded too serious and it was making her uncomfortable. He reassured her there was nothing to be worried about. Rade's heart pounded in her chest despite the reassurance.

The evening found a tense Rade at home. She was jumpy and waited impatiently for Zach's arrival. Something in her gut told her she wasn't going to like what Zach had to say.

She opened the door sometime later to an equally tense looking Zach. He responded to her "hi" with a kiss on the forehead, and she clung to him momentarily before asking if he was ready to eat. He inhaled the warm smell of the baked potatoes, gravy and grilled chicken wafting in from the kitchen.

He shook his head, "Please can we go somewhere?"

"But I made dinner!"

He repeated his question impatiently, and she cautioned him not to bite her head off, and he apologised profusely explaining that he just needed some air. They could return and have dinner later on as he had been looking forward to eating the meal she had gone out of her way to cook. She didn't believe a word of what he said and wanted to suggest they could sit outside at her parent's garden, but he took her palms in his larger ones and ushered her to the car.

He drove to a familiar destination in silence.

"Zach is everything alright?" She asked anxiously.

"Yes, everything's fine," he replied with a reassuring smile, brushing a knuckle over her cheek.

Rade heaved a sigh of relief. Yes, being outside was great, the fresh air relaxed her a bit as he found seats for them and ordered a bottle of red wine.

He asked if she wanted something to nibble on; she nodded in affirmation, and he placed the order as she waited in silence. Gosh; the suspense was killing her.

The sound of the trickling red wine as it was poured into their glasses by the waiter, the dismissive "thank you" by Zach to the lingering waiter followed by a slow twirl and a slow sip made Rade squirm in frustration. She was done being patient.

"Spill Zach!" She snapped impatiently.

"I may be travelling soon," he declared.

"But I know that already; you mentioned it when we spoke this afternoon remember," she responded questioningly.

"I am not talking about the local trip; about that one, it's been rescheduled for next week."

"Where are you going then?"

"South Africa first…" She was frowning in concentration. "Please Listen and hear me out. It's not a visiting business trip; I am going to work there."

"Work!" She exclaimed, "But your work is here."

Zachary sighed deeply, his head in his palms.

"I've been offered a one-year renewable contract as a Consulting Architect with the firm I used to work with in the United States. The first phase, which is six months, is for a project in South Africa. They are building one of the largest Dams in the world, and the bid for this project has been ongoing for a while. I'll fill you in on the tiny details later."

"How come I've never heard about this?" She interjected. "You know nearly everything there is about me; I tell you all my plans even before I've finished thinking them through, but you've never even mentioned this to me in passing." She said, hurt.

"Well, the discussions were initiated during the period we weren't really speaking to each other. Everything was still inconclusive and you know I never talk about things until I'm certain. The firm has another project in Abu Dhabi, then Dubai that they also want me to be part of; that one is over in another six-months; so it's back to back.

They've also offered me a permanent job as a partner if I want to remain with them after my contract expires. That offer has been in the pipeline for a while."

Rade was in shock; she wasn't surprised they wanted him on board. Zach had a brilliant mind, she had been blown away when he showed her the proposed design for the Goldmine but sceptical about practicality until his partner reassured her that Zach was renowned for his remarkable concepts but even more so for how practical they were.

"Unbelievable! This is major, Zach! You can't tell me you only knew about this today; you must have had an inclination in what direction they were leaning."

"Actually, I've known for about a month."

His words knifed through Rade, jolting her to a jaw drop. The look of dismay on her face wrenched his heart.

"That's before you proposed to me," she said softly, blinking away tears threatening to fill her eyes.

"But nothing was conclusive," he answered quickly in defence. "You are a businesswoman; you know how these talks are initiated and go on for ages. The bid for this job was before we even met. And there were and still are many factors to consider; I have my own firm, and there's the Goldmine project. The timing is a bit off as it is. It was the incessant calls asking me to revert as soon as possible on the reviewed contract that made me realise it is for real. My mind has been in a whirlpool since then." She stared at him in silence.

He begged her to say something, no matter what it was, but there was nothing to say; she was finding it hard to process the new information. She took a large gulp from her wine glass. She reconfirmed he said it was a one year contract and he nodded in affirmative. "With short breaks in between, of course," he added.

The order came, and it didn't look appealing anymore. She asked that it should be packed for her to take away, and the waiter's suggestion that they eat it hot and freshly prepared died on his lips when he saw their expressions.

There was silence as the waiter hurried away.

"So when do you have to leave or what's the plan exactly?" she asked.

"If I accept the offer, I'll have to leave in ten days, a fortnight at the most," he replied.

Rade's eyes grew hot, a contrast to the cold weight crushing her lungs, she couldn't breathe. This moment was killing her; then something snapped inside her, and she went off on him.

"You are a jerk, Zachary! How can you do this?

How can a two-week notice suffice when you plan to be away for a year or perhaps even more? I've watched this scene in movies too many times, someone goes away, and that's the beginning of the end. We need to make some serious decisions regarding this relationship. This may be a good way to end it."

"Don't be dramatic, please don't say that," he muttered picking her hands in his which she promptly snatched away.

She felt betrayed. She didn't understand how he could have failed to mention this to her at some point. She would have been mentally prepared at least knowing that there was a possibility he would be going away. She was beginning to wonder if there were other things she didn't know about him. She, on the other hand, shared everything with him; his lame excuse that she was more talkative angered her even more. He apologised for the umpteenth time and watched her in silence. She suddenly felt exhausted after venting and asked him to take her home. It seemed that when things were going too smoothly, something drastic always happened. He drove her home in silence.

"Rade, I love you, and I would never do anything to hurt you deliberately."

"That's a lie, Zach, withholding the information

about this job was deliberate, and you've hurt me; I share everything with you, I see now that the honesty isn't mutual. You know how I feel about long distance relationships; we've talked about it before, I hate them and I don't think they work. If I'm going to be in one, at least prepare me! Now I understand why you were reluctant about going into business with me; you had this huge project on your mind, at least some part of you hoped it would come through."

He let out a huge sigh as she twiddled the engagement ring on her mid-finger. She let herself out of the car before he got round to her side; they walked to her door in silence.

"I'll see you tomorrow," he said softly after her terse "Goodnight."

She could feel the tears clogging her throat; she was angry and hated the fact that she was so angry. She paced around her bedroom for an hour. She had an uneasy sleep and woke up with the same thoughts.

A year seemed like forever, but it really wasn't, she thought. She needed to talk to Zach; she needed reassurance everything would work out, though she doubted it. She rang him.

"Rade?" He asked enquiringly knowing it was her but couldn't help asking.

Rade plunged in immediately, "Zach, I am so sorry about last night. I don't want you thinking I am not happy for you, but your news caught me off guard." "I know, Rade; if only you know how I feel, you're one of the best things that have happened to me; you didn't say a quarter of the things I expected and deserve. I apologise for not being as open as I should have been. There's honestly no malice behind it, and I couldn't have found a more understanding life partner and friend."

Rade sighed. He always had the right words, but it didn't change the fact that she hated long distance relationships.

He said he would come over in the evening so they could talk to her parents. She refused and said she would mention it to them at some point; the relationship was theirs, not her parents'. It wasn't a big deal, she added; though she had no plans of mentioning it to them.

"It is, Rade! Please stop pretending it isn't; it's okay for you to be upset," he said.

They argued for a while before she agreed to tell her parents on her own.

Her parents didn't like the news at all, especially Mrs. Doherty.

"What rubbish!" Her mom exclaimed. "I can't wait to see Zachary and give him a piece of my mind.

I thought him a very responsible young man; how can he be going away on such short notice?" Her mom wasn't making things easy for her.

"Mom, Zach is responsible; he suggested we go to the registry and get a marriage license. That's how responsible he is, but that isn't an option for me at all. I reminded him how we had decided we would have a beautiful courtship; there is something sweet and romantic about this phase. I'm not having that taken away from me to be replaced by a rushed wedding because of Zach's work."

"How do you propose to have this sweet romantic courtship with someone miles away?"

"Mom," Rade shook her head in dismay, reminding her mother it was her fiance leaving, not hers. Her father interrupted the women, telling his wife to hold her peace and that this obviously wasn't going to be easy for Rade. Mrs. Doherty was chastised and went over to hug and apologise to her daughter.

Chapter Twelve

"Good evening," Zachary's eyes roamed over his fiancée's frame as he greeted her. She looked at him inquiringly wondering what he was up to; he had insisted on coming to speak with her parents a couple of days later and brushed aside her excuses that their relationship was personal; therefore, they didn't need any one's approval or disapproval. It was then she noticed the small group behind him, which surprisingly included his father. She ushered them in quickly and exchanged pleasantries with the group, comprised of Zach's father, Muhammad Bello, his brother, a family friend, Maimuna's Aunty Asabe, Maimuna, Buba and Simi. Zach had come to introduce his family to the Dohertys properly. Rade's mother, who loves playing hostess, was walking on air. Her parents were happy with the introductions, albeit impromptu.

Then Zach's family presented their gifts; Rade had never seen such an assortment of fruits in her life before. Aunt Asabe made a speech while they presented the gifts, craving their indulgence at the suddenness that did not in any wise diminish the importance of the meeting.

Rade's father was impressed by Zach's display of commitment to their daughter and expressed his pleasure at meeting Zach's father, who arrived in Lagos that afternoon.

"It's like you folks just did a year's grocery shopping for my parents; look at these fruit baskets! Did my mom secretly send you a shopping list?" Rade jokingly asked Simi, who shook with silent laughter and glanced at Mrs. Doherty, who was smiling contentedly and wondered what she would say if she heard her daughter.

"You are really naïve about the marriage culture. When families from both sides are introduced formally, the groom's family brings gifts to the bride's. You're correct, as ordinarily, your family would actually send a list of supplies before the traditional marriage, and some families go all out even for the introduction."

She went further to explain that if given more

time, the introduction would have been more elaborate and formal. This informal, impromptu one was arranged at Zach's insistence to introduce the immediate families upon Rade's approval; anything more than this would have been unnecessary.

Simi, who was the most knowledgeable person on Nigerian history and culture that Rade had ever met, went on to give a narrative of what she thought her parents would expect of them if they were to have a traditional marriage ceremony, commonly referred to as the engagement. Being from different tribes would make it even more interesting; she wasn't sure what the bride price would be though.

"What do you think a bride like Rade would be worth?" Simi asked Maimuna tongue in cheek.

"You've got to be kidding me! So they still offer money for brides. No one's going to come and pay for me like some slave."

Maimuna and Simi ignored her and continued debating on how much they thought she was worth, and they both agreed they probably couldn't afford it.

"Don't worry, it differs for each tribe, but I do know that majority ask for a bride price, that's aside from all the other gifts the grooms family is required to present. It's now majorly a symbolic gesture as most families usually return the money. I don't think the intention is that the cash is a direct representation of the woman's worth."

"Of course, it is!" Maimuna interjected. "Anyway, back then, it was. Haven't you heard Helen reminisce bitterly on her childhood and how her father jabbered almost all through her parents' tumultuous marriage on the amount he paid as bride price for her mother and how she wasn't worth a Kobo of it."

"Wow! That's awful. No wonder she's cynical about marriage," Rade said.

"Please, Helen is cynical about everything, but I hear you Maimuna. And you, Rade, have to also know that when a woman gets married, it is not only to her husband but to the whole family, so when you and Zach get married, we will address you as our wife."

"Our Wife indeed; I don't see who I'll be marrying with Zach from your family except Zach himself; I may consider inviting you over for lunch at our house occasionally Simi," Rade said mischievously.

The three girls dissolved into laughter as Simi threatened to start retrieving all the items they had just brought to her parents if Rade wasn't going to agree to be called "our wife," with

Maimuna as the referee of the verbal spar, even though she was biased and leaning towards her cousin's side. Rade's mom looked over at them disapprovingly and motioned that they be quiet.

"Oops! Mrs. D's got her eyes on us, better behave yourselves, girls," Maimuna muttered under her breath.

The rest of the evening was a pleasant one, and after Zach and his family left, Rade stayed back to talk to her parents.

"I always knew that boy had good blood in him."

Rade and her father exchanged amused glances at her mother's comment.

"So it took him bringing his father over here for you to decide he was serious and has good intentions; yesterday you had decided he was irresponsible," Rade said to her mom.

"The younger generation take a lot for granted and have little or no regard for our culture, family values or opinions of the older generation. Marriage for us is more than both of you getting together, living happily ever after and all your romanticised ideas. There is a bigger picture, such as family, which is an integral part of marriage. And to answer your question, yes, Zachary bringing his family here has scored him higher points with me; I've always liked him, and nothing will change that, but now I respect him even more because he has shown respect to us as your parents."

"Mom, there is no bigger picture aside Zach and me; the marriage is about us as husband and wife…"

"Rade, stop arguing with your mother; I'm sure we know a bit more than you do about marriage."

Mrs. Doherty looked gratefully at her husband and sighed.

Rade decided to let go and apologised to her mom. They spent the rest of the evening regaling their daughter with stories of their introduction and traditional marriage. The stories were interesting and colourful, but a bit much in her opinion. She excused herself and left for her apartment, after which Zach called eagerly to ask for feedback.

The following day, after Church service, Rade drove hurriedly out of the Church; they were all meeting at Buba's place. It was his uncle's birthday and the end of the Ramadan fast. The whole gang was there except Maimuna who was on call but promised to join them after work.

Buba asked for suggestions on what they could call their group, maybe "council meeting?"

They had the best times together and had great conversations, and someone else jokingly proposed that they nominate a secretary to take down minutes. Everyone had settled into his or her various positions in Buba's living room; his uncle was entertaining at his own wing of the house.

"I agree with you, Buba, and we need to start paying Simi for all the delicacies she puts together for us," added Rade

Everyone chorused their approval as Simi walked in with Buba's nephews, dishes and cutlery in tow. Rade got up from where she was curled up beside Zach to help. Simi reeled out some of the unfamiliar dishes they were having and Rade was so excited she almost spilt a bowl of peppered sauce. Buba had a man come in to grill some *Suya*, the popular skewered meat and chicken. Rade was chewing with deep concentration into one of the starters, *Wara*, which Buba just explained, was curdled cheese. She was trying to decide if she preferred the fresh one or the other fried golden brown one. The others were tearing into the Pitta bread and dipping into the garlic paste and chickpeas paste. Simi had also made some *Massa*, pan-fried Rice cake. They were having Couscous served with lamb and cabbage soup as a main dish. Rade peered at the rich redness of the *Zobo* juice as Buba helped himself to some and motioned that she try a glass of *Kunu*. She had decided she was going to visit Simi's state of the art kitchen and learn how to make some simple local dishes.

Maimuna arrived soon after and announced she was famished and that she "hated Nigerians sometimes." There were a few protesting grunts from the others, and Buba reprimanded her for making such a malevolent statement, adding that he didn't realize she had changed nationalities.

Maimuna insisted she was at liberty to speak as she wished and said she was sure he knew it was just a manner of speaking, not to be taken literally. She added, tongue in cheek that the thought of changing nationalities and race, if possible, wasn't a bad idea though. Maimuna was constantly analysing the African continent and expressing her misgivings. She didn't understand how a people so rich in human and natural resources kept falling short of the desired expectations. It hurt and angered her at the same time. She narrated the ordeal at the clinic that had just sparked her current episode. She was vague and didn't want to go into details but summarised that there was a major administrative problem, which could have been prevented, but the people responsible didn't take the initiative to nip it in the bud at the time. It was allowed to spiral out of control and blow out of proportion. Now the hospital management had instructed a committee should be formed with Maimuna as the chairperson and that a full report with recommendations be submitted in the next seven days.

Maimuna was working at being more patient and was known not to suffer fools gladly. She was upset and said the obvious way forward was to hold someone or the people responsible for the problem accountable. Why did they need to set up a committee for something so straightforward? That department was renowned for its bureaucracy, and she had never met a group so sluggish! She found the whole process laboriously ridiculous and said so; watching the administrative staff assemble themselves in the Chief Medical Directors office and make a show of being remorseful only irked her the more.

They asked her to say something but the whole charade was a bit much for Maimuna, so she announced angrily, "Light is synonymous with knowledge. Allow some light into your black minds people. This is why Africa is still in this backward, deplorable state." After which she left, and there she was sitting with them and still fuming.

Everyone stared at Maimuna in surprise; they didn't see the correlation.

"That's an overreaction; I would never have put you as a white supremacist, the people "blessed" with the warped mentality that the white man is superior and infallible. You lashing out at the whole black race because of a problem at the clinic is ridiculous. I started getting suspicious of you when you told someone you didn't like being called black. You're a racist bigot!" Buba said as the room went into an uproar; everyone was chorusing their different opinions at the same time.

"I'm entitled to how I feel Buba. Racist and Bigot mean the same thing by the way, and I'll try not to be too offended you called me that. You don't know what racist means; if you did, you wouldn't call me that."

"Can someone check the dictionary!" Zach injected playfully in an attempt to lighten the mood.

"I definitely do not think the white man is infallible; I wasn't even talking about the white man. I was talking about the African race, and even your eavesdropping is faulty. All I said on the day you're referring to is that I'd rather be referred to as 'African' because even the word or the colour 'black' usually connotes gloom, darkness, evil, and that I understood to a certain extent why the African Americans wanted to be addressed as such and no longer as 'black'. It's my prerogative."

"It's very annoying that you keep putting down your people at each turn; you and your slavery mentality."

"Slavery mentality is a repression of the mind. It is seeing a problem and not wanting to acknowledge or admit there is one but always on the defensive and blaming other people instead of finding a solution. The bondage is in the mental realm and affects the entire outlook. Doesn't this describe you in some ways, Buba?"

"You are so off point," he fired back.

The others couldn't believe the two were going at each other so viciously. Maimuna was Buba's idol. "My goodness! You guys take it easy. All these black, white terminologies are man-made. Man is responsible for labelling himself with the intent and purpose of identification and for differentiating. I, for one, have no issues with being called black; black is beautiful! I don't think God sees colour when he looks at humanity. We are all just one to Him, and the mixture is great as far as I'm concerned; imagine the whole world being just one race; very boring!" Rade stated while dusting off the chilly from her Suya before popping it into her mouth and chewing with her eyes shut, one foot shaking to an unknown beat and the other on Zach's knee as Maimuna's eyes shot daggers at her.

Zach chuckled and kept massaging the foot on his knee.

"You're not totally correct, Rade," Zach began, "I'd often wondered why God created different races if He knew there would be so much discord until I read the Bible again and heard a sermon from one of the deepest preachers of our times on how 'Nationhood' is part of God's plan. We are not all the same in God's eyes as you put it; generically as mankind, we are the same, but He recognises our individuality. He dispersed the people at the Tower of Babel and confused their language for the purpose that they would spread out. Diversity is good, and racism is man-made. Now, talking about racism, Africans are tribalists and Nigerians are at the fore. What really peeves me is when we complain about being discriminated against by someone from a different race, yet in this country, we have people from one tribe who will not marry people from a different tribe. Some tribes believe they are superior and will have no dealings with people they don't speak the same language with. Government parastatals are the perfect breeding ground for tribalism. In the corporate and private sector, I've witnessed nepotism based on tribalism.

People awarded contracts not on merit but by their state of origin. Tribalism is even worse in my eyes than racism. I'm so lucky with Rade's family, no such issues there."

"And vice versa," she added.

"Some people may not agree with you. You are from the north, and to most, we get the best of everything without working much for it," Maimuna replied.

Simi came back in with dessert, "I don't understand what all this talk is about, all I know is that Africans suffered intolerably in the hands of the white man. The slave trade went on for almost four hundred years. Can you imagine the debauchery — the inhumane, brutal way our people were treated? The suffering and degradation; abused and treated no better than animals." She spat the words like she had gravel in her mouth. "I can arrange a group visit to the slavery port in Badagry, so you all can experience a small part of our history. Let's visit the subject of the irregularities in the annexation of land in the African continent by the white man in all his wisdom and the colonisation that violated and sullied the African culture and invariably birthed the colonial mentality, which Maimuna may be suffering from…" She interrupted herself when she glanced in Rade's direction; "Rade if you keep eating that *Suya*, you won't have any room for dessert!"

Everyone was relieved she was distracted. No one could hold the fort to Simi when it came to knowledge on African history. She was sure to depress them with the gory details of the black man's sufferings; they were familiar with her graphic storytelling method.

"Simi, it appears that you and Buba may be plagued with the so called colonial mentality since you recognise the symptoms so well. Colonial mentality can also be extended to mean your fixation on the white man and how you blame him for everything that has gone wrong with your race. You empower him when you go on about how much he was able to alter your existence. You blame him for giving you his religion, though it isn't his, he just brought it to you. You blame him for corruption, for the failure of your leaders to perform well long after independence, for his language. You admit how stupid you are when you agree he outwitted you on your own land. You can never accept responsibility but keep blaming him for your own failures; you've accepted that he has that much power over you. From my definition and perspective, you and Buba have a severe case of colonial mentality, Simi. This started as a straight forward conversation, but you decided to twist it out of context. We weren't talking about what the white man did to the black man, but if we want to go there, let's do that: If the white man did anything to the black man, it was with the support of the black leaders who were drawn away by their own lust and greed. Why are you filled with so much bitterness?" Maimuna fired back.

Simi was ready to start verbal combat with Maimuna, but Rade's mouth was now empty, and she rejoined the conversation.

"As far as I'm concerned, the black people helped sell their people into slavery, and enough with the self-pity and whining already. Isn't it time we moved on from the past and started doing great stuff. The Jews were sold into slavery too, they are still discriminated against, but you don't hear them complaining as we do. Most civilisations have a history of slavery. I agree this race has gone through the wringers, and we are still being discriminated against, but it's the fixation on being the victim I don't understand. In my opinion, we are a great race blessed with everything. Talking about slavery, since my return home, I've seen some families even in Church with underaged maids; they maltreat them, don't send to school and don't allow them any freedom; that's some kind of slavery to me. Are we going to blame the white man for that too?"

The room went up again, and Zach excused himself to go to the bathroom as they all tried giving their opinion on the new subject matter. The discussion had morphed to discrimination against blacks, especially in modern-day America. "I think it's quite simple; you should act the way you want to be treated, my friends and colleagues in the UK never treated me differently, nor did I treat them any differently. I was and still is, treated with respect wherever I go in the world. I agree, but I think the discrimination mentioned is a bit exaggerated…"

Buba interrupted before she could finish, "you do see life through rose-tinted glasses, Rade; I wish you could be more realistic. Blacks suffer discrimination at every turn, whether they be black British, black Americans, Caribbean's, etc. We see, read and hear about police brutality against blacks, the segregation in corporate America, the continual struggle by blacks for their rights, even in South Africa. Good for you if it never happened to you or you didn't notice where you've come from, but to undermine other peoples experiences by saying you don't believe in discrimination is nonsense."

Rade's eyes widened in shock.

"You see how intolerant of other people's opinion he is!" Maimuna screamed.

"Have you read the book, 'Blink' by Malcolm Gladwell? Discrimination is human nature and comes in different forms: Race, gender, social status, religion, and so forth."

Buba and Maimuna continued with each other, and Simi was reprimanding Rade for daring to undermine and underrate the slave trade, the sufferings blacks had endured, discrimination against black people in current day America and Rade argued she had never implied such. Simi went on to back some of Buba's arguments against Maimuna with facts and continued harping about all the injustices against the black man till she got red in the face.

Maimuna shook her head and added that some of the " blacks" she so vehemently defended would not see her as one of them considering her fair mixed race colouring and probable Arab ancestry. "The skin is the largest sensory organ in the body, and its hue is the basis by which some people judge, differentiate and treat people to a large extent; you, Buba, Zach and I are Fulani. Do you know some people don't even consider us Nigerians? Forget the cloak of Northerner you hide behind."

The cousins burst into laughter and started taking digs at each other. Someone mentioned that

Africans had no problems with accepting mixed race people as a mixed race; it was the Caucasians who didn't recognise them as a mixed race; any slight taint of the white blood with black makes it invariably black.

"That's an American point of view!" Fresh arguments ensued that led to a unanimous decision to change the topic after they all agreed they were saying the same thing albeit in different ways. Africans had been ill-treated. Rade loved her friends, everything always ended on a lighter note, though everyone was given a chance to voice their opinion, one way or the other.

Zach returned to the room and asked what he had missed as he went over to Rade and pushing her hair, kissed the nape of her neck.

"Nothing!" They all chorused as she leaned into him.

Buba accused Rade and Zach of making them single people feel weird with the entire "lovey-dovey, touchy, feely."

Simi said it was her opinion that Zach overcompensated because he didn't get enough motherly love.

Maimuna and Buba laughed as Rade threatened Simi with her hands and eyeballed her.

Rade declared that she loved her man. She admired

a strong man who can wear his heart on his sleeve so unabashedly; it was refreshing. She loved him overcompensating because she, like a spoilt cat, craved and lapped up all the attention. She, in turn, reciprocated all the loving she got in large doses.

Buba sighed in resignation.

She called out to Zach who, very sweetly, two glasses in hand, hurried over to his fiancée. She stretched out her arms and enclosed him in a bear hug.

"Awwww," the girls chorused.

"What?!" He asked squirming under all the attention as they all smiled at him, except for Buba, who was shaking his head in pity.

Buba pulled out the paperback novel almost falling out of Maimuna's satchel and groaned. He couldn't believe how many times she had read that particular book from her favourite author. Perhaps that's what triggered her mood. "There are many other books waiting for you to read them, Maimuna. What's the fixation on '*A Thousand Splendid Suns*'?" The heroine, Miriam's sufferings always triggered something in her.

She shrugged as Simi shook her head; she had gifted Maimuna the novel several years before. Most people knew the way to Maimuna's heart, a book by Khalleed Hosseni, Kahil Gibran and

Paul Coelho. They decided to ask if anyone else was reading a book and what. Perhaps it would explain their state of mind.

Rade was still on her African literature path and was reading '*The Famished Road*' by Ben Okri and '*Second-Class Citizen*' by Buchi Emecheta. Zachary, '*The Last Outcast*' by Chris Okotie, and Simi, '*Secrets About Men Every Woman Should Know*' by Barbara De Angelis, which made the men snigger. Helen reiterated that she hardly read fiction; she was constantly arguing with writers point of view. They pressed that it didn't have to be fiction. The last book she had read was '*The Brain That Changed Itself*' by Norman Doidge; Buba was reading too many things at the same time.

Rade thanked Maimuna for treating Lateef for next to nothing, as his insurance could definitely not cover the extensive work he needed done on his teeth. Maimuna waved it aside and told them Lateef was probably the most interesting patient she'd had in a long time. He had come into the clinic after the initial consultation and was visibly nervous. She had spent some time just chatting with him, and he had plied her with stories of the lovers' spar between him and his wife and asked her opinion as to what women really wanted. His wife was prone to jealous bouts, and he didn't understand how to placate her. She also blamed him for their childlessness and everything that went wrong in the universe.

He told her in his broken English about his one time proposed migration to Canada; he mused on how his life may have been better if he had completed the form after going for an interview with an Immigration expert firm who were recruiting truck drivers for a haulage company in Canada under the unskilled migrant programme. Lateef said he had seen his life mapped out in front of him but hadn't understood any of the details on the form, though he had been reassured he was qualified seeing he had the relevant driving experience and had driven larger moving vehicles than the ones stated in the application. He was unable to come up with the application fees, and he believed his wife started resenting him from that moment. And despite telling her that the application may not have been successful, she had convinced herself and believed he had taken away her "American dream," though he kept reminding her it was Canada. He'd also told her that she probably wouldn't have survived the cold days seeing that she would be "shaking like a leaf" when he just as much as turned on their home ceiling fan to the lowest. Maimuna had laughed her head off.

He said his life had been pretty much dull until he met Rade and everything changed for the better; she believed in him and had gotten him a job as a head driver at Doherty's, and now he was able to spend more money on his wife. He had been enduring the discomfort from the aches he got whenever he chewed due to several cavities and the excruciating pain from the completely bad teeth, but here he was, having his teeth checked out by the beautiful Doctor Maimuna. He was living the 'Nigerian dream' as far as he was concerned, and his wife would have to deal with it; after all, they now lived in a better house and he was having his teeth cleaned and whitened which would have been previously impossible. They all laughed, and Buba asked Rade how she met Lateef. She told them about the first encounter and that subsequently, she couldn't help but observe how reliable he was. Lateef would keep to his word if it killed him and it was easy recommending him seeing he was also a skilled driver. He drove and operated heavy machinery with an innate uncanny skill.

Simi urged Maimuna to tell the others the other reason, aside from the fact that he was Rade's protégée, Lateef had enjoyed the complete pro-bono dental treatment. She rolled her eyes at Simi as everyone urged her to spill.

Two weeks before then, Maimuna had gone to one of the ghettos with a Psychiatrist, her partner on an independent research into recreational drugs abused by children and teenagers in the ghettos. It was a project dear to Maimuna' s heart, and they were near completing the documentary. It was Lateef's former neighbourhood, and he still lived not too far away, so Rade had asked Maimuna to call him for support when they arrived there. Maimuna had called, and Lateef had offered support of a different kind when the rumbling in her stomach had refused to quieten while she was talking to a teenage girl with codeine addiction. She'd felt a cold sweat break all over her, and her mouth had gone dry as she fought the battle with her bowels which was threatening to unravel all the mysteries in her stomach. She tried in vain to remember what she had eaten while tightening her legs together and clenching her bottom, they were in a rough area, and she couldn't see any house with a decent toilet in sight. Lateef had been there in a flash. He must have had the same experience at some point in his life, as he understood what she was experiencing the moment he saw her. He pointed to a friend's place, but she didn't think she could make it to the house he claimed she would find this half decent toilet. Her bowels won the fight, and he improvised. She felt immediate relief and some shame wash over her as a slight wind hit her bare bottom at the cleared area of someone's backyard. Lateef's face had been impassive as he kept watch over the area and listened to the disgraceful sounds she couldn't contain.

Rade, Zach and Buba stared at Maimuna in disbelief while Simi chortled on the floor with laughter. She was being horrible; she had heard the story first hand after the incident and promised not to tell anyone. The others couldn't help but join in the laughter as the thought of beautiful Maimuna with her long, slender limbs crouched, bare bottomed at some backyard in the middle of town and guarded by Lateef was a bit much. They apologised to her afterwards as nearly everyone could relate.

Simi said she was always warning Maimuna about her sensitive stomach, but she never listened, she told them Maimuna had a similar experience in University and Maimuna groaned. Apparently, she had eaten some beans at a canteen outside the school, and on her way back, her stomach had begun to rumble. She had accepted a ride from a friend who had been asking her out when there was no bus in sight, and she'd prayed all the way back to school for the rumbling to stop while the guy kept chattering away, happy to finally get a chance to be alone with her. He'd asked if she would like to stop somewhere for a drink and she would have plunked something on his head if she had the strength. She was using all of her strength to steel the poop from coming out. She had been quiet while he kept pushing until the first wave of the putrid smell of her fart permeated the confines of the small car; then he became speechless and gave her bewildered side-glances. Simi was visiting Maimuna at school and said she would never forget the horrified expression on the guy's face when Maimuna flew out of the moving vehicle just before he got to the front of her room and made a dash for the bathroom. She barely made it, and Simi had feared for her cousin when she came out afterwards looking like a peeled tomato after having a vigorous bath, requesting for several paper bags in which she tied her jeans and underwear and discarded them. Maimuna wasn't sure she could ever face the guy anymore but did eventually. He was quite happy and relieved that beautiful girls like her did 'shit' after all. They all groaned.

She was glad Lateef had been there to be of assistance, and he was equally pleased with his teeth. His famous infectious grin was now near perfect.

Days later, Rade took a day off work to be with Zach; she got more apprehensive as the days went by. They had waved aside all his protests and decided to have a send forth dinner in his honour. That evening, he sat on his bed helplessly while she helped him repack a suitcase. They had gone shopping earlier in the day to buy a few essentials. She was quite deft at packing the essentials into the suitcase, and Zach watched her refold a shirt into a perfect square, noting from her slightly fuller arms, she had put on some flesh. She did a final check then brought out her favourite shirt of his; Zach always looked so handsome whenever he wore that shirt.

"Please, can I have this?" She asked.

"You can have the whole suitcase," he replied.

Rade laughed until she became teary. Her reaction to the thought of him being away scared her more than the actual thought of him being away. She didn't understand the now familiar hollow feeling inside her, nor the sheer panic that would follow afterwards. It wasn't like he was going away forever, he would have breaks in between to visit home, and she would also visit him. They would video call, and before she knew it, he would be back. He sensed her turmoil and pulled her to him, rocking her and stroking her hair. Rade started sniffling back tears.

There was a tentative knock on the door, then a peep; it was Simi asking them to come get something to eat. She pulled away from him and told him she would join him shortly. He stared at her worriedly and left the room at her insistence. Simi gave Rade a gentle back rub that was reciprocated, then excused herself to see to the happenings in the living room. Rade decided to rest a little on Zach's bed, and it was the insistent shake of Maimuna's hand on her shoulders that made her realise her little rest had turned to full sleep.

"What on earth happened to you? Everyone's wondering where you are!"

The gathering was reminiscent of the one that her friends had organised when she was leaving London. She had been pleased but had teased them when they started giving their teary good-bye speeches on how she'd be sorely missed. She had made her speech and thanked them for the party but chided them for all the melodrama. She was sure she would probably not spend more than six months in Lagos and hurry back. How wrong she had been! She had come and would be around for a while. What if Zach decided to accept a permanent position with his former firm? It was bigger in every way than his. What would happen, then? She knew she was overthinking things but couldn't help herself. She was beginning to enjoy her life here and didn't think she would be uprooting herself again, not to America in any case, which is where Zach could end up.

"I wonder why everyone's talking like I'll be gone forever, it's beginning to irritate me," Zach said to Buba, looking at Rade where she stood talking to friends.

Buba smiled, thinking it was just a while ago, the day at his party when he had stood with Zach looking across the room at Rade.

"Everyone's going to miss you and just expressing their feelings, nothing wrong with that," Buba replied.

It was a pleasant evening regardless, and quite late when the last guests left. Maimuna and Simi got on to different things and left Rade and Zach to themselves.

"I think it's time I went home," she announced.

"Home! Zach exclaimed, "I thought you'd stay over tonight."

"Zach you and I know we won't be able to keep our hands off each other, it would be foolish of us to think so."

Zach begged her to stay.

She insisted she couldn't stay the night; she knew they would make love like it was the end of the world. She couldn't deal with that kind of emotion; she felt unstable enough as it is.

He smiled at her.

"Sometimes I wish I wasn't such a good guy."

She smiled and told him how much she appreciated him.

"It would be nice to make love, then go to sleep in each other's arms, and to think that we won't be seeing each other in a while," he grumbled.

"I understand how you feel Zach; I feel the same way, but please let's try and stay on course, let's continue the relationship that isn't based on sex; we've done well so far."

"I'm glad you said so far. How realistic do you think this is?"

"What do you mean? Do you plan on being with someone else?"

He stared back at her and moved closer. He started kissing her neck and ears; Rade felt her knees buckling and sighed. Then his phone rang, she peered over at the screen, it was Mandy, she was at the dinner and one of the last guests to leave so Rade wondered why she was calling. He answered after excusing himself, and Rade tried in vain not to eavesdrop on the conversation.

"Mandy says hello. She has a message for someone in S.A; she was just calling to remind me to make a note of it like I asked her to."

"She obviously calls you this late normally. You know I'm an understanding person, but what is it with you and Mandy?"

Zach shook his head, "look, let's not bother about Mandy right now."

But Rade just continued to stare at him.

"You know the story Rade; we met through a mutual friend when she just came to Nigeria. We dated on and off for a little over a year or maybe nearing two."

Rade kept staring at him.

"We've worked together on a few projects as you know and she's amazing at her job. Since we didn't work out, our relationship got purely physical more recently."

"Please spell out, what purely physical means."

"Rade!" He exclaimed, but she kept staring into his eyes, Zach couldn't resist them.

"We've been having sex on and off as the need arises."

Rade stared back at him in shock. "Sometimes I actually feel I don't know you Zach, and it scares me silly; little things just keep popping up now and then, like this job offer. Are you sure there aren't any more things I still need to know? Have you been with her since you met me?"

Zach exclaimed and voiced his anger at her line of questioning. She reminded him of their promise to be open to one another and added that he didn't have to answer if he didn't want to. He silently cursed the phone call that had led to this conversation.

"Okay, I'll give you the truth if you can handle it. I have, but that's before you and I got serious, just a little while after we met actually."

"I don't understand men; it's so easy for you to have meaningless sex and with several partners if need be. They say if a guy is not going with you, he is going with someone else. Are you a cheating man? Because I can't deal with that. I know you are human, and may make mistakes but to go out deliberately to betray me, I won't tolerate it. I want you to be truthful with me at all times, whatever happens, you have to promise me that right now."

"I love you, Rade, and I want to be with you only; I'm not a cheating man, but I am human, and I'm weak sometimes. That is what a relationship is for; attempting to get to know the person you intend to spend the rest of your life with, but you must understand me and the different sides to me. You know me as a friend, a business partner, a boyfriend/fiancé now; you will get to know me as a husband, then eventually as a father. However, as we go on, you must get to know me as Zach, no roles attached, just a spirit being living in a treacherous body which I must learn to control; so I may make mistakes, but I promise I will never lie to you. I am trying not just for you but for myself also. I haven't been with any other since I asked you to be my girlfriend and I intend to keep it that way, a relationship must be based on trust, and you have to trust me."

Her eyes were moist. He pulled her to him and hugged her tightly then sighed as he disengaged himself from her.

He went over to announce to Simi and Maimuna he was taking Rade home, they expressed their surprise. They both had also assumed she was staying over for the night.

The drive to Rade's house was a silent one; Zach saw her off to the door.

"You're going to take care of yourself and no seeing or talking to any strange men," he added.

"Aye, sir!" She replied, giving a mock salute. He laughed, and then he kissed her lips. Rade felt the beat of their hearts pounding in unison. It was a beautiful kiss. He kissed her closed eyelids, her forehead, and then pulled back.

"Goodnight Rade."

She could only smile back and nod. She watched him walk away and hugged herself, he turned and waved, and she waved back frantically like a teenager on her first date.

She stood outside her door for a while, just staring into space then went to bed; her mind stayed active all through her sleep.

Zachary couldn't sleep. His thoughts were of Rade. He always told himself he would never marry someone he didn't love; it had to be someone he could truly love, but he never thought it would be quite like this. She brought out more than the protective feelings he felt towards his sister and female friends. He had a very clear picture of the kind of life he wanted for both of them. Watching her repack his suitcase had struck a cord in his core, and he had shocked himself at almost blurting out he didn't want to go anymore. He knew that if she had asked him not to take the offer for whatever reason, he would have obliged her; he didn't understand why, they weren't bound to each other or even married, but he would have. It surprised him how soft he was getting; he pondered on the complexities of human emotions as he drifted off to a short sleep that was cut off by the sound of the alarm clock.

He had a long chat with his sister and left the house, noting that even Rade's car looked nice parked beside his. He was on his way to pick her up and drop her at work since he had driven her home the previous night.

She came out right on time; he loved that about her, she was always punctual, looking very lovely in a dress shirt and one of her famous silk scarfs, hair tied back into a chignon. She had on a pair of peep toe pumps, her well-shaped legs glowing. She looked somewhat different, and he told her so.

"It's the heavy makeup; I woke up with some nasty bags under my eyes, consequences of a few days of lack of proper sleep; my face just knows how to wear my hearts sorrow, it's so annoying."

Rade tried to get some work done after Zach dropped her off at work. He was running some last minute errands and came back later in the evening to pick her up to the airport. He'd checked in and so had enough time to spare. They went to a restaurant on the first floor at the Airport where Simi, Maimuna and Buba came to join them. As he stood at the bar to inquire after an order that was taking so much time, he got into a conversation with a man who was seated at the table beside them with an elderly woman he bore a striking resemblance to.

"You are a lucky man," the man commented, glancing over at the three girls.

"I am? Why so?" Zach asked with a grin.

"Com'on man; you're with three beautiful women, please don't act like that isn't a big deal."

Zach chuckled, "you're not doing badly yourself," motioning at the attractive elderly woman sitting at his new acquaintance's table.

The two men introduced themselves, and made their way back to Zach's new acquaintance, Danladi's table and he introduced Zach to his mother; Zach bowed to her. She smiled back at him warmly, and then her face took on a conspirator's expression as she asked. "Who are those striking ladies?"

He looked over at the three girls chatting and noted with pride that they were indeed striking. Danladi's eyes widened in embarrassment at his mother's forwardness. "Mother!"

Zach brushed aside his protest and called the girls attention and asked that they come over to be introduced. Mrs. Danjuma was quite engaging and expressed surprise the girls weren't models. She further embarrassed her son by demanding the prize money for winning the wager they had made. She had placed a bet on the "petite one" being Zach's partner; her son had bet on Simi.

Rade couldn't stop smiling; even her mother wasn't this forthright. The son looked exasperated as he counted some money and handed it over to his mom. There was no denying the close bond between mother and son. To their delight, Zach and Mrs. Danjumma were going to the same destination and were on the same flight. They exchanged more laughs, paid the bill, and it was time for the travellers to head out. They parted at the immigration checkpoint. Zach exchanged hugs with Maimuna, and then Simi, as Danladi and his mother argued quietly.

"Mother, please remember to take your medication."

"Ah, stop bossing me around *jare, mo ti gbo*." She answered back in fluent Yoruba. He nodded and hugged her. Zach promised Mrs. Danjuma he would take good care of her.

Then he turned to Rade and kissed her lips.

"I love you," he whispered into her ears.

"I love you too," she replied, trying hard not to cry.

Zach and Danladi reached for Mrs. Danjuma's tiny hand luggage at the same time.

"She's with me from here on," he said to

Danladi, who smiled back gratefully. He was visibly worried about her.

"She's with Zach; he'll take care of her," Simi reassured him. The two cut a pair as Zach led her, arm on her elbow, past the checkpoint after she had scoffed at the wheelchair offered. She was talking while Zach listened patiently.

The three ladies headed home after exchanging business cards with Danladi. It was quite an evening for all three ladies and their new acquaintance who couldn't stop worrying about his mom. She had just recovered from a minor heart attack and had scoffed at his fears over her travelling unaccompanied.

Chapter Thirteen

Time seemed in a hurry and carried everyone along with it. Rade and Zach were immersed in work, but they tried to speak with each other every day despite their busy schedules. Lately, it seemed like they were constantly playing phone tag, every time Zach called she would be in one meeting or away from her phone and when she returned his call he too would be preoccupied or away from his phone. They kept in touch through video calls, texting, voice messages and whatever way possible. Zach's workload was quite heavy; he still had to keep up with the projects he had back home. He had resolved that day to speak with his sister, whom he had slightly neglected.

"She's become a workaholic! She should be here any minute; I threatened to revoke our friendship if she didn't find time for me. It seems with you away everyone has suddenly become very busy."

Simi filled him on the events he had missed. She was garnering a lot of attention, and her colleagues heralded her as an innovative Chef; she had carved a niche for herself by pushing the local Northern dishes and creating new menus. She had just returned from the capital city where she had catered at the wedding ceremony of a prominent Northern leader. They were pleased with the variety of local dishes on display added with creative presentation. She announced Rade's arrival when the doorbell rang, and Zach asked to speak with her if it was okay. She handed the phone to Rade upon her entry, who mouthed a silent, "who is it?"

Rade said hello, but there was no reply until she heard the familiar chuckle.

"Zachary!!!" Zach pulled the receiver away from his ear a little, grinning. They hadn't spoken in two days.

"No wonder your phone has been engaged, I've been trying to reach you!" She told him how much she missed him, and Zach couldn't forget the words she used: "I miss you like my own body."

He chided her for abandoning Simi which drew a cry of protest and "Simi the snitch" from her. He had also heard she had taken to wearing his T-shirt every other Friday; he liked that very much. Rade promised to deal with Simi who was laughing from the kitchen. She was looking forward to a great girly time with Rade who had come to stay the weekend. She told Zach Simi was taking her to the Fulani community in Lagos where she was going to have her hair braided like the Kanuri women and was looking forward to it excitedly. He cautioned her not to be adventurous with the food. They spoke of the near future and their individual and joint plans.

Another three months passed by in a whirl. Simi and Maimuna travelled to Mauritius, and Rade's ears had been full with plans for the trip, which unfortunately she couldn't make with them because of work. She missed them terribly and was plied with pictures she could swear were taken every minute to document the jolly good time they were having. The next proposed travel destinations were Egypt and Morrocco, and Rade had been instructed to make herself "available for that one or else…"
Before their departure, Danladi and Simi seemed close. They were all friends now, but the girls knew whom he had eyes for. Simi always ignored the winks and knowing smiles Maimuna and Rade gave her. He was obviously interested in her, but

Simi was not having any of it; she was relishing her freedom. She didn't want to be romantically involved with anyone. He seemed like a patient man, and they hoped they were right about him.

Rade's phone rang, and she started to search for it frantically in the "world of her bag" as Zach often teased. She had just looked at pictures her annoying friends had sent to torture her on the good fun she was missing. She knew it was Zach ringing. She grabbed it in time.

"Hi, darling, phone lost in the world of your bag, aye?"

"How did you know?" She asked, laughing.

"Well, you picked up, or I guess your bag did, and I heard all the rustling as you searched for it in the mayhem of your make up purse, wallet, and general bag junk."

She called him names, laughing heartily.

"I met your sister today, quite different from you. Whatever happened to you?" He asked teasingly.

Rade laughed and continued with the name calling, telling him to go for her sister if he was so taken and he replied he would just suck it up and make do with her, chuckling as Rade promised to make him eat his words.

"They discussed the Goldmine property; things were going smoothly but slower than anticipated.

His partner was on ground, so he was up to speed on what stage they were. The place was attracting quite a bit of speculation, and several people called every day to make enquiries about space and pricing. He wasn't surprised.

"Alright then darling, are you coming home for Christmas?"

He couldn't say; he was still in England from where she had just returned visiting him for a few days, but he was returning the following day. His stay in South Africa looked like it would be extended by a few weeks.

"Christmas is still some time away anyway; I'll know closer to the time. We're just in August."

"It's not that far off, Zach; you know time goes by so quickly, and I hope you remember it's my birthday next month."

"Like I can ever forget my girl's birthday. My, we are getting old, aren't we?"

"Zachary!" She exclaimed, and he laughed.

"Why are some women so touchy about age? It's just a number even though it brings you closer to your dying day."

They both laughed, and Rade still had a smile on her face long after she hung up.

Maimuna and Simi returned from their trip with

stories that made Rade green with envy. She had heard all the stories repeatedly, and she sometimes forgot she hadn't made the trip with them. She knew everyone they had met on the trip by name. She was looking forward to December excitedly; they were planning a family reunion since everyone was coming home. Her sister and her family, her older brother whom Zach had met at her sister's place in South Africa, and her dear Aunt Jo.

Mrs. Doherty was buzzing with anticipation.

Three days before Christmas, Rade was still expecting Zach until he called to announce he wouldn't make it down for Christmas. There was simply no available seat on any flight; he had waited until the last minute and was unpleasantly surprised at the turn of events. She was so upset tears sprung to her eyes.

"Zach, I asked you several times if you had booked your ticket when you were certain it was okay to leave SA; I even volunteered to do it for you, but you called me mother hen, now look! You more than anyone knows how crazy travels get at the end of the year." Zach felt so bad that he didn't know what to say.

"I am so sorry Rade; you know there's no other place I'd rather be than your side at this time. I'll keep trying; I'm on standby... I didn't think Christmas day flights would be fully booked."

She told him not to bother, and he felt rotten. Everyone was disappointed when she told them Zach wasn't coming for Christmas, especially Aunt Jo, who desperately wanted to meet the man that had swept her favourite niece off her feet. She was away in Spain on Rade's last visit to England to see Zach.

Rade asked her Aunt if she'd heard anything about Phil, who answered in the negative and expressed how sad she was regarding Phil's disappearance, she had been quite fond of him. Rade had convinced herself that Phil had travelled someplace far where there was no telephone or Internet so he couldn't reach anybody, thinking of her friend as dead was unthinkable for her.

Rade, her friends and family had a wonderful Christmas, it was filled with a lot of catching up, plenty of laughter, family dinners, presents and the only thing missing was Zach's presence. He was alone out there, and he missed out on being with family. The new year was ushered in with a lot of joy and excitement; Rade had started the count down to Zach's return. It would be exactly a year in February since he left.

The next time Zach called, she found she wasn't surprised when he said he wasn't coming home in February; it would be sometime in the middle of the year. She had a sneaky suspicion Zach would accept the offer from his old firm; she had tied herself up in knots wondering what she would do if it came to that. She had to keep reprimanding herself to stop jumping the gun. He had asked her to start thinking of the part of town she would like them to live after their wedding, which seemed quite far fetched to her now.

A few weeks, later Zach called Rade, "Guess what?" He exclaimed.

"I love guessing games," Rade answered excitedly.

"Listen to this," he continued "I'm reading an excerpt from a tabloid: *London playboy who went sailing with his now deceased girlfriend some time ago who was presumed dead or missing because there were no traces of his body has been confirmed alive.*"

She didn't quite get it, and then it hit her, "Phil! Oh, my goodness!" Rade exclaimed, her hands shaking, "you said it, Zach, not to lose hope."

"Listen," he continued, "Phil's unconscious body was found ashore by a reclusive old couple, after the exertion from swimming endlessly and hyperthermia. He remained in critical condition for a worrying period, and after he regained consciousness, they found he had suffered partial amnesia."

"What a farfetched story! This sounds like something out of a movie! Did Phil's family make this up?" Rade said.

He continued, telling her about the couple's only son who had been away to Australia at the time and returned to find a recovering Phil in his parent's house and reported the case to the police which the old folks hadn't done all this time as he still wasn't in optimal form especially mentally. "They say he has been moved to an undisclosed hospital, but he's alive and getting better."

They both agreed the story seemed curious and she wondered why no one had called to inform her; they would eventually find out what really happened, but the most important thing was that he was alive.

"I am so happy, Zach!" Rade exclaimed.

"I'm ecstatic," he replied, surprising them both.

"I miss you sweetie, and let's start planning the wedding immediately I return."

"What if I am not ready?" She answered.

"Then I'll just have to drag you off to the altar without your consent."

"Caveman," she replied.

The rains came, and while being driven to work in the mounting Lagos traffic, Rade realised it was the first day in April. She smiled as a thought came to her, and it progressed to a full grin to her driver's surprise, who usually spied on her through the rear view mirror whenever he thought she wasn't looking. She was usually one of the earliest at the office and had ample time to ring Zach.

"Zach," she started, "I don't know how you're going to take this, but I've given this some thought and concluded I can't continue with the relationship. You said you'd be away for a year, now a year and two months later, you still haven't rounded up. What if you decide not to return? Let's go our separate ways, I've had a good time, and I'll never forget how wonderful you've been to me."

There was silence on the other end.

"You're joking, aren't you? Are you serious Rade?" He asked again when she didn't respond.

"I'm as serious as a heart attack," she replied, stating other reasons why she wanted to end the relationship.

"Where is this coming from? Look, don't make any rash decisions," Zach's heart was thumping so hard, he didn't know how to start.

"I love you, and that hasn't changed; it's not been easy for me too. I promised I would be back and nothing's going to change that."

There was silence on the other end. Then he began a line of questioning Rade didn't even get a chance to answer. The last one she heard before the line cut off was, "Is there someone else?"

She knew it was time to call off the hoax, but she was getting a busy tone as she tried to ring him back. Why had the line cut off? She wondered and then realised he was probably trying to ring back, and so she stopped redialing. She was distracted all day by the lack of communication; she had sent several messages that remained undelivered and were still pending in her outbox. What could have happened in between the call drop and several hours later? She made a mental calculation of what time it was in Abu Dhabi. She was worried and couldn't stop blaming herself for playing such an expensive prank. She tried to no avail to reach him that night, and by the next morning, Rade was as tense as a string. She couldn't tell anyone what she had done. She called his office and was asked to call back after his phone went unanswered and she had been put on hold for a few minutes. She called back and was told Zach had taken the day off, as he wasn't in optimal health. She was confused and distracted; his mobile phone was still switched off.

The second evening was spent like the one before it, pacing around her sitting room. Where on earth was Zack?! She had prayed and known she should have peace, but her conscience ate at her. She couldn't believe how immature she'd been. The voices in her head argued with each other; everyone played pranks. Why had it been when she was about to say "April fool" that the line cut off? She was sure Zach hadn't hung up on her, but his phone was still off by the second day. He could at least call her to conclude the conversation.

By her bedtime, she was wondering if she would get any sleep when her door buzzer went off.

"Oh, not again," she thought.

The old man at the gate had informed her earlier that she had forgotten to turn off her headlights after returning from the gym where she had gone to try and work out her frustration. She went unhurriedly to open the door and got the answer to why Zach hadn't called. He was at her doorstep in person!

"Zach!" She drank in the sight of him and flew

into his arms, and they hugged each other tightly, Rade felt tears prickle her eyes. She pulled him inside, and they held each other again in silence.

She ushered him into a seat which he took tiredly pulling her with him. Rade held his face between her palms and kissed him gently on the lips.

"What was she going say to him now?"

The buzzer brought them up straight; the taxi man was waiting to be paid, the gateman announced. Zach explained he didn't have any cash on him, and she dashed in and out of her room to make the payment.

Chapter Fourteen

Rade sat on her favourite chair, chewing a well-manicured nail. Zach had gone in to have a hot shower. She still hadn't gotten over the shock of seeing him and jumped when he captured her uneasy fingers in his hands and stooped in front of her.

"I know a lot of things have been going through your mind, but I'm here to make you see how wrong you are," he started.

Rade interrupted him before her shame and guilt reduced her to tears.

"I don't even know how to start, but I've been very silly."

"I understand Rade, and I don't blame you."

Rade had to yell to make him keep quiet; he was making things more difficult for her.

"What I said on the phone was just a joke."

He smiled and rubbed her cheeks; he told her he knew she was only trying to make him feel better, and he appreciated it.

"No, Zach, listen to me without interrupting," she continued, "I have behaved foolishly," she explained to him, "it was only an April fool prank."

The look of disbelief on Zach's face made Rade's heart bleed.

"You put me in a state of panic with that news and completely disorganised my work schedule the last few days, yet you were only fooling around?! How can that be? You sounded really serious! I could hear the pain in your voice," he continued as she sank deeper into her seat.

He stood up and paced across the room irritably. She looked at him pleadingly, but he refused to meet her eyes. He sat down opposite her and glanced intermittently at her while shaking his head. Then he began to laugh. Rade looked at him worriedly, the look of remorse on her face fueling his laughter. She looked like a chastised puppy.

"You really are a mischievous girl and should be punished for playing such pranks. I mean, it wasn't even April first in Abu Dhabi Rade," he said in exasperation.

She nodded quietly in agreement.

She got him something to eat, and he asked if he could sleep over; it had been a long flight. He couldn't get a direct flight at short notice, so he had to fly to Doha and picked a connecting flight to Lagos where there had been a delay because of the bad weather.

He needed to ring Simi. The voice filled with sleep turned to one filled with surprise when Simi heard her brother's voice. Simi asked why he had come without telling anyone to pick him up from the Airport and asked Rade if she was in on it.

"It was a spur of the moment decision; there was something urgent I needed to attend to which I have done already."

"Really, are you sure you arrived today?" Simi said puzzled. She promised to pick him up later that morning as it was well past midnight.

Zach went to sleep as soon as his head touched her goose feather filled pillow. She had a little trouble sleeping; she was shaken by Zach's flying down to speak with her, and of course, it was quite unusual to have him in her bed.

He was around for three days, all of which were filled with checking the progress at the site and spending time with Rade.

Rade had a smile on her lips on her way to work the morning following Zach's departure. She had

314

begged him not to mention the joke to anyone. When Simi asked him for the umpteenth time why he had really come, Rade pleaded with her eyes as he assumed a pained expression, looking almost ready to tell, then with a wink explained he had just missed his girl so much he had to get away albeit for three days. They were still trying to decide between them what her punishment would be; she had offered to reimburse half of his ticket money, and he had disdainfully waved it aside as "darn to easy."

He promised to come up with something befitting as she pleaded with him to be gentle with her.

****

The end of his contract had finally drawn near, and Zach was rounding up to return home; the remaining months were spent flying between the USA and the Uk. On his final stop in London to attend a dinner given in honour of an award given to the firm he was working for, he went in search of Phil at Rade's insistence; she was reunited with her friend though they hadn't spoken much.

Although he had regained his physical strength, he had gone into depression over his girlfriend's death; he was having great difficulty getting over it. He was fixated and couldn't get past the day of the incident, her suggestion they go sailing, and the cautioning voice he heard restraining him, but he hadn't listened and his girlfriend had paid for it.

She knew from their brief conversation that Phil was a changed man, and he and Zach had taken a liking to each other when they eventually met. The woman they both loved was something they had in common. It was hard not to like either man anyway; they had obviously found each other irresistible, she'd said when she spoke with Phil after Zach's visit. His chuckle encouraged her; the old Phil was coming back, and she prayed he got over the difficult period soon.

"It's a miracle I'm alive, but I don't understand why God chose to save me?" Phil kept asking.

It was amazing how some people had to learn the hard way she thought. Phil had to go through a painful experience to finally acknowledge God, but for others, the journey to God was easier. He was delighted to learn that she and Zach were getting married.

On Zach's birthday, Rade called him first thing in the morning to wish him a happy birthday, but it rang out. He called her back sometime later. He told her he was going out for drinks with some acquaintances later that evening.

Two days later, she realised they hadn't really spoken since his birthday; there were issues regarding the Goldmine property she wanted to discuss with him. She eventually got to talk with him after several messages between them.

"Wow! I finally get to speak with you," she announced. He seemed quite distracted, and she told him so. Zach's mind was in turmoil; the past few days had been a torture for him. He had been avoiding her, and he told her so.

"Why; is there a problem?" She asked, warning her heart not to skip a beat.

Zach didn't know where to start; he didn't even know if to start.

A month ago he had bumped into Clarice at the Mall of the Emirates on a trip to Dubai; seeing his ex-girlfriend from the States was uncanny, though they had both been so excited at seeing a familiar face. She had moved to Dubai to work with an oil company two years before. They met up for drinks that evening and had kept in touch; text messages were exchanged, and hers were beginning to get a tad bit flirtatious, and he told her so. He was in love and engaged to be married to the most special woman in the world. She told him it was harmless. She was single, lonely and seeing him had brought back a flood of memories. He checked up on her from time to time; she was a nice girl, and it was nice to have a friend around to chat with sometimes. He knew now that he had underestimated the situation and had ignored the warning signals. He was confused as to whether he had subconsciously wanted it to happen, but the remorse was overwhelming. He couldn't keep it to himself any longer; he had been avoiding Rade for a few days, and he knew she would notice something was amiss.

"Please don't tell me you're not coming home any longer."

He winced and started to think of the best way to convey the information. He was due back in Lagos in a few weeks; they were going to start making plans for the future.

"Zach!"

"Rade, please, I need you to hear me out; I feel horrible! I never thought you and I would have this kind of conversation ever."

"What is it? You're scaring me."

The silence was deafening. Zach could feel his

heart pounding in his ears.

"I've been with someone else."

The silence continued until she asked, "What does that even mean? I don't quite understand."

He was at a loss for words as he tried to explain. The incident had played in his mind over and again; his birthday, going out for drinks, Clarice coming back to his penthouse flat, the music, the sudden change in the dynamics of things, and the sudden physical need that had overwhelmed him. The girl's eagerness had been a huge turn on; she had never hidden the fact that she still wanted him; they weren't strangers. The last minute where he could have still backed out, but had gone ahead and taken the plunge towards satisfying his physical craving. He had been overconfident, quite sure he couldn't be tempted, as he had passed up several advances from women in the past.

The response he got scared him even more. Rade's peal of laughter filled his ears. "Oh, Zach! This is so banal. Is this what you've been cooking up all this time? I honestly thought you'd come up with something more interesting and less obvious." She was still chuckling, and he was confused.

There was another spate of silence until she apologised for not playing along, but she didn't want history repeating itself, like the phone line cutting off when he was only joking and retaliating for her April Fool's day joke on him. This was going to be harder than he thought. He briefly contemplated the new available way out, thinking, like he had many times that day that perhaps, she was better off not knowing, but he just couldn't.

He tried to make her understand there were no excuses and that he took full responsibility. She was numb as she began to realise that this wasn't a joke but a reality; that a few weeks before he was to return home, he was calling to say he had slept with someone else. He had mentioned bumping into Clarice and them keeping in touch but not this. His voice sounded distant to her as he continued to speak words she couldn't really hear. She hung up on him. A few hours later, she was still trying to understand her feelings; she didn't quite feel anything. She wanted to feel something, disappointment, anger, but nothing came, just emptiness. He kept ringing her, but she didn't even bother to pick; she just kept trying to imagine Zach with another woman. Like anaesthesia, the numbness eventually wore off, and the reality of his words knifed through her, causing different emotions to race through her in a mad rush. She is howling alone; things are creeping into her body, draining all her strength. Her mind is on fire; thoughts are burning; she can smell the ashes of betrayal. Her shoulders are tremendously heavy, weighing her down, leaving her paralysed. The betraying words of the man she loved left her heart abandoned and deep sadness hovering over her mind. She couldn't breathe, clutching her chest tightly, she doubled over in a gut-wrenching cry.

One day had ended, and a new one was already halfway through, Rade stood by her window staring at nothing; other than the occasional noise of the birds chirping in the compound, her scattered thoughts covered all traces of sound. The excruciating pain of his betrayal felt palpable; perhaps she could extricate it from her core with something swift and sharp, she thought as it sat heavy within her, stretching her heart taut. She cast her eyes upward, the dark clouds peeking out of the light grey skies; her heart beat faster to see the dark clouds, it strangely felt like seeing a traitorous friend, one who had been deeply loved. The skies seemed to paint a portrait of Zach's words as she envisioned another wrapped in his arms; how he'd so easily betrayed her without a thought, with Clarice, a blast from the past who seemed to have sprung out of nowhere.

Days became weeks and weeks stretched further apart since Rade spoke to Zach. She'd rejected all calls from him and every attempt to reach her. Mostly lost in thought, but she was doing well picking up the pieces of her broken heart. She hadn't spoken to anyone about it yet; she couldn't bring herself to tell her best friends and family that Zach had hurt her in ways she could never have imagined. She kept herself busy with everything and anything else, including having dinner with her parents every evening and enjoying the easy banter between them, which often lingered till late into the night.

Tonight, at dinner with her parents, Rade chuckled as her father sneaked a little salt on his food, as he occasionally did if he could find the salt canister his wife hid away ever since she had decided salt wasn't good for his health. Then she sighed and watched them in silence; thirty-eight years of marriage, and still devoted to one another. How did they do it?

Mrs. Doherty guessed what was running through her daughter's mind, she knew something was wrong with her relationship, but Rade wasn't saying anything. She prayed everything would get back to the way it used to be. They got into a conversation after the dishes had been cleared.

Rade asked her mother how they had stayed strong together all this time. She had become very reflective since breaking up with Zach.

"A relationship, any kind for that matter, must be based on trust; you have to trust that the person is in it for the same reason as you are, you play your role and trust that the other person plays theirs too."

"What if the person isn't worthy of the trust, mom? What happens then; how can you give someone something they don't deserve?"

"Faith my dear, you have got to believe! Besides, there are many things we all have we don't deserve." Rade sighed as her mother continued, "Your father and I have had our issues, but we have always overcome them. He is the husband, and I am the wife; the roles will never change. There is freedom in knowing what is expected of you and simply doing it. It helps that we are best of friends, no one has come between us, not for lack of trying though, even you children never managed to do that; the relationship we have is exclusive."

She mused on the conversation with her mother while lying on her bed later that night and remembered another conversation she and her friends had about relationships. Buba was of the opinion that a man could never be faithful to one woman to the chagrin of the girls.

"How can you say that Buba? That is so untrue," she'd responded then.

"I'm being realistic; it's difficult for you to accept because women are idealistic. It is almost impossible for a man to be monogamous, the man wasn't made to be monogamous."

He had asked Zach to back him up. Rade had asked Zach to be very careful about what he said because it could be held against him in future. He'd simply grinned and said he understood what Buba was saying clearly. The girls may never be able to appreciate how a man's body functioned, how separated it could be from their reasoning and how it led them astray sometimes, but to say it was impossible that a man could have a monogamous relationship all his life was an exaggeration. There are priests, monks, and men who have learnt to control their body and it's sexual urges.

"Exactly! Simi had said. "Buba, you really worry me sometimes. Where do you get all these funny theories you postulate? Take women, for example, we have desires too, but we learn to control them. Men just look for excuses to cover up their weaknesses. It's worse in this part of the world where our culture aids infidelity. God wouldn't ask you to do something if it wasn't possible. You are just too lazy to exert your will power but don't blame the way you're made for your desires."

It was a sore point for Simi.

"Men are very different from women, Simi," Maimuna raised her hands in defence and had asked to finish before Simi attacked her. "A woman's desire is largely linked to her emotions, so a woman will usually, (I know there are exceptions) desire someone she is attached to emotionally. Men think with their bodies; it is very common to hear a man desire a woman he doesn't even like or one he will not talk to the minute he's done having sex with her. 'Men are fountains, while women are wells.' They are moved by what they see. Their sexual urge is like other urges they have; hunger, the need to go to the bathroom, and they give in to it, like animals really."

The men had protested vehemently.

Rade had then asked Buba why men got married if it wasn't possible for them to be monogamous.

"Because marriage is a good thing; it enhances a man's social status; he can bear children and have a family. Besides, the man does want to be faithful to a woman in some cases, however, intent is different from reality."

"Some cases?" Rade had interjected.

"Yes, in some cases," he'd reaffirmed. "Not all men

want to be faithful to one woman; some want to be with many women, some are born polygamist, some self-made womanisers; it will be useless to expect such men to be faithful."

He'd gone on to say that he believed womanising was genetic, most womanisers had sons who inadvertently turned out to be womanisers. He likened sexual desire to Pandora's box that monks, priests and others like them had left shut, but once it was opened, it was hard to control. Once a man started to have sex with one woman, he would automatically start to desire others.

Simi had stared at her cousin in awe, and he'd reassured them he was fine when she asked him for the umpteenth time if he was okay.

"I don't know about womanising being genetic. I think it's a case of nurture over nature. A boy raised in a home where the father practices infidelity may be more likely to be influenced negatively. Buba, with all these opinions you have, it's no wonder you don't have a girlfriend, my dear cousin," Maimuna had said.

"My not having a girlfriend has nothing to do with my opinions that are largely true, by the way. Most men think this way but are afraid to say it to women, for fear of being terrorized. Truth be told, men are afraid of women. The wrath of a woman should be avoided at all cost,"

Zach had chuckled and shaken hands with his cousin adding that the Bible even suggests that it was better to dwell in the corner of a housetop than with a brawling woman in a wide house, and in more extreme situations, even the wilderness than with a contentious and angry woman. Buba was intrigued and asked Zach for the particular Bible passage as they guffawed, and the ladies stared on, unimpressed.

"What kind of man are you then, Buba?" Rade had asked slyly, going back to the topic, "a born polygamist?"

"On the contrary, though I am Muslim and permitted more than one wife if you can love them equally, I'm the kind of man that desires to be with the right woman for the long haul."

The girls cooed.

"That being said, marriage is a cultural thing; the rules differ with each culture, what is acceptable in one culture is unacceptable in another.

"God's laws supersede any man-made laws, culture included. I don't understand how men have multiple relationships, being with one person is hard enough as it is, I guess it's an acquired high, fueled by greed and lust. And Buba, not all priests control their sexual urges," Simi had said.

"Why do you keep going on about men, women have multiple relationships too, what's their excuse? People have the ability to love more than one person because each person is different. What they don't realise is that love is a decision and not an emotion; you can decide to put a value on a person, place them above all else and love them. It's hard for me to comprehend, but in the past week, I've met two married women who claim they love their husbands yet are cheating on them. How can you love someone and continue to do things to hurt them? Love does not seek its own and puts the other before oneself. They defended their professed love vehemently and thought it okay to regale me with their stories; I think they mistook my dentist chair for a shrink's own. I can understand that behaviour from single people but..."

"Are you saying it's okay for people who are not married to cheat on each other?" Rade had interjected before Maimuna finished.

The guys began to enjoy the conversation; it was nice when the women turned on one another.

"Don't take that tone with me, Rade, and don't twist my words out of context; a relationship is very different from a marriage. The rules of engagement are different and no matter what people say, marriage is more than a social contract and more than a piece of paper that binds two people together. Infidelity in marriage is a serious thing."

Rade asked the question again.

"You're clearly not getting me, of course, it's not right to betray anyone's trust in a relationship, but the bottom line is that a relationship is different from a marriage."

"Exactly! And for men to think they can cheat on their partners when they are single and stop when they get married is foolhardy. Men are creatures of habit, more so if we follow Buba's warped pandora's box theory. Once they start, marriage cannot stop them; it has become a habit now aided by familiarity."

"You can't make such assertions," Zach said to his sister, "I've known a few ladies men who have settled down after marriage."

"If it's the same people I know you're referring to, only time will tell; they will be tested, and then you'll know for sure."

"Simi, that is so judgmental!" Zach answered.

"No, it's not. Who am I to judge anyone? Everyone's relationship is as peculiar as the individuals in them differ. Look at the couple in Paul Coelho's book, Zahir, for example, they had some sort of open marriage, and it seemed like it worked for them until it all fell apart, and I was going to marry a pathological cheat and try to make it work. But I know that the Bible says a man should leave his mother and father and cleave to his wife, and then they become one flesh, so it is possible for a man to be faithful to a woman; his unwillingness to do so is another matter entirely. God did not make the man a polygamist; the fall did. God had made a reference to polygamy when He told the woman that the man would rule over her in Genesis. For a person to rule, the people being ruled are usually greater in number than the ruler. However, I still stand by my opinion that God made one Adam and took one Eve out of him; He could have made two, so He must have known one woman was more than sufficient. In any case, marriage is the physical representation of the spiritual union between Christ and his bride, the Church. There's only one Church."

Maimuna had smiled; she was right behind her on this one.

Rade wondered where they got some of the spiritual insights they had. They had a good teacher of the Bible. Buba looked very thoughtful and asked why some of the great men in the Bible had married multiple women if that was the case.

Zach had answered that the fact that they did didn't make it right.

"So what kind of man are you, Zach?" The girls posed the same question they had to Buba earlier to him.

"Come on ladies, no need to ask, what do you think his answer will be? His girlfriend is here, didn't you just hear what I said earlier about a woman's wrath and he, Zach, confirmed it with scripture. What sane man will put his foot in his mouth after what you girls, especially our dear Simi has said this evening?"

The girls had laughed as the men shook hands again.

Now in retrospect, she thought that he had gotten off too easy.

On the day of Zach's arrival, she awakened from a troubled sleep and rubbed her temples. One strange dream after another had troubled her sleep. She had made a decision, but it didn't give her any peace. The weeks leading to that were anxious ones for her. She fretted. She missed him but only a small part of her; no, she lied, a big part of her resented him for betraying her, and she couldn't let it go. Zach had resigned to his fate; he couldn't force her to be with him. Even though his heart ached, and he kept asking himself if he had been indeed stupid for telling Rade the truth of his stupidity;

her reaction was a revelation. Love was meant to cover a multitude of sins. Not in this case obviously. His uncountable "I'm sorry" couldn't wash this away.

It's sad how things had taken a turn for the worst in such a short period.

After much deliberation on her part, she decided to meet him at the Airport. She held on to her anger and allowed it to quell her fluttering heart when she saw him. She felt awkward as he attempted to pull her to him in a tight embrace. He tried to get through to her, but she had erected a barrier between them that only she could take away. She didn't allow any conversation between them, and Zach was frustrated beyond measure. He had hoped her coming to meet him was a good sign, but she said she only did it as it would be awkward otherwise.

It was obvious to their friends and family after a few weeks that things were not the same, yet no one dared to ask any questions; to ask was to acknowledge something was wrong.

Mr. and Mrs. Doherty was worried about their daughter; her father had restrained her mother from interfering.

"Give them some space, let them try and face their challenges on their own."

Mrs. Doherty didn't agree but hearkened to her husband. She longed to talk some sense into her daughter's head and told her husband so. She vowed to do so if things remained the same much longer.

Rade's birthday was approaching, and it was two years since they promised her the deeds of the Goldmine property. What they hadn't told her was that they had hoped she and Zach would have been married by the time and they intended to bequeath them with the deeds as a wedding present. Being married to Zach was the unspoken prerequisite to receiving that particular gift. Nothing seemed to be going according to plan.

Zach was very unhappy; the break-up marred the joy at the success of his work and his return. He hadn't even told her his model floor lamp and recliner had been shortlisted for the award for the most innovative designs at the Europe Design Fair. He had messed everything up, and he hated the feeling. He had condemned himself over and again. He was tired of blaming himself and the guilt alongside. Time, on the other hand, had no problem passing by, they talked, and he waited, hoping and losing hope. She told him she wondered if he had been with other women he wasn't telling her about and that she still loved him but couldn't be with someone she couldn't trust. He didn't even understand what that meant anymore; he had told her everything.

"What if I hadn't told you? He asked.

She had no response to that; the point was that she knew and that was it.

He reminded her of his promise before he left that they would always tell each other the truth, the pledge to be open at all times.

He asked for her forgiveness for the umpteenth time, though she claimed she had given it already, but she couldn't forget. He decided to let her be and hoped in the fact that at least she hadn't returned his engagement ring.

The next morning, Rade stared at her reflection in the mirror as she applied her foundation. She missed Zach very much. She had taken his friendship for granted. They were still in business together, and her respect for him in that regard had increased in droves despite everything going on between them. It was hard to find committed people and Zach was one of them. But why did men cheat, why, why, why?! She knew most of the reasons by heart, but it didn't make it okay. He had messed everything up.

"Cheating on you is not the worst thing a man

can do to you."

She turned swiftly; who and what was that? Her heart pounded loudly in her chest; the voice had been loud! She stared intently at her reflection when she realised it had come from her. She had to sit down.

Then the tears came, she didn't understand herself anymore; what impelled her and what kind of person she really was. Had she always been this unforgiving, how could her heart have stayed so hardened against a man she claimed she cared about, even after she had lashed out and punished him? Why did evil seemingly carry more weight than good? Why had one mistake from Zach dimmed all the good things he had done for her? And the fact that he was a good man, Zach's love was apparent whenever she looked into his eyes. This experience was opening her eyes to her own shortcomings and how less than perfect she was. She wasn't even sure she was ready for marriage; her mom had told her marriage was about forgiveness, yet forgiving was hard for her. If she couldn't forgive now, would there be things she would consider unforgivable when they were married? Even if she didn't want the relationship any longer as his actions hurt her, her hostility and the deep malice towards him shocked even her sometimes.

She was certain there were things about her Zach wasn't pleased about, but he had decided to love her anyway. She remembered the morning after he arrived from Abu Dhabi courtesy of her prank, he had begged to make love to her, abstaining was difficult for him he'd said; he used to be a sexually active man, now they were both trying to grow as Christians in every area. Though they had decided to wait until marriage, it seemed harder in a long relationship, though but not impossible, they both agreed. She needed to stay focused, "sex beclouds a woman's judgment," she reiterated. She had reassured him he wasn't alone, they were in love and attracted to each other, besides they had done it before, the memories of that evening in Ibadan still drove her into a frenzy, but they still had to try. After a lot of fondling and giggles, he had lain on top of her duvet-covered body and told her she was his "missing rib."

"That's a first! How corny, Zach!" She had scoffed.

He smiled at her, "that's what being in love does to you; it makes you say corny things. However, it doesn't undermine the sincerity."

She smiled and asked him never to stop saying cheesy things to her.

She asked God for forgiveness. It was clear to

her that she was seemingly strong in one area but weak in another, yet she dared to judge another. She didn't commit fornication but would get a plaque in unforgiveness and many other wrongdoings. She had to look for Zach and talk with him.

Two months later, she dreamt they had a beautiful wedding ceremony. They wore their traditional outfits and a minister joined them in the beautiful garden at her parent's house. It was followed by a grand ball later that evening. She looked regal in a cream coloured lace gown that showed off a lovely décolletage, a miniscule waist and flared hips before flaring out at the bottom. But it was her face that captivated everyone, including the groom. It glowed. Zach looked like the cat that had eaten the whole cream; he was proud, happy and feeling very lucky. He cut a dashing figure in his Damask Tunic, a very eligible bachelor who was glad and very anxious to change his status.

Mrs. Doherty outdid herself with the flower arrangement; dozens of crystal floor vases carried a wide array of exotic fresh flowers, so did the centrepieces. The exquisite tall floor lamps, tea light candles and chandeliers cast a warm glow in the marquee. Beige, cream, gold and ivory; everything at the venue was layered in those colours in varying textures of crushed velvet, lace, soft linen and delicate silks. There was diamond glitter everywhere. The flatware glistened and gleamed, the wine glasses sparkled and glimmered almost fairytale-like, and she and Zach were the Prince and Princess. A blend of ethnic, rhythm and blues, soul and jazz music, filled the air. Simi provided world-class catering. Buba commented he had never seen so much food in one place at the same time; they had over thirty main intercontinental and local dishes; it was almost impossible to choose. Phil, who never backed away from a challenge, drew the ire of a particular stewardess. She was his appointed hostess, and he saddled her with the responsibility of explaining some of the local soup dishes he was attempting to eat.

"*Tause* or *Kuka*?" He asked, peering at the menu that bore the northern dishes.

She looked at his handsome face distractedly before Simi came to the rescue.

Afterwards, they drove to an "unknown location" to many except a few. It was a replica of the model he had given her for her birthday. Their first night together as a married couple would not be spent anywhere else. He carried her into their new home filled with the alluring fragrance of her favourite Oud scent diffuser mixed with the floral, wispy scent of fresh flowers. The fresh flowers were a tradition she would gladly continue from her mother.

He proceeded from the foot of the stairs to their bedroom; the king-sized bed was covered with the finest beddings Zach could find. Silk, satin and intricate damask would be the backdrop for the long overdue, erotic love dance they would perform shortly. He set her on the bed and proceeded on one knee to take off her five-inch stilettos. Her feet dug into the plush rug by the bed as he led her into the breathtaking, luxurious, fully fitted bathroom. She winced as her feet met the cold marble floor before he sat her on an ottoman with a kiss then went on to fill the Jacuzzi after pouring in some bath salts with flourish. There was a bottle in an ice bucket by the side; she eyed him with amusement.

He pulled her into his arms as they danced to their own music, and then he began to unzip her dress slowly.

"Let me show you what you've been missing," he said, and Rade laughed, her heart thumping in excitement.

Rade woke up with a stretch. "What a dream!" She thought. How could a dream be this real; she wanted to stay in bed and bask in it but willed herself to get out of bed. Her bones felt languid; it must have been a long night she thought again as she sighed, then smiled as she felt a familiar hand run over her form.

Realisation dawned, it was noon, and she was lying in her husband's arms the day after their wedding, and yes, it had been a long night. She snuggled back into him contentedly as he proceeded to make up for all the period of abstinence and wondered if they would be able to make the night flight to their honeymoon destination.

Epilogue

The attractive living room in Zach and Rade's vacation house was in silence; the only noise was that of the ticking clock. Zach was slumped in a chair, in front of him was a half-drunk cup of coffee. He heard the muffled ring of his mobile and sprang up, but as he dashed to pick it up from where it had dropped in between the opposite chair, he crashed into the table, the mug and coaster flying in different directions. He thought of his wife's expression if she saw the mess and grimaced. He hurried over and answered the phone and didn't wait for the caller to finish before hanging up; all he heard was his wife was awake. He hurried out of the house like a man chased. He had stayed with her all night, and the doctors were still observing her. The delivery was exceptionally easy, but unprecedented fatigue had engulfed her afterwards. It had been two days. They were keeping a close watch over her and sent him home to take a shower with a promise to call if she woke up. He had gone home and tried to pray but had been at a loss for what to say. Eventually, he said a little prayer, "Lord, infuse Rade with strength in Jesus name, amen."

He went into the private ward and saw her; she still looked tired but was feeling much stronger. He pulled her into his arms and kissed her passionately; it was the sound of someone clearing the throat that broke them apart. It was the midwife, and she sent Zach a disapproving look, which he returned. Zach and Rade embraced each other tightly again. He smiled to himself, to think that it was just about two years ago since the grand opening of their mall called "**Wura Ola.**" It had and still received accolades for its exceptional design, amongst other things.

Three years now since they had been married and a few people asking coyly, Nigerian style, when the babies would start coming, and here they are. He peered at the two bundles: Twins! Being a father was strange enough as it is, but being a father of two children at the same time! That was still mind-blowing for Zach.

The original plan was to have the babies in Lagos, but he was glad he took the last minute decision that they would have their babies abroad because Rade had refused to take things easy and often overworked herself. The staff in the office was relieved, as they didn't understand why their pregnant boss kept showing up at the office when she was supposed to be on leave. They didn't know how to deal with a pregnant, shouting woman.

Several weeks before her due date, he had arranged a house, bought their tickets and informed her of their departure date. She knew she had been badly behaved and didn't bother protesting. She still managed to commission new frames for the bestselling Doherty prints that lined the reception wall a day before their departure.

He had told her before their wedding, when she had asked him why he had never given up on her, that he had made a promise to himself, after all considerations, her unforgiving attitude included, he wanted to get a reward for being the best husband and father on judgment day. He was proving it. Rade didn't think there was any man alive who could be as attentive as Zach was, from the day they got married and through her pregnancy and the light in his eyes told her nothing would change, whatever happened over the years.

Someone once told her, "Marriage is the ultimate step of faith; you not only marry who the person is, you marry whom the person will become." She understood the different phases their marriage would go through, but she was confident that the core of her husband would not change. He stared in awe at his wife and her stomach, thinking what a mysterious being the woman was. What an exceptional design of God; a great blend of beauty and practicality. She deserved more credit than was given to her. He watched Rade try and suckle one of their babies and leaned over to kiss her cheek. He was excited.

"Your breasts look like balloons, how does it feel to have the baby suckle your nipples? I'm kind of jealous," he said.

"Oh, Zach!" Rade replied as she drifted off into a short nap, he watched her and kissed her fingers intermittently.

There was a knock sometime later and a grand entry by Mr. and Mrs. Doherty, Simi and Maimuna. The Doherty's usually travelled during the summer, and it was perfect timing with the delivery of the babies.

The family exclaimed and gushed over the babies, with Mrs. Doherty boasting about her genes; thus the twins.

There came the usual bantering when they were all together. Maimuna told Simi to start taking notes as she knew she loved twins and has been dreaming about having two sets since they were little girls. She and Danladi were getting married in two months.

Zach's mobile phone rang; it was Goke calling to congratulate his sister and Zach. After speaking with his sister, who was awake now, he asked to speak with Maimuna to Rade's surprise. Maimuna was talking in hushed tones, and Mrs. Doherty took on her gossipy tone and told them that when Goke had come home the last holiday, he and Maimuna had seemed close.

Rade's eyes widened, and Zach commented on the fact that Maimuna was practically beaming.

"Don't be such horrible tease," Simi said pinching Zach and giggling.

Maimuna ended the conversation with Goke and came back to join the circle.

"Goke says he's coming to Nigeria soon," she announced.

"That's good news; I wish he'd just settle down someplace and stop moving around so much like a gipsy; he told me he would a few years back," Mrs. Doherty said wistfully.

"Me too," Maimuna replied, looking at everyone and daring them to say anything. Mrs. Doherty glanced at her daughter and winked.

"I've always wanted a beautiful sister-in-law," Rade said.

"You have one!" Simi exclaimed as they all laughed. There was silence, and Maimuna said, "I've always prayed for a loving, caring, beautiful sister-in-law too."

They awarded her a round of applause.

"People are going to think we are a cult very soon if we keep marrying one another. Why can't that brother-in-law of mine find another woman instead of planning to come and sweep my cousin off her feet; I just know how this is going to end," Zach said with mock anger as they all laughed.

"Let us pray," Mr. Doherty said, "and commit the lives of these precious little gifts from God. We ask for wisdom for the parents that they raise them in the way they should go, and when they grow older, they will not depart from it."

Zachary and Moradeyo looked into each other's eyes and knew they were blessed. Rade still found it hard to understand the path her life had taken, the things that had been planned for her without her knowing. Her walk with Jesus had taken a new turn; she was starting to understand grace and unconditional love a little better. She had received the gift of friendships from the wisest women in the world as far as she was concerned, namely Maimuna and Simisola. She would never have guessed her life's lesson instructors would be Fulani women from the north, who had the courage to convert from their family religion and had been ostracized by many for it; who left the safety of their home region for the west to pursue education and career while still maintaining their cultural traditions. The life lessons she had learnt and was still learning were remarkable. Zachary was another matter entirely. She had found a new best friend and life partner.

Her life before she came to Lagos had been nice, but her life in Lagos was incomparable. Returning home was the best thing that could have happened to her. She remembered scoffing along with a friend when she asked, "Is there anything good in Lagos?" The same friend had nearly broken her neck from craning it incessantly at her wedding, almost swooning when she saw Zach and taking in all the proceedings at the ceremony.

"I'm jealous," she had whispered in Rade's ear while congratulating her.

Rade didn't blame her; even she had been foolish

and doubted what good she could find in Lagos, Nigeria. Little wonder it is said that what makes the desert beautiful is that somewhere it hides a Well, and the possibility of discovering that Well makes life interesting. Sometimes we are the antagonists in our own life's story. She remembered how she had often stood in the path of her own progress. She now knew that God's purpose could find you wherever you're located, the less obvious, the better.

The nurse on duty peeped in and shook her head in wonder. "This family is exceptional;" she muttered. "There's something about them;" she repeated to herself as she found herself responding to their prayers.